NURSING WOMAN

SARA FRASER

Nursing Woman

WARNER BOOKS

A *Warner* Book

First published in Great Britain in 1987 by Futura
Reprinted 1988
Reprinted by Warner Books 1992
This edition published by Warner Books in 1994
Reprinted 1995, 1996

A CIP catalogue record for this book
is available from the British Library.

ISBN 0 7515 0672 9

Printed in England by Clays Ltd, St Ives plc

Warner Books
A Division of
Little, Brown and Company (UK)
Brettenham House
Lancaster Place
London WC2E 7EN

Introduction

In the England of the early nineteenth century the sick-nurse was of low repute. Regarded as drunken, ignorant, dirty and brutal, she was seen at best as a necessary evil, at worst as an added curse on the suffering.

But there were some women who wished to make the nursing of the sick a reputable and honourable profession, and who were prepared to fight for the welfare of their patients against all odds. This is the story of one such woman – a young girl named Tildy.

Chapter One

The Parish of Tardebigge, Worcestershire.
August 1821

The huge covered wagon drawn by twelve horses advanced
along the sunken wood-girt lane like a ponderous juggernaut, its massive wheels crunching the dirt and stones,
leaving broad flattened tracks to mark their iron-rimmed
progress. Tildy Crawford with her child in her arms and a
heavy bulging sack tied across her slender back heard the
jinglings of myriad harness bells and turned. She caught
her breath at the sight of the mammoth vehicle which so
filled the width of the track that its wooden sides gouged the
grasses from the banks, and its hooped canvas top caught
and tore free the leaves of the overhanging branches of the
hedgerow trees. Her dark eyes flicked from side to side
searching the steep banks for a way of escape from the path
of the oncoming monster. The sides of the banks were
almost sheer at this point, and Tildy hurried on down the
lane, the combined weights of child and sack bundle
dragging painfully upon her body. Some distance further
on a bush growing out from the bank offered handholds
and Tildy gratefully seized them to pull herself up to the top
of the bank, where she stood to wait for the juggernaut to
pass.

The be-smocked, leather-gaitered waggoner rode

postillion on the nearside lead horse, his long whip in his hand and his low-crowned wide-brimmed hat pulled low on his forehead. He studied the young woman as he neared her, and softly whistled his appreciation of what he saw. His own fat-bodied woman sprawling upon the cargo in the capacious open mouth of the wagon was also studying the girl on the banktop and envying the glossy dark hair, the pretty face and the shapely body which could be discerned beneath the shabby grey gown and shawl.

'Whooah! Whooah! Come up now . . . Come up . . . Whooah!'

The team came to a standstill, and opposite Tildy, his head level with her own, the waggoner asked,

'How far to Redditch, pretty gal? 'Tis my first trip to these parts.'

'About two miles to the centre,' Tildy told him in her soft voice tinged with a rustic burr. 'You'll not be able to take any short cuts with a cart that size.'

'I'm wanting the Unicorn Inn,' the man said. 'D'ye know where it lies?'

'You must go to the Chapel Green; it's very close to that.' She hesitated a moment, thinking of the walk ahead of her, and added hesitantly. 'I'm going that way myself. If you could give me a ride, I'll be able to show you directly to the Unicorn.'

The man grinned at her with tobacco-stained teeth. 'That's a fair enough bargain, pretty gal, jump in wi' my old 'ooman.'

He jerked his head backwards, indicating the wagon behind him, and with a smile of thanks Tildy moved along the banktop until she was able to step across into the great hooped opening.

'Set yourself down, my wench, and make yourself easy.' The fat woman welcomed, and puffed out her plump cheeks, noisily expelling a gust of wind. ''Tis too bloody hot to walk when a body con ride, arn't it?'

'Indeed it is, Ma'am.' Tildy agreed, and with a grateful sigh sank down upon the heap of cloth-wrapped packages that almost filled the interior.

The great vehicle lurched into motion and Tildy called, 'Stay on this road, Master, until I shout you to turn off.'

The man lifted his whip in acknowledgement without turning to look at her. The fat woman stared curiously at Tildy, noting how clean she appeared in her body and clothing, and noting also the pink, newly healed pockmarks smattering the skin of both the woman and baby's cheeks and foreheads.

'I see your babby had the smallpox recent,' she remarked.

Tildy nodded. 'Yes, he and I both. But we're well over it now, thanks be to God.'

'Amen to that.' The fat woman agreed cheerily, and glancing at the ringless fingers of the younger woman, questioned, 'Wheer's your man then, gal? Why arn't he helping you to carry your load on a hot day like this 'un?'

Tildy flushed, knowing that the other had noticed her lack of a wedding ring. 'I've no man,' she replied quietly. 'I've got a husband, but I've not set eyes on him for nearly a year.'

The fat woman clucked her tongue sympathetically. 'A runaway, is he?'

Tildy nodded, and the fat woman grimaced comically. 'Then count it a blessing, my duck. I wishes many a time that my bugger 'ud run off. All he's good for is getting drunk and filling me wi' kids that we can't hardly afford to feed, ne'er mind clothe. That's in between the times that he's beating me black and blue for nothing at all. They'm all bad buggers, men am, so they be. We'd stifle the sods at birth iffen we'd a peck o' sense in our noddles.'

Tildy could not help but smile wryly at the other's words, but held her own silence.

'So you lives in Redditch by yourself now then?' the fat woman probed.

Tildy felt no irritation at the constant prying. It was the way of her world.

'I'm hoping to live there,' she answered. 'I've been in the parish poorhouse you see, but I left there today and now I want to get work and a place of my own to dwell in.'

The fat woman lifted both hands high and rolled her eyes dramatically. 'Poorhouse, is it? You doon't need to tell me what it's like in theer, my wench. I bin inside a score o' the buggers since I married that bastard out front theer.' She abruptly cackled with laughter. 'And I doon't doubt that I'll see the innards of a hundred more afore I'm in me grave.'

Tildy warmed towards the cheerful manner of her new companion and smiled broadly. 'That one has been sufficient for me,' she answered. 'I pray to God I'll never have to go back inside its walls.'

'What sort o' work will you do in Redditch, gal? That babby might be a hindrance iffen you was thinking o' going into service.'

Tildy paused for a moment, as if considering the point, then said, 'I'm not going into service if I can help it. To tell truth, I'm thinking of working for myself in a manner of speaking. I'm thinking of hiring myself out as a sick-nurse. I learned a fair bit about caring for the sick when I was in the poorhouse.'

'Sick-nurse, is it?' The fat woman pursed her lips judiciously as she considered the idea. 'Yes, it might well serve, my duck. You'm a very clean and presentable-looking gal. You could work for a good class o' people, right enough.' She winked slyly, and grinned. 'I'm told there's all sorts o' things can be gained by a good-looking young nurse-'ooman . . . Mayhap even a rich old man laying on his final bed.' She laughed salaciously. 'My oath! That u'd do you all right. Catch some rich old bugger in his sick-bed, and arter he'd signed all his worldly goods over to you in his will, then pulling his pudden for him, until he died o' joy.'

Her ribaldry was so totally devoid of malice that it carried Tildy along with it, and she joined whole-heartedly in the other's laughter.

'You've no kin, then?' the fat woman asked abruptly, and Tildy shook her head.

'None that I could call on, at any rate,' she replied quietly. 'I was left orphan when I was still but a child, and me and my brother were separated then. I've got an aunt hereabouts, but there's no love between us, and I've not seen her for a long time.'

'You doon't look much more than a child now, gal,' the woman joked. 'Got a skin as smooth as a babby's arse, so you have.'

'I'll be twenty next month.' Tildy was almost defensive. 'And being a mother as well, I can't really regard myself as a young girl still, can I?'

'That's true enough,' the other admitted, and they lapsed into a companionable silence.

Before very long the woodlands ended and rough pastureland replaced the ancient oaks and elms. To the south-east across a broad shallow valley rose the hills on which Redditch town was built. Tight-clustered groups of crooked-gabled houses, and tall-chimneyed manufactories stretching down the hillsides interspersed with gardens, patches of greensward, coppices of trees, the whole presenting a curious mélange of modern industry and ancient pastorality. It was a town which boasted a peculiar distinction; it was the world centre of the needle and fish hook manufacturing industry. From this distance Redditch looked pleasant and peaceful in the shimmering somnolent air, but Tildy knew well what horrors of noise and filth, of ignorance and brutality existed in the clusters of buildings, and for a brief moment she doubted the wisdom of her plans to live and work in the town. With an effort she quenched those doubts.

'I've no choice in the matter,' she accepted. 'I need work to support myself and my Davy, and this is where the work can be found.' She bent her head and lightly kissed the soft hair of her sleeping child. 'But the first thing we'll need to find is shelter for the night, won't we, my honey? A place for us to live. Where will that be, I wonder . . .'

The horses strained to draw the great wagon up the steep Fish Hill, their iron-shod hooves striking sparks from the stones beneath them as they scrabbled for purchase. The waggoner cursed vilely and lashed the foam-streaked hides with all his strength, his long whip drawing flecks of blood

11

to mingle with the sweat that sprayed out from the impact of the blows. Finally the flat plateau of the town centre was gained and the team halted, breath gusting from their frothing muzzles, flanks heaving, muscles trembling and twitching.

The waggoner dismounted and looked back down the hill. 'God's trewth, but that's a real ball-breaker, that 'un is,' he grunted, then called to Tildy. 'Wheer's the Unicorn, then?'

She clambered down on to the roadway, her child clasped in her arms, and looked about her. The town centre was a large triangular open stretch of sparse-grassed, hard-trodden earth pock-marked by holes where sand and gravel had been dug out. It was surrounded by houses, rows of cottages, inns, shops and a couple of blacksmiths' forges. On the far side of the triangle stood the single-storeyed greystone chapel of St Stephen surmounted by a squat-towered cupola. Just beyond and to the front of the chapel was a crossroads.

'Turn right at the cross there, Master,' Tildy pointed. 'The Unicorn is just a little way down on the left-hand side of the road.'

He nodded and without further words took hold of the lead horses' bridles and whipped the team into motion. Tildy waved goodbye to the man's wife and turned to accost a woman passing by.

'Your pardon, Mistress, can you direct me to a lodging-house?'

The mob-capped, aproned housewife stared specu-latively at Tildy. 'Theer's two such hereabouts, but they'm terrible rough, my wench.'

'That's no matter,' Tildy answered. 'I'll only be stopping there for a short while.'

The woman frowned doubtfully. 'You looks to be a respectable body. 'Udden't you be better putting up at one of the inns?'

Tildy shook her head. 'I can't afford inns' prices, Mistress.'

The doubtful frown remained on the other's face. 'Well,

like I say, the lodging houses hereabouts am terrible rough, but they'm chape, no doubt on that iffen that's what you'm looking for.. Goo along theer behind the chapel. Keep on that way and look out for the sign o' the Red Lion pub. Theer's an archway to its side that leads into Silver Street. Goo along the street until you comes into the Silver Square, you'll find both the lodging houses theer. But like I said afore, girl, I'd not want to see any kin o' mine in either on them . . . '

Chapter Two

'Noo, Benny! Noo!' the pregnant woman begged franti-
cally and then screamed as the man's fists pounded against
her body and face, bruising flesh, breaking skin, bringing
blood spurting from mouth and nose. She fell to her knees,
her hands desperately cupping her swollen belly as if to
shield her unborn child, and screamed again as iron-shod
clogs crashed into her chest, cracking ribs and sending her
sprawling, gagging with agony upon a heap of rotting
refuse and wet ashes.

'Gerrup you fuckin' cow! Gerrup!' the man bawled
dementedly, and again savagely kicked and stamped at the
shrieking woman as she tried to scrabble on hands and
knees across the foul heap to escape. He lunged forwards,
grabbing her long hair in both hands and dragged her
bodily along the ground raving and cursing in his drunken
frenzy.

All along the narrow thoroughfare frowsty heads popped
out from windows and doorways to stare avidly at what was
happening, but no one moved to intervene between man
and wife.

'You fuckin' cow! You fuckin' cow! I'll larn you, you
fuckin' cow! I'll larn you to fuckin' mouth off at me.'
Slack-lipped, spittle dribbling down his chin, the drunken
man dragged his shrieking woman upright by her hair and
punched her to the ground again, then stood over her with

clenched fists, voiding a stream of verbal filth upon her bloody face.

Sick with horror, Tildy pressed against the wall and held her child close to her breasts, terrified in case this drunken animal should turn on her and her baby.

He dealt out a final vicious kick, then swung about and lurched towards Tildy. She flinched as he staggered past her and vented a shuddering sigh of relief as he went on down the alley. A trio of ragged, raddled women came to the moaning victim and lifted her between them to carry her into a house.

'God's curse on the wicked bastard!' one of them mouthed over and over again. 'God's curse on the wicked bastard! God's curse on the wicked bastard!'

Badly shaken by what had so suddenly confronted her, Tildy hurried on along the fetid alley until it abruptly widened out into a square. Like the alley the ground here was thick with refuse and animal wastes and the air was heavy with an all-pervading rancid stench. She halted and gazed about her, her eyes mirroring the quickening of a fearful dread within her as they measured the mean hovels and tumbledown houses with their broken, rag-stuffed windows and splintered doors that crammed around the confined space. This was Silver Square, and behind her was Silver Street, and Tildy was to wonder many times about the identity of the satirist who had given them their names.

Small, half-clothed children played barefoot in the filth, some dragging old shoes on pieces of string, others carefully constructing mud-forts, and yet others skipping and chanting in rhythm. Slatternly women and rough-looking men lounged in doorways and leaned over window-sills smoking clay pipes, exchanging gossip, arguing, joking and laughing raucously. In the big ashpit in one corner of the square some youths were hunting rats with barking mongrel dogs, while in another corner young girls were dancing to the fluting notes of a tin whistle. Despite the abject poverty there was a vitality about the scene that suggested spirits uncowed by hardship and deprivation.

15

A group of men were sitting on the ground directly before Tildy playing a noisy game with a pack of dog-eared cards. One of them, a haggard-featured, middle-aged man wearing a broken-brimmed top hat noticed the young woman and grinned up at her with black stubs of teeth.

'I bid you welcome to our noble square, young lady.' His gin-hoarse voice was that of a cultured gentleman, and Tildy stared at him with nervous surprise.

'Whom do you seek here, lovely lady? Can it be myself, I dare to hope?' he questioned mockingly, and his companions laughed and made loud lewd comments.

Tildy flushed with embarrassment as his unwelcome questions focused the attention of the square upon her, but she forced herself to stand her ground and speak civilly.

'I'm seeking Mrs Readman's lodging house. Can you tell me which one it is, please?'

The haggard-featured man rose unsteadily to his feet and removing his hat from his greasy shoulder-length grey hair made a courtly bow. 'Indeed I can tell you where that establishment is, lovely lady, since I patronize it myself.'

He was a grotesque scarecrow with broken boots, ragged pantaloons and an ancient coat with no shirt or undervest beneath it to cover his scrawny sunken chest. Yet his bloodshot eyes were gentle as he studied Tildy. 'I pray you do not be afraid of the Silver Square, my dear young lady. Rough and uncouth it may be, but no one will harm you here. There is Mother Readman's house, over there, and it is a veritable palace I do assure you, patronized by a most select and accomplished clientele.'

'Sit down, you bloody old fool, and leave the wench be,' a woman jeered from a window.

'Many thanks to you,' Tildy told the man, and picked her way among the refuse towards the tall ramshackle building that she now saw carried a sign above its decrepit entrance.

'Beds Twopence. Bench One Penny.'

'A room you wants, is it? A whole room to yourself?' The

gigantically fat, scarred-faced harridan who went by the sobriquet of 'Mother Readman' almost filled the doorway with her bulk.

'Yes, I want a room for me and my child,' Tildy told her. Despite the fearsome appearance of the proprietress Tildy felt no fear of her. The small eyes almost buried in puffs of fat held no viciousness, although they were hard and shrewd as they examined the young woman standing on the doorstep.

'You doon't look to be a whore, girl?' It was more statement than question.

'I'm no whore!' Tildy exclaimed indignantly. 'My baby was born in wedlock, and I don't sport with men.'

The pendulous cheeks quivered and the woman's brown teeth bared in laughter. 'All right, my wench, no need to bite me yed off.' Her tone was placatory. 'But you must know that most o' the younger women who comes to me seeking a room to themselves be "tails", and it's their customers and fancy men who pays the rent for 'um.'

'There'll be no man paying my rent,' Tildy stated firmly, 'and I've money enough of my own to be going on with.' She became uncomfortably aware of the small crowd gathered to listen to their conversation and asked with a touch of impatience, 'Well, Mrs Readman, do you have a room for me, or not?'

The vast tallowy face was still grinning. 'Ohh aye, my wench, I've got a room that might do for you, but it'll cost three shillin's the week, and that paid in advance.' She jerked her several chins back over her shoulder. 'Come on in and take a look at it.'

Puffing and wheezing, Mother Readman clambered laboriously up the rickety flights of stairs, and Tildy followed, trying to disregard the myriad stinks and curious eyes that materialized from every gloomy nook and cranny of the rambling building. At the very top of the house Mother Readman halted on the narrow landing to catch her breath, her massive, shapeless breasts wobbling as she panted.

'There's three rooms up here, wench. This 'un's yourn.'

She led Tildy to the rear room – a tiny boxed-off space beneath the gable end of the roof, its ceiling sloping so sharply on both sides that only in the centre of the room could the women stand upright. It was lighted by a small broken-paned window and the sole furnishing was a narrow plank-bed with a straw-filled palliasse and a single threadbare blanket.

Tildy looked about her and her heart grew heavy. Mother Readman noted her expression.

'Beggars can't be choosers, my wench,' she said gruffly. 'The roof doon't let no rain in like the hedges does, and that's a softer bed to lay on than dead leaves in a ditch. When you'se shoved a bit o' rag in the window to keep the draughts out, you and your babby 'ull be as snug as bugs in a rug.'

Tildy's shoulders and arms ached fiercely from the weight of baby and bundle, and her heart also ached as she stared at the squalid room. 'I need only stay until I find somewhere better,' she told herself. 'This need not be a permanent dwelling-place for me.'

'Well?' It was Mother Readman's turn to inject impatience into her voice. 'Does you want it or not, my wench? Iffen you does then let's be seeing the colour o' your rhino.' She held out a fleshy hand thick with ancient dirt.

From the small cloth bag tucked inside her bodice Tildy took out a silver florin and a shilling piece and gave them to the woman. Mother Readman grinned in satisfaction.

'You must provide your own candles, but you can cook in the kitchen when you've a mind to, my wench, theer's always a good fire theer, and the pump's out the back o' the house. The water tastes a bit sour, but it arn't killed anybody yet, not to my knowledge anyway.' She turned to leave, then paused and pointed at the child. 'Iffen you wants to leave the babby any time then I knows a woman as farms 'um for a tanner a day. They gets fed for that as well.'

Tildy's doubt showed instantly in her face and Mother Readman cackled with laughter.

'Be you one o' them mothers who dotes on her darling

18

child, my wench, and can't abear to be parted from it? Well, when you'se birthed and buried as many o' the little buggers as I 'as you'll get over that nonsense, you see if you wun't.'

With that she left, and Tildy slumped thankfully on to the musty smelling mattress and laid down her burdens. Despondency threatened to flood over her, but she fought it back.

'I'll only be here for a few days,' she told herself determinedly, 'just until I get work arranged and find somewhere nice for me and Davy to live.'

She stared fondly at her child still soundly sleeping. That morning before leaving the poorhouse she had given him a dose of the soothing mixture called 'Godfrey's Cordial' – a mixture of sassafras, treacle and laudanum universally used by mothers to keep their infants quiet. Tildy was uncertain about the cordial, not liking the deeply comatose state that it created in children, but since all the women of her acquaintance swore by its efficacy she tried to dismiss her misgivings as groundless. Now, satisfied that the baby would remain asleep for some considerable time Tildy decided to leave him here and go to shop for food and drink for them both.

'I'll need candles also, and some pots and pans.'

Carefully she arranged her child's limp arms and legs so that he lay comfortably, and with a fond kiss on his smooth brow, left him. From the lower landing came the sounds of voices arguing and as Tildy rounded the sharp angle of the staircase she saw Mother Readman standing on the landing with two sombre-coated men, both wearing low-crowned top hats. At sight of Tildy all three fell silent, the two men staring at her with expressions of mingled suspicion and hostility.

'Who be this then?' the elder man, tall, spare-framed and hard-featured demanded to know, and as he spoke moved to block Tildy's way.

'Her's a newcomer,' Mother Readman hastened to explain. 'Her's rented one o' me attics for herself and her babby.'

'What's your name, girl?' the man questioned harshly.

Tildy was forced to halt. Puzzled by his attitude and made nervous by his aggression, she answered softly, 'If it please you, my name is Matilda Crawford.'

His cold stare moved up and down her body then locked on to her eyes.

'Did you hear aught o' what we was saying, girl?'

Tildy shook her head. 'No, I did not.'

'Does you know who I be, girl?'

Again Tildy shook her head. 'No.'

'Be you sure you heard naught?'

Stung by his hectoring she told him impatiently, 'I've said already that I've heard nothing . . . now, will you let me pass?'

Anger sparked in the cold eyes before her. 'Don't take that tone wi' me, girl, or you'll bloody soon have cause to wish you hadn't.'

'Leave the wench be, Jonas,' the thick-set and tough-looking younger man interrupted. ''Tis time we were going.' He reached out and gripped the older man's shoulder.

The older man jerked free of the restraining hand and without taking his eyes from Tildy's told her warningly,

'Remember girl, whilst I'm about it's best for people to be like the Three Wise Monkeys. Does you get my meaning?'

Wordlessly Tildy nodded, and apparently satisfied, the man swung on his heels and went stamping down the next flight of stairs followed by his companion. As the hollow echoes of their descent died away Mother Readman gusted a sigh of relief.

'Thank God that bugger believed you when you said you'd heard naught, Tildy.'

'But how could he not believe me when I spoke the truth?' Tildy answered forcefully. 'All I heard was your voices, but I couldn't make out any words. Who are those men, anyway?'

'That's Jonas Crowther and the young un's his son-in-

20

law, Ben Fairfax. Crowther's an evil sod. The whole bloody district goes in fear of the bugger. Him and his bloody gang. ''The Rippling Boys'' is what they'm known as round here. There's no devilment the buggers arn't capable of. If there was any justice in this world then Crowther would ha' bin hung years since – ahr, and his bloody bully-boys wi' him as well.'

'If he's so bad, why haven't the constables put him in jail?' Tildy wanted to know.

'Because the bastards be fritted of him, that's what I reckons anyhow.' Mother Readman's jowls shook as she waggled her head. 'I'll tell you summat, Tildy. I'll toe the line wi' any man or woman, and take my lumps without skrawkin', but Jonas Crowther puts the fear o' Christ up me, so he does. I reckon that the bastard is in league wi' Old Nick hisself, and that's the truth on it.'

Tildy fought to suppress a smile, but the other woman was shrewd enough to recognize the effect her words had had on her companion.

'Ohh yes, my wench, you may well laugh and think me a silly bugger for saying such, but mark my words, there might well come a day when you smiles on the other side o' your face . . . Anyway, let's forget about that evil sod now, shall us? Come on down wi' me, and I'll show you wheer the kitchen and pump be.'

Mother Readman waddled heavily down the next flight of stairs, the wooden boarding creaking loudly beneath her weight, and Tildy dutifully followed after her, her thoughts busy with what she had been told.

The kitchen was a large gloomy room, the low-beamed ceiling smoke-blackened, its walls greased by countless transient bodies, and its very fabric impregnated with the smells of those bodies and the odours of stale cooking. Rough-made wooden benches lined the walls and a great ancient wooden table, its surface thick with the dirt and stains of constant use dominated the centre of the room. Built into one wall was a huge ingle-nook hearth on which a fire now blazed, its flames creating an atmosphere of over-heated, eye-watering fug. A great iron cauldron hung from a chain above the fire and from the bubbling mess it held came the steamy stench of tainted meats.

Mother Readman noted the direction of Tildy's gaze and cackled with raucous laughter. 'That's me old stewpot, girl. Penny a dish I charges, and it's rich ateing I'll tell you. Iffen youm hungered I'll gi' you a bowl for free, seeing as how you'se rented a whole room to yourself.'

Hungry though she was the thought of tasting the rancid mess caused Tildy a distinct sensation of queasiness, so smiling she politely declined the offer.

The fat woman led her to the outer door and opened it to disclose a small rubbish-strewn yard surrounded by tall, crumbling brick walls. A long-handled water-pump leaned drunkenly in the centre of the yard. In one of the opposite corners of the walls reeked a huge sodden midden-heap, in the other corner a broken-doored privy reeked equally strongly.

'There arn't a brew-house, Tildy, no wash-copper neither. There used to be one wheer the midden-heap is now, only it fell down years since,' Mother Readman explained. 'I gives out all me washing to Widow Miles up the Back Hill theer. She's chape and honest enough. You'll need to do the same.' Her pendulous cheeks and jowls quivered as she cackled raucously, 'Mind you, you'll be one o' the rarer sorts iffen you does send out washing. Most o' my lodgers arn't washed hide nor hair sin they was birthed, I reckon.'

Tildy nodded. 'I can well believe that, Missus Readman.'

There was no sarcasm contained in her words. In Tildy's world the poor were dirty in body and habits. The poor stank. That was the reality she had lived with and accepted all her life, just as she had accepted that she was of a small minority in struggling to maintain high standards of hygiene, ignoring the gibes and insults she garnered by doing so from those of her fellows who considered that she was putting on airs, and trying to ape the manners of the superior classes.

From inside the kitchen came a gin-hoarse voice.

'Mistress Readman, will you be good enough to serve me with a bowl of your admirable pottage?'

It was the haggard-featured, grotesque human scarecrow who had accosted Tildy in the Silver Square. Now he faced them and removing his hat again essayed a courtly bow towards Tildy.

'So, we meet again, Ma'am, and may I say that for my own part it is a most pleasing encounter.'

Tildy could not help but smile at his droll manner. Mother Readman was not so easily amused.

'My stew youm wanting, is it, you scrounging bastard?' she growled. 'You owes me for ten nights on the bench and ten bowls o' vittles already, so let's be seeing some o' what you owes me, my bucko.'

The half-drunk man struck a theatrically haughty pose and his haggard features assumed an exaggerated expression of scornful contempt.

'Merciful Heavens, hark to the woman!' He rolled his eyes skywards, then glared at the landlady. 'Mistress Readman, must you forever badger me about a few paltry pence of reckonings? Have I not told you repeatedly that I have expectations? Have I not told you that as soon as the next company of Thespians arrive in this district then I shall be playing some of the most important roles of my entire career? My star will shortly be in the ascendant, my good woman. I am a great artiste, a great actor. Soon I shall be recognized as such and shall receive my rightful dues.'

Mother Readman was unimpressed. 'Well, until that day comes, Cully, you needs must pull your belt in tighter because you'll get no more vittles nor shelter in my house until you pays your reckonings wi' me. So gerron out o' my house, you useless drunken bugger, afore I takes me fists to you.'

The haughty posture disappeared instantly to be replaced with supplication. 'Mistress Readman, I'm nigh on starving. All I ask is a bowl of stew. I swear upon my honour as a gentleman that soon I shall be in a position to pay you all that I owe. My good woman, remember what the Swan of Avon, great William himself said, "Sweet mercy is nobility's true badge" - *Titus Andronicus,* Act one, Scene two - I scored a veritable triumph in Norwich in that play, my dear,' he informed Tildy with a satisfied preening, and she could not restrain a giggle at his posturing.

'I'se heard enough o' your nonsense. Gerron out of here this minute.' Mother Readman advanced upon him, clenched fists raised.

He waved his stick-like arm above his head. 'Do not offer me violence, woman,' he declaimed. 'Remember, "The smallest worm will turn being trodden on" - *King Henry the Sixth, Part Three,* Act one, Scene two.'

She aimed a blow at his head, and he ducked and shouted,

'A horse! A horse! My kingdom for a horse!' Then he turned and scurried along the passage to the street shouting as he went, '*King Richard the Third*, Act five, Scene Four.'

Tildy's giggles became unrestrained laughter, and when Mother Readman turned her own raucous cackling burst out.

'He's a saucy bugger, arn't he? Marmaduke Montmorency he calls hisself. He come to Redditch wi' Fentons Players, and fell in love wi' a local girl, so he stayed on, but the girl died and he took to the drink. Leastways, that's how the story goes.' She sobered and sniffed loudly. 'Takes a bit o' believing, but I suppose it could have happened so.'

Tildy, remembering the gentleness in his eyes thought silently that it really could have happened, but made no comment.

'Does you fancy a drop o' tay?' Mother Readman asked. 'I always has a sup on it about this time o' day.'

Without waiting for a reply the woman bustled about the kitchen, and soon she and Tildy were sitting before the hearth sipping from bowls of the fragrant dark liquid. Tildy found herself enjoying this unlooked for hospitality and relaxing in the warmth.

Mother Readman's eyes, half-buried in their puffs of fat,

regarded the younger woman shrewdly. 'I'se placed you now, my wench,' she stated suddenly. 'Youm the poor'us woman as was brought down to Ivy House on the green theer to look arter Anna Coldericke – her that's gone to Devon now.'

'That's right, Missus Readman. I was brought from the poorhouse to look after her. In fact, I only left the Ivy House and went back into the poorhouse a couple of days since.'

'Did her pay you well for what you done for her? Seeing as how it was you stopped her house being burned down.'

Tildy nodded. 'Yes, she did. She gave me ten guineas. That's how I was able to get my ticket of release from the poorhouse.'

'Phewww!' Mother Readman vented an impressed gust. 'Ten guineas! That's a tidy sun, that is. You can live on that for a good few weeks iffen youm careful. Mind you, be careful that you don't spread the news that you'se got such a sum wi' you. It's all right telling me, because I'm a straight living 'ooman, and close-mouthed wi' it. But some o' the bastards who comes through this house 'ud cut your throat for ten guineas – cut it for ten bloody shillings, come to that.'

Tildy found herself both liking and trusting the older woman, and she smiled. 'I'll take care. There's no fear of me doing aught else, not with my baby to think on.'

'What be you planning on doing now then, Tildy? What sort o' work?'

'I thought of hiring myself out as a sick-nurse,' Tildy told her. 'I learned a bit about caring for the sick when I was in the poorhouse.'

The lips in the tallowy features opposite pursed doubt-fully. 'It might serve, girl, though you'd need regular work, and that from the gentry. Us ordinary people couldn't pay sufficient for you to live on doing that. We can't even afford to see the doctor. But a pretty cratur like you, surely you could easy find a man to look arter you and your babby? Wouldn't that be better than slaving your guts out and risking catching all manner o' things from them what's badly?'

'No!' Tildy's . vehement rejection caused Mother Readman to look at her in surprise. 'No! I want no man to care for me and my child. I'll take care of us both without any man's help.'

The older woman grinned knowingly. 'Had trouble wi' men afore has you, girl?'

'More than enough,' Tildy nodded. 'And I want no more of it.'

'Well, don't you moither about that, my duck.' The woman's pudgy hand reached out and patted Tildy's knees reassuringly. 'There'll be no man 'ull dare to pester you whiles youm under my roof.' The pudgy hands raised and clenched into fists. 'Iffen any of 'um tries it on wi' you, then you come and tell me, and I'll soon put 'um to the right about turn, fuck me blind if I wun't.'

Again Tildy experienced a surge of trust in the older woman, and she smiled her gratitude. 'I'll much appreciate that, Missus Readman. All I want is to be left in peace, and to do the best I can for my child.'

'You'll be all right here, my wench,' Mother Readman stated positively. 'I knows that the Silver Square has got a bad name in the town, and that this house has got a wuss 'un. But you'll be safe enough wi' me, and that's a fact.'

'I believe you, Missus Readman,' Tildy murmured quietly, and meant it. She finished her tea and rose. 'I must go and do my shopping. My thanks for your kindness.'

Mother Readman waved her hands in dismissal. 'Lissen, Tildy, I'se got pots and pans in plenty, so you can take what you needs to carry your milk and such.' She hesitated a moment, then added, 'And I arn't trying to meddle in your affairs, but iffen youm thinking o' working as sick-nurse to gentry, then youm agoing to need a character. They'll not take you into their houses wi'out one.' Her brown stubs of teeth bared as she chuckled ruefully, 'I'd gi' you a character meself, but coming from me it 'ud be a damnation in the eyes o' them stuck-up buggers. Does you know anybody suitable hereabouts as 'ud vouch for you?'

Tildy pondered a moment, then said slowly, 'Perhaps the parson will, Reverend Clayton. I met him when I cared for Mrs Coldericke and he spoke very kindly to me always.'

'That's the style; he'd do very well,' Mother Readman encouraged. 'You goo and get your necessaries now, and settle yourself and the babby. Then fust thing tomorrow morning, you goo and see him.'

Tildy nodded. 'Yes, I'll do that, Mrs Readman – first thing tomorrow morning . . .'

Chapter Three

Gusts of wind rattled the rotting, ill-fitted casement of the room, and rain drummed heavily upon the roof tiles above Tildy's head. Beside her, nestling in the crook of her arm on the narrow bed her child moved restlessly and whimpered in unquiet sleep.

The candle on the floor beside her cast a wavering glow, and Tildy lifted her head and glanced down to see how much remained of the stubby tallow stick. The extravagance of keeping a light through the night was forced upon her. Three times she had been woken by the biting of bed-bugs, and each time had been forced to rise and hunt down her tormentors by the wavering light of the candle, catching the small, flat mahogany-brown bodies between her nails to crush them, smelling the peculiar musky odour as their life-juices smeared upon her skin.

Now she lifted her fingers to her nose and grimaced as that odour penetrated her sleep-dulled senses.

'When I have my own home,' she promised herself, 'then all shall be clean and fresh within it. Sheets smelling of lavender and rosewater shall cover my bed, and never a flea, bed-bug or louse shall ever find a haven under my roof.'

Beneath her gentle face and manner Tildy Crawford possessed a tough inner core of courage and stubbornness which had enabled her to survive the harshness of her existence without deadening or coarsening her spirit. But she suffered from periodic attacks of self-doubt and inferiority, and one of those attacks now began to assail her as she lay gazing up at the shifting shadows.

'I'm so glib, telling everyone that I'm going to work as a sick-nurse.' Her dark eyes became troubled. 'But in all truth, what do I really know of nursing the sick, or of anything else, come to that? I'm an ignorant woman, born poor, lived poor, married poor, and shall die poor.' For some minutes despondency weighed down upon her, but then her stubborn spirit rallied. 'I nursed Anna Coldericke and the children and myself as well through the smallpox, did I not? And I nursed well in the poorhouse in the short time I was at the work. And I've taught myself to read and write, have I not . . . not easily, I admit, yet still I can scribe slowly, and read all but the very hardest words.' The despondency began to lift. 'There must be books which can tell me what I need to know about sickness and cures, and I've money enough to buy those books. After all, doctors have to learn from books, do they not, so why cannot I . . . '

With a lightened heart she gently drifted back into sleep, and the drumming of the rain became a soothing rhythm in her ears. 'I'll see the parson tomorrow. He'll help me,' was her last thought. 'He'll help . . . '

Chapter Four

'It is foul weather, Crawford, most unseasonable for the time of year, is it not? Come, warm yourself at the fire.' John Clayton, curate of St Stephen's Chapel, was a young man who possessed an attractively ugly face and an exceptionally fine physique, the muscles of his body bulging against the sombre clerical garb that he favoured.

Tildy gratefully did as he invited, and steam rose from her shawl and gown as the heat of the flames warmed the sodden woolstuffs.

From his chair beneath the rain-lashed window of the book-lined room the clergyman studied the pretty young woman at the fireside. His profession did not inhibit his appreciation of her slender, full-breasted body, and her dark hair dressed in a long thick glossy plait which curled gracefully to the front of her soft white throat.

'Now Crawford, how may I serve you?' he enquired in a kindly tone.

Encouraged by that kindness Tildy explained her reason for calling on him, and he heard her out in silence. When she had done, he steepled his forefingers in front of his chest and bent his head for long moments.

His delay in answering caused Tildy a tremor of anxiety and she kept her dark eyes fixed upon his white short-queued wig, willing him to make a favourable reply. He coughed to clear his throat, and the sudden sound in the silence of the room made Tildy start slightly.

'So, you wish me to stand as guarantor of your character, Crawford.' He looked up at her. 'But I know so little of you, young woman. You do not attend my chapel. How can I reconcile my conscience to give you a character, when for all I know, you may well be loose-living?'

Her heart sank, and to her chagrin she felt a flush spreading upwards from her throat. She coughed nervously and the flush reached her cheeks. When she began to speak the words came hesitantly, and inwardly she was angry at herself for that hesitance.

'Sir, I only ask you to recommend to the doctors hereabouts my work at the poorhouse as a sick-nurse, and my service to Mrs Coldericke when I nursed her.'

'Mrs Coldericke was something of an eccentric, Crawford, and looking after paupers cannot really be deemed a qualification for the nursing of gentlefolk,' he stated sternly. 'Besides, even if your previous service was such as to render you suitable for the type of employment you desire, gentlefolk prefer to be cared for by those well known to them, such as faithful servants or relatives. Nursing is not a profession, Crawford, after all. It is a task that any competent goodwife should be capable of fulfilling.'

Tildy's innate stubbornness burgeoned. 'With all respect, Sir, you and I both know well that good sick-nurses are not easy found.'

A suggestion of a smile quirked his lips. 'I can accept that there is some truth in that, Crawford.' Abruptly he went at a tangent. 'Why do you not seek other types of work. Domestic service perhaps? Or the soft-work at the needles?'

'I know naught of needle-making, Sir, and apart from that, people tell me that the trade is very slack at this time, and many needle workers are without employment. And as for domestic service, I have my child with me. People are not willing to take a woman with a small child into their house and service.'

He gestured impatiently and Tildy noted how clean and well-manicured his soft hands were.

'He's never had to work at a rough trade,' she thought with a touch of asperity.

'Your child need be no hindrance to your gaining domestic employment, Crawford. It can be farmed out. There are women in this parish who keep such establishments.'

Resentment at his casual dismissal of her beloved Davy flooded Tildy's mind. 'Baby-farmers have a bad name, Sir, and rightly so,' she affirmed forcefully. 'The children in their care sicken and die all too often.'

Her reply struck home, and the clergyman conceded her point.

'Regretfully there is some truth in what you say, Crawford. There have been instances of neglect by some women, but not all are of that nature, and there is most certainly a pressing need for those women who are conscientious in the discharge of their trust, if only to relieve the burden upon the poor rate and the poorhouse. But, we are straying from the point, are we not?' Again he steepled his forefingers and bent his head as if in deep thought.

This time the silence lasted so long, that Tildy moved restlessly, and Clayton looked up frowningly.

''Pon my soul, girl, if you cannot refrain from jumping about for even a brief period, how will you serve in a sick room where all must be still and peaceful?'

The realization that he would not aid her came to Tildy even as he spoke. Momentary despair was overlaid by a feeling of defiance. 'If he won't help me, then I'll manage without it,' she thought.

'I am greatly troubled by your request to me, Crawford. I am troubled by your motivation,' he told her pompously. 'I do not believe that your desire to aid the misfortunates of this world comes from a Christian sense of compassion and duty. Rather it springs from the sordid desire for mercenary gain. Therefore, I cannot in all conscience stand as a guarantor of your character. I would strongly advise you, young woman, to pray to the Lord for the strength to overcome that sin of greed which appears to dominate you so . . .'

As she heard his words Tildy's fiery spirit rebelled, and she could not hold back from a heated reply.

'You accuse me of greed? Because I wish to be paid for the work I do? You, who sit here well-fed and well-clothed, knowing nothing of what hunger and cold and hardship really mean. You, who grow rich prating of holiness from your pulpit to hypocrites who have no spark of human kindness in their bodies.' She became increasingly angry as her mind's eye pictured those devout worshippers from among whose ranks had come so many of her persecutors throughout her bleak life. 'Save your damn sermons for those who have need of them, Parson.'

Close to tears, she ran from the room, leaving Clayton staring after her with open-mouthed astonishment.

Hurrying up the Fish Hill, shawl-wrapped head bent against the stinging wind-blown rain, Tildy berated herself with a sinking heart.

'What a stupid fool I am. Why cannot I learn to hold my tongue before my betters? The parson will never ever aid me now after what I've just said to him. He'll give me a bad character to all and sundry. Of a surety he will. God's curse on my temper. I'd do well to bite my tongue off, so I would . . .'

The weather had driven people indoors and Silver Street was deserted as Tildy hurried along its sleazy length. From a darkly shadowed covered passageway in a row of cottages a hoarse voice called weakly.

'Help me, young woman! Please . . . help me!'

Tildy halted and saw the haggard features of Marmaduke Montmorency, peering at her from the covered passageway. He looked deathly pale, and his eyes glittered feverishly in deep bruised-black sockets. A racking bout of coughing shook his frame, doubling him over so that his hat fell from his long greasy hair to the floor of the passage. The coughs eased, and gasping for breath, eyes streaming, he begged,

'For the love of God, help me, young lady, I'm sorely ill.'

Faced with this pathetic, grotesque figure, Tildy felt pity

whelm over her. 'Come.' She held out her hands. 'Come with me.'

He stepped haltingly out from the passageway, his claw-like hands spreading against the streaming wet bricks to steady himself.

'Come. I'll help you.' Tildy put her arm around him and he sagged against her. The dank stench of his body and mouth filled her nostrils so that she physically flinched from its miasma. Forcing herself to disregard the fetid odours, she half-carried his skeletal form across the Silver Square and into the lodging house.

The kitchen was full of wretched-looking men, women and children: trampers, tinkers and the homeless flotsam of the town. The air was steamy and thick with the smells of toasting bloaters and cheese mingling with the ever-present bubblings of the huge stewpot. A noisy hubbub of argument, laughter, song and talk was a counterpoint to the lip-smacking, sucking and slurping of eating and drinking as people filled their bellies with whatever they could find to satisfy their hungers.

No one paid any attention to the newcomers – no one except for Mother Readman, enthroned before the wide blazing hearth in a massive battered chair, like some beggar queen surrounded by her ragged courtiers. Her slitted eyes fixed upon Marmaduke Montmorency.

'Out, you scrounging bastard!' she bellowed, and the hubbub miraculously hushed as if a queen had spoken. 'Out! Afore I pitches you out on your fuckin' neck!'

Tildy ignored the shouts and the staring eyes and gently eased the sick man on to a wallside bench, then went to Mother Readman.

'Please, can he stay, Mrs Readman? I'll pay his dues,' she asked quietly.

The slitted eyes were speculative. 'And what about the money he already owes me?'

Tildy hesitated for only a moment. 'I'll pay that as well, only please let him stay. The poor man is sick. He needs food and warm shelter.'

The huge fat shoulders rose in a dismissive shrug. 'Iffen

34

you wants to throw good money away on rubbish, then that's your business, girl. He can stay.' One fat hand appeared from the multi-layered swathes of clothing that covered the massive amorphous body. 'But I takes the rhino in advance.'

Tildy reached within her bodice for the small bag that nestled between her full firm breasts. Without disclosing the bag she extracted a golden guinea and placed it upon the grubby, sweaty outstretched palm. The fingers snapped shut like a trap on the coin.

'I arn't got the change to gi' you now,' the fat woman said.

'No matter. I trust you for the change when you have it.' Tildy smiled, happy to have ensured that the sick man had shelter. She turned about to look at him, only to see the eyes roll upwards in his head as he tumbled from the bench to sprawl face downwards on the floor. She pushed through to him and knelt by his side. Her hands trembled as she pulled him on to his back, dreading what she might see. His lips were livid, his deathly white face tinged with a greenish hue. The breath rasped in his throat and she could see the pounding of his heart against the stick-walled ribs of his naked chest. She stared down into his glassy open eyes and a sensation of utter helplessness overcame her.

'What can I do?' she thought desperately. 'What's wrong with him? What can I do?'

'Clear out o' the way, let the dog see the bloody rabbit.' Panting wheezily Mother Readman waddled to Tildy's side. Tildy stared beseechingly up at the great tallowy face, and the old woman chuckled breathlessly.

'Don't fret yoursen, my wench, the bugger's only having one of his turns. Push him back on to his face; he'll swallow his bleedin' tongue else.'

Tildy did as she was bid and Mother Readman went on.

'Does you want to rent a room for him?'

Tildy nodded.

'All right then.' The fat woman issued orders, and some of the men lifted the limp body and shuffled out with it. Tildy would have followed, but Mother Readman held her back.

'Leave it now, girl. They knows how to lay the bugger down. He's thrown more turns than I'se ate hot dinners. He'll lie for an hour or more afore he comes to his senses. You can do your Lady Bountiful piece then. I'se told 'um to put him in the room next to yourn. You can keep your eye on him easier there.'

'Many thanks.' Tildy was touched by such thoughtfulness, but the fat harridan quickly dispelled any illusions that the girl might have.

'As long as youm willing to pay, then he can stay there, girl. But the very minute his rent is owing, then out the bugger goes. It arn't a charity ward I'se got here, you know, it's my bread and butter.'

'I know that Mrs Readman and I'm not asking for charity. I'll pay.' Tildy spoke quietly but firmly, and the other woman's manner softened.

'Listen to me, Tildy Crawford. The money you'se got might seem a small fortune, but believe me it wun't last long iffen youm agoing to throw it away on every pitiful cratur that comes to your ken here in the Silver Square. Times be cruel hard, girl, and you must learn to look for yourself, fust, second and always. You'se got to harden your heart and close your eyes to other folks' sufferings. Iffen you don't, then you'll be pulled down into the gutter wi' 'um. And mark my words, there's precious few in this world who'll reach their hand down into that gutter to pull you out on it.'

Tildy recognized that the woman meant well in advising her so. 'I know you're right, Mrs Readman, and that you tell me only what is best for me, but I just can't stand and do nothing when for a few pence only I can help some poor soul who's in such sore need.'

Irritation hardened in the puffed, slit eyes. 'A few pence only, is it? Let me tell you, girl, a few pence here and a few pence there can soon amount to a good few guineas.' The hanging jowls quivered in a disgusted rejection. 'Well, I'se told you, and iffen you wun't listen, then be it on your own yed.'

Ponderously she waddled back to the fireside and

wheezily settled her vast body back on to the creaking chair.

Tildy went upstairs to her attic, but first peeped into the room where Marmaduke Montmorency had been placed. He was chest down on the narrow bed, face turned sideways. Again pity whelmed over Tildy as she saw the corpse-like, skeletal features with saliva trickling down the slack jaws from the gaping mouth.

'You poor benighted soul,' she murmured, and turned into her own room. As she pushed the door ajar she called softly. 'Davy, your Mammy's back, honey.'

The child lay peacefully, only the gentle rise and fall of his chest showing that he lived, and Tildy leaned over the pillow, anxiety tugging at her heart as she saw how pale the small delicate face appeared.

'Davy?' She spoke urgently. 'Davy, what ails you?' His skin was chill and moist to the touch. 'Davy? Wake up!'

The blue eyes opened and drowsily focused on her, then the perfectly shaped lips curved in a smile, disclosing tiny white teeth, and she sighed shakily with relief.

'Oh Davy, Davy.' She crooned his name over and over again and rocked him gently in her arms. 'You frightened me, you naughty boy. You frightened me, lying so still and cold.'

The rain drummed on the tiles and wind rattled the casement. She hugged the child closer, enveloping him with the warmth of her body. 'This room is too cold and damp, honey. I'll needs get us a better place to live in.' Waves of love brought a choking thickness to her throat, and she covered the small face with soft lingering kisses. 'Don't die and leave me all alone, Davy,' she whispered fervently. 'Grow strong and tall, never die and leave me . . .'

Chapter Five

Doctor Charles Taylor, physician and surgeon, prided himself on his lavish table, and now, replete to bursting, he sat with a straining waistband and surveyed the ravaged remains of salt-fish, boiled leg of mutton with capers, roasted loin of beef, cold ham and chicken, plum puddings, apple tarts, cherry pies, almonds and raisins, and the honour guard of empty claret and port wine bottles, and belched contentedly.

His guests, likewise replete, sprawled upon their chairs around the dark-polished oaken table, their faces sweat-glistening and rubicund in the light of the wax candles.

'Thomas, bring in the punch,' the old man instructed his manservant, and scant moments later the great silver bowl steaming with the aromas of rum, brandy, oranges, cloves and lemons was placed in front of him. Silver cups were ladled full of the hot drink, long-stemmed clay pipes and tobacco were distributed, and for a time the only sounds were of lips sucking pipe-stems and punch.

His powdered head wreathed by strong-smelling smoke, Charles Taylor watched his guests – all men, for the doctor did not enjoy the company of women, unlike his son, Hugh, whom critics had been heard to describe as 'all stays, scents and whiskers'. His son was seated facing him at the bottom end of the long table. Six other men were ranged, three at each side, between the pair. Charles Taylor addressed one of them, the Reverend John Clayton.

38

'This foul weather will play the very devil with the harvest, John. I fear Lord Aston's tithe barn will have much empty space in it this year.'

John Clayton sipped his aromatic punch appreciatively, then smiled. 'I think your fear will be justified, Sir, but I must confess that as a humble curate who receives no tithes, I cannot find it in my heart to worry unduly about the contents of the vicar's barn. Whether it be full or half-full my purse remains lean.'

A ripple of laughter ran around the table. Reverend the Lord Aston, Vicar of Tardebigge Parish, was notorious for the meagre stipends he allowed his curates, of whom John Clayton was one.

William Bellamy, attorney at law, a small, pouter-chested pigeon of a man, giggled drunkenly. 'How can it matter whether the barn be full or empty, Reverend Clayton? You know well the old saying, ''Poor harvest in the field, rich harvest in the burial yard''. My Lord Aston gleans rich pickings whatever the weather.'

John Clayton's smile faltered. 'I'm quite sure that the hardships a poor harvest brings in its train gives no pleasure to Lord Aston. He is a most humane gentleman.'

A spiteful gleam came into Bellamy's eyes. 'Oh, indeed he is a most humane gentleman. Does he not recommend constantly a good plain diet for the parish poor?'

The smile on John Clayton's lips had now disappeared completely. 'What exactly are you implying, Mr Bellamy?'

The plump little man's head bobbed excitedly and the spite now entered his voice. 'Why to be sure, Reverend Clayton, I thought my indication was perfectly clear. 'Tis well known that our benevolent vicar believes that a dinner of plain bread and water topped off with a fine sermon is a most wholesome diet for the poor; far more good for their souls than meat and ale.'

Before John Clayton could reply another man intervened. His bluff weather-beaten face and heavy broadcloth coat and breeches were the badges of his trade of farmer.

'Goddam the bloody tithes, say I,' he growled, the drink

39

he had taken causing him to slur his words. "'Tis bloody robbery, so it is. Plain and simple daylight robbery, and iffen I had my way . . .'

'Come now, Master Horton,' Hugh Taylor interrupted him, 'and you other gentlemen also. Are we not all good friends and boon companions here? I beseech you, do not let us have high words at my father's birthday dinner.'

The younger Taylor was a remarkably handsome man, tall and strongly built with silky blond hair and side-whiskers, fresh complexioned and blue-eyed. His clothing was ultra-fashionable, his gilt-buttoned blue dress coat puffed and padded at shoulders and chest, his starched white cravat rising almost to his earlobes, his waistcoat and undervest a gaudy rainbow, his pink knee-breeches and white stockings skin-tight, and his body exuding a heavy fragrance of expensive perfumes.

John Clayton bent his close-cropped, unpowdered head. 'My apologies, gentlemen.'

And William Bellamy lifted his cup of punch. 'I drink to your health, Reverend Clayton, and to Reverend the Lord Aston.'

John Clayton acknowledged the toast by lifting his own cup and the two antagonists drank, while the table applauded them.

The elderly William Field, needle master, factor and merchant trader, held up his cup and the manservant hastened to refill it. Field took a deep drink then smacking his lips with satisfaction observed, 'That's a bit o' good, that is, and talking about tithes, Master Horton, it arn't only you farmers as suffers, you know. This bad weather might be affecting your harvests, but it's hard times for the needle trade as well. Me sales be only half what they was this time last year, and not a quarter o' what they rose to in the war. These days I can hardly keep me mill working, and me outworkers be moaning summat cruel because I arn't got no work for them at all.'

The talk became general.

'I see the vestry must needs levy another poor rate this month.'

'Ahrr, and the last 'un levied not two weeks since, and that was a stiff 'un, warn't it?'

'It arn't only the idle who be on relief these days. There's good steady men claiming it as well.'

More than half of the men present were needle masters - self-made men for the most part, and like their product, tough and sharp. If men like these were hard put to survive, then times were most certainly hard.

John Clayton remained silent, toying with the silver cup he held in his strong fingers. Turning it to catch and reflect the pale golden flames of the candles. His thoughts turned to the pretty young woman who had called on him that day, and when Hugh Taylor bantered,

'Now John, what's amiss? Are you thinking of a lost love?'

Clayton smiled, and shook his head. 'No Hugh, not of a lost love, but I was thinking of a woman . . . ' He went on to relate the story of Matilda Crawford's visit and its ending. 'And dammee, if she didn't near bite my head off and run from the house. Times may be hard for the lower orders, but that has had no effect on their impertinence, or their impudence. I fear that will never be cured or curbed.'

Hugh Taylor was intrigued by the clergyman's account of the young woman's unusual ambitions to become a sick-nurse. He acted as his father's assistant, and it was largely due to his considerable charm and business acuity that their practice flourished in the district. He was a 'country doctor', which meant that instead of studying for his profession in a university teaching faculty, he had served an apprenticeship to his father for several years, then spent one year practising anatomy, dissection and physiology at a London infirmary, and a further year walking the wards of that hospital.

'This young woman, John - it's unusual for young 'uns to want to be sick-nurses - is she any good for the work?'

'Why yes, I should say that she probably is so.' The cleric was trying to be fair. 'Although in all honesty she lacks long experience of the work, at least that is what she told me. But she is a deal too forward and independent in

41

her manners, Hugh. It don't do for a pauper-woman to be so impudent to those whom the Lord has placed in higher stations in life.'

'Would you say that she is intelligent?' Hugh Taylor pursued his line of thought.

John Clayton pondered for a moment. 'I should say that she is. Intelligent in comparison with other women of her class, at least. Doctor Pratt's scapegrace nephew, Lucas Royston, was quite taken with her quickness to learn, as I recall.' He grinned suddenly. 'But why all these questions, Hugh? Are you thinking of employing her yourself?'

The young medical man returned the grin. 'It's a thought, John . . . but I doubt that I will. Our old pauper goodwives come cheap and docile enough to suit us. We've no need for young women who are forward and independent in their manners.'

Chapter Six

Charles Burke Bromley was first and foremost a dreamer. He was also a printer, stationer, bookseller, druggist, medicine vendor, bookbinder, grocer, music-seller and dealer in sundries. His shop in the New End, which was the bottom of the Front Hill rising from the southern end of the town centre plateau, resembled an Aladdin's cave of goods pertaining to his many and varied business interests, all jumbled together in what appeared to be a hopeless confusion. Yet he was unerring in his ability to immediately seize upon anything that his customers might ask for from among the confusion.

A tall, slender, weak-bodied man invariably swathed from chin to ankles in a long white apron, his threadbare, rusty-black clothing, broken-soled boots and frayed linen was a mute testimony to his perennial poverty. For despite his many accomplishments, high intelligence and variety of business lines, Charles Burke Bromley was too given to day-dreaming to be a successful merchant.

His thin face was badly pitted with the blue scars of childhood smallpox and, although only thirty years of age, he had already lost most of his hair, the few oiled strands brushed across his shiny pink scalp only serving to emphasize that loss.

Blinking his watery, red-rimmed eyes he fumbled for his thick-lensed spectacles and placed them on his long thin nose. He then smiled, displaying his only physical asset, his perfectly proportioned white teeth.

'Yes miss, can I help you?' His voice was high-pitched and squeaky.

Tildy, struck by the incongruous perfection of those white even teeth in such a woefully plain face, smiled back, and her earlier diffidence about entering the shop on such an errand left her. 'If you please, I wish to buy a book.'

'Yes, I have books here,' he told her encouragingly, and his gentle heart began to quicken its beating as he saw her beauty. 'What sort of book do you wish for, Ma'am? A novel, perhaps, or a book of poetry?'

Tildy hesitated, and looked helplessly around her at the jumbled interior, and her nostrils filled with the confusion of smells that came from onions and inks, cabbages and paper, spices, potatoes, ointments, leathers and a myriad other items. She grimaced and spread out her hands. 'I'm not exactly sure what sort of book I want.'

'Oh!' His watery eyes, hugely magnified by the spectacle lenses, gazed blankly at her, and then blinked rapidly once, twice, three times, four times as his always drifting thoughts clarified. 'If you could explain what it is you need the book for, Ma'am, I could then possibly advise you on a suitable work.'

Tildy smiled gratefully. 'Yes. Yes, that's it . . . Well, I want a book that will help me to care for sick people.'

'To care for sick people,' Bromley repeated vaguely. Already his fertile imagination was constructing romantic dreams centred on glossy dark hair, oval features, and large soft limpid eyes.

'Yes, that's it,' Tildy nodded, thankful for his apparent understanding of her needs. 'I need a book that will tell me all about sick people.'

She waited for the shopkeeper to move, but he only remained standing gazing at her, his face a dreamy blankness. After a while puzzlement caused her to enquire, 'Do you have such a book, Sir?'

He made no reply, only remained in his dreamlike daze, and Tildy wondered, 'Is the man a natural? A simpleton?'

44

A touch of apprehension entered her head. 'If he's a loony, perhaps he's dangerous.' This disquieting thought caused her to ask sharply. 'Your pardon, Sir, but have you understood me?'

Her voice punctured the dream bubble that enclosed Charles Burke Bromley, and abruptly he returned to reality, reddening with embarrassment.

'Yes, I have such a book,' he flustered. 'In fact, I have several such books. A moment, if you please, Ma'am.'

With unerring accuracy he swooped on to several volumes, plucking them from under cabbages, behind glass bottles, beneath reams of paper, from shelves of stone jars and even nestling within the strings of a battered old fiddle. Now fully roused, he was eager to help this delightful girl.

'May I enquire, Ma'am, if you wish to nurse a sick relative or friend?'

'Well no, I have only my child for family, and he is quite healthy at present, I thank you,' she told him artlessly. 'But I intend to work as a sick-nurse, and I've a great interest for knowing the appearance of different diseases and the way they must be treated.'

He gravely considered this information, then his beautiful teeth gleamed happily. 'I fully understand Ma'am, indeed a most laudable ambition, if I might say so, and I venture to affirm that I have the very books for you.' With a flourish he selected three of the volumes and casually pitched the rejected ones back amongst the jumble. Pointing at two of the selected books he explained, 'These comprise the "Complete English Dispensatory" in two parts, theoretic and practical, compiled by John Quincy MD. Within them are the descriptions of every medicinal ingredient and compound known to science, together with the methods of extracting, distilling, mixing and administering those ingredients and compounds. A truly monumental work, and here,' he pointed to the third book, 'here we have the "Domestic Medicine" of William Buchan MD.'

'But I've heard of him,' Tildy uttered, surprised and pleased.

'Have you indeed, Ma'am?' Charles Burke Bromley beamed delightedly. 'Then of course you will already know what a profound and worthy gentleman William Buchan was.' He opened the book and peered shortsightedly at the lettering. 'This is a treatise on the prevention and care of diseases by regimen and simple medicines. It also contains observations on the comparative advantages of vaccine innoculation, with instructions for performing that operation . . . '

'I've had that operation performed on me and my baby,' Tildy could not help interjecting.

'Have you, by God!' he exclaimed admiringly, and his excitement increased as he went on. 'Oh, and look here, Ma'am, it says here that it contains an essay enabling ruptured persons to manage themselves, and a family herbal . . . plus to which are added . . . ' His voice grew even squeakier as his excitement went on increasing. ' . . . such useful discoveries in medicine and surgery as have transpired since the demise of the author!'

The thin face wore an expression of triumph and the watery eyes blinked so rapidly that they became a blur of movement behind the thick lenses. 'They are the very thing, Ma'am. The very thing for your purpose. There is no doubt on it. No doubt at all.' He laid the book down on the cluttered counter. 'Well Ma'am, do they suit?'

Tildy nodded. 'Yes, and I shall need a dictionary also.'

Beaming with happiness the bookseller swooped on yet another dusty volume. 'Here's one, Ma'am, Morgan's ''Dictionary for Scholars''.'

Carefully he parcelled the four volumes in brown paper.

'If you please, Sir, how much do they cost?' Tildy was tremulous with excitement at the thought of owning such magnificent books, the first she had ever owned in her life.

'The dictionary is fifteen shillings, the dispensatory is two guineas, and for Buchan I'll charge only sixteen shillings. It should be nineteen shillings and sixpence, but since you are buying four books I shall forgo my profit on Buchan. So that makes three pounds and thirteen shillings in total. A sound investment, Ma'am, very sound indeed.'

Tildy swallowed hard. Three pounds, thirteen shillings! An immense sum. She thrust the immensity of it from her mind. 'I've sufficient money to afford the books,' she told herself defiantly, 'and even more books if I should wish them.'

For the first time in her life the joyful recklessness of spending golden guineas seized her, and with barely restrained impatience she extracted four gold coins from the bag between her breasts and laid them on the counter. She snatched up the change and the neat brown parcel, and with a word of thanks hurried from the shop, leaving Charles Burke Bromley staring wistfully after her, saddened by the abrupt disappearance of this beautiful girl from his life. He sighed, and leaning against his counter gave himself up once more to his dreams.

The day was warm and sunny as if the weather wished to make amends for its previous surly outpourings. Making her way along the noisome alley towards the Silver Square, Tildy cradled her precious new possessions as if fearful that the lounging roughs she passed would snatch them from her hands. Suddenly a desire for clean air and the sights and scents of woods and meadows overcame her.

'I'll take Davy with me,' she decided. 'We'll enjoy a holiday.'

The mental conditioning of long years of servitude to toil caused a stirring of guilt. 'But really speaking I should be searching for work, not going gallivanting around the meadows.' Her hand unconsciously moved to her breasts and her fingers touched the small pouch beneath her bodice. 'Damn it! I've still lots of money left. It's too nice a day to spend going cap in hand for work. A walk in the meadows with Davy will do us both a power of good.' Rebelliously she battled and overcame her sense of guilt. 'We've been stuck among these filthy hovels for days; we need a breath of fresh air.'

Her mind made up, she smiled happily and ran into the lodging house.

Chapter Seven

The stream from which Redditch took its name rose from its springs in the Lickey Hills some miles north-west of the town. It followed a winding course through the wide estates of the Earl of Plymouth, feeding that noble gentleman's ornamental lakes in the grounds of his mansion, Hewell Grange, then flowed eastwards, northwards and eastwards yet again through the low ground skirting the spurs of the hills. On its final eastwardly thrust it powered the machinery of needle mills standing on its banks on the northernmost edges of Redditch town, then joined its waters with the Arrow River and flowed southwards to meet the mighty River Avon in the fertile Vale of Evesham.

Pigeon Bridge straddled the stream half a mile from the bottom of the Fish Hill and served as the northern boundary marker for Redditch. With Davy in her arms Tildy crossed its shallow hump and turned east along the narrow road which parallelled the stream for some distance before curving back on itself to head west through Alvechurch village and finally north to the city of Birmingham, some fifteen miles away.

Ancient cottages studded the stream's banks, and to Tildy's left the green meadowland, covered with grazing sheep and cattle, was ribbed with the medieval strip-cultivation of the town's forefathers. Ahead of her lay the mysterious humps and mounds and hollows of the Abbey Meadows, where once the mighty Cistercian abbey of

48

Bordesley had raised its towers to the glory of God. Strange tales were told of these grass-covered ruins – tales of secret subterranean passages, of buried treasures, of goblins, ghosts and ghouls – and people were loathe to cross this ground when the nights were dark and stormy and the clouds scudded across the face of the moon to cast eerily writhing shadows over the tombstones of the ancient burial ground surrounded by sombre black-green yew trees.

The fish-ponds of the monks still existed and fat carp still swam in their dark, rush-shrouded depths. Tildy, tired from the weight of her baby, sank down at a point where the stream entered the ponds. She unwrapped the happily-gurgling child's swaddlings and changed his clout for a clean one she had brought with her. She then washed the soiled clout in the pool and spread it out on the grass to dry. With cupped hands she gave her baby clear stream water to drink, then drank deeply of it herself, and laved her head and arms, delighting in the cold freshness of the water against her hot skin.

Some distance from her the close-set twin buildings of the old forge needle mill reared their high bulks and the soft breeze carried to her ears the deep-pitched rumblings of the great iron water-wheel trundling upon its mighty axle between the buildings, powering their myriads of cogs, cranks and pulleys, and setting spinning the grindstones of the pointers. A slight frown creased the smooth skin between Tildy's brows at the thought of the needle pointers; they were a breed apart from normal men, dry grinding the points of needles, and with every breath they drew destroying themselves. The dust of steel and stone penetrated their lungs, tearing at the living tissues year in, year out, puncturing the hairlike capillaries until flesh and blood merged in soggy ruin and the victim drowned in his own lungs. They were men careless of their own lives and health, seeking only to earn the exceptionally high wages paid for the work, and spending those wages on drink and debauchery because they knew that they were doomed to die young from what they termed 'the pointer's rot'.

Tildy feared the pointers, and she was not alone in that fear. Most other people feared them also because their brawling savagery was a by-word throughout the length and breadth of the Midlands. They came to their trade at around twenty years of age, and most lay in their graves before they reached thirty.

Tildy shivered slightly and turned to her child, now sitting upright on the grass solemnly gazing at a brilliantly coloured butterfly fluttering around him. She reached out to touch his silky dark hair.

'You shall never become a pointer lad, Davy. I'll do anything rather than see you in that murderous trade.' A fond smile curved her moist red lips. 'You shall be a gentleman, my honey . . . I'll make sure of that.'

She took a long length of strong cord from her gown pocket and tied one end of it around her wrist, and the other end around Davy's ankle. 'There now, honey-lamb, you can crawl about, and if I should fall asleep then you'll not be able to go far without waking me.'

She lay back, closing her eyes and breathing in the scents of sun-warmed grasses and flowers, and the heavier fecund smells of the rich earth that nourished all growing things. The murmurous songs of insects and the humming of bees were soothing in her ears, and imperceptibly she gently drifted into sleep while beside her the child chuckled its delight as the beautiful butterfly softly alighted on his chubby hand.

'Well now, youm a fine little chap, arn't you? And what might your name be?'

The man's voice snatched Tildy to instant wakefulness and she pushed herself upright, her sleep-dazed eyes searching wildly about her. Laughter sounded in her ears as she focused on the man seated two yards away from her, with Davy on his knees.

'Now doon't you be afeared, Missus, I means you no harm.'

He was young, near to her own age Tildy judged, and as

her senses fully returned she felt a twinge of fear. The young man was wearing the distinctive 'pointer's rig': a red shirt beneath a sleeveless leather waistcoat, a rolled apron about his hips, cord knee-breeches and thick-ribbed woollen stockings, heavy iron-shod clogs, and on his long tousled hair a square hat fashioned from brown paper.

Davy was chattering happily in his unintelligible baby-talk and tugging with both hands at the ends of the brightly coloured neckerchief the young man wore carelessly knotted around his unshaven throat. His body looked lean and wiry with muscles writhing like ropes on his neck and arms, and his black-stubbled face was tough and brawl-scarred, while his wide-set hazel eyes held the gleam of recklessness.

Instinctively Tildy came on to her knees, reaching out for her child. 'Davy?' she called urgently, but the child paid her no heed, so intent was he on his game.

'Now don't fret yourself, Missus, I'm only aplaying wi' your nipper. I'd not harm him for the world.'

She saw the gentle way his hands were supporting the small wriggling body on his lap and felt abashed. 'I'm sorry,' she muttered, 'but you startled me so.'

He grinned, and although he lacked a front upper tooth, his grin held a piquant charm. 'Harry Mogg is my name. What's your name, pretty 'un?'

'Tildy,' she answered, a trifle reluctantly. 'That's to say, Matilda. Mrs Matilda Crawford.'

He nodded. 'Ahr yes, Missus it 'ud have to be. Youm too pretty to be single still . . . But I think I likes Tildy best.'

Little Davy tugged wildly and chattered excitedly, and the young man grinned down at him. 'You likes me well enough, doon't you, young 'un? You arn't afeared of Harry Mogg. But I don't reckon your mam cottons on to me so well.'

'You're a stranger to me, Master Mogg.' Tildy had recovered her composure by now. 'So I've neither liking nor disliking for you because I know nothing of you as yet.'

'As yet.' He repeated, and throwing back his head burst

into full-throated laughter. Frightened by the loud noise little Davy's face twisted and he looked ready to burst into tears.

The young man noticed the change of mood instantly. 'Now then, young 'un, theer's no call for you to start askriking.' He spoke softly. 'Here, you go and talk to your mam.' With a single lithe motion he rose and deposited the baby back into Tildy's arms, then remained standing in front of her. Not liking his posture of dominance Tildy also rose to her feet, and found that she matched him in height.

'Wheer be you from, Tildy? I arn't seen you afore round these parts.'

'Well, I live here now.' Tildy was beginning to feel easy with him. His manner radiated friendliness and despite the toughness of his scarred face, his reckless eyes held no suggestion of brutality or menace. 'I'm staying at Mother Readman's house in the Silver Square.'

Surprise showed clearly in his expression. 'Living at Old Ma Readman's, be you? I should never have thought it, iffen you hadn't told me so. How long has you bin theer, then?'

'Not long,' she replied. 'And I doubt I'll be staying there long, either. I want to find a place of my own.'

He nodded understandingly, then informed her, 'I'm from Headless Cross meself. I lives in them cottages nigh on the White Hart.'

Headless Cross was a mile south of Redditch at the top of the long rising ridgeway known as Mount Pleasant.

'I works at the pointing, over at the forge theer.' He waved towards the nearby mills.

'I guessed you were a pointer,' Tildy remarked, and his piquant grin returned.

'Ahr, I expect that's what made you a bit afeared o' me when you first opened your eyes, warn't it?' he observed shrewdly.

'Truth to tell, it was,' she admitted.

He shrugged wiry shoulders. 'Ah well, I can't blame you for that, I suppose. Theer's a load of folks what's afraid of the pointer lads, and concerning some on 'um, there's good

52

cause to be afeared. But all us pointers arn't tarred wi' the same brush, Tildy. We arn't all the mad beasts that folks hereabouts makes us out to be.' His momentary gravity was displaced by his infectious grin. 'Most on us just wants a short life and a merry 'un, Tildy. We don't really mean no harm to others when we'em enjoying ourselves.'

'That's as maybe,' Tildy said reflectively. 'But it does seem that when the pointers go on the spree, then other people do get harmed, more times than not.'

Harry Mogg only shrugged in reply and Tildy could not hold back from pressing her advantage.

'There now, your silence shows that you know I'm right.'

He laughed easily. 'O' course you be. And now I've admitted to it, why doon't you and me go and share a pot of ale. There's a beer-ken down along the stream theer towards Pigeon Bridge.'

Tildy's colour heightened and flustered she shook her head. 'I'm a married woman, Master Mogg, and a respectable one. I don't go to beerhouses with men.'

He stared meaningfully at her ringless fingers, and defiantly she told him. 'I know I've no marriage band. That was pawned for food long since, but I am married, and that's the truth.'

'Wheer is your man, then? What trade does he follow?'

Tildy smiled mirthlessly. 'He claimed to be a nailmaker, and I've no idea where he is these days. He ran off from me and the baby nigh on six months past.'

'He run off from you?' The young man was doubting. 'He must be a bloody queer sort o' man to run off from a good-looking woman like you. You must ha' give him a bloody good reason to go from you.'

For a few moments the memories of her violent, loveless marriage crowded into Tildy's mind. 'I can't blame him for doing so.' She spoke absently, her thoughts still back in the Sidemoor. 'We were never suited to be man and wife. I never wanted him, and I made that fact plain enough. I suppose in some ways we were both to blame for what happened . . . Still, it's over and done with now.'

53

'How can it be over and done wi', iffen you still reckons to act like a married 'ooman?' Harry Mogg questioned forcefully.

Tildy faced him, and staring levelly into his eyes told him, 'I'm not a religious woman, Master Mogg, and I'm no hypocrite who goes round swearing that she can't abide men. I like men. I'm a normal woman with all the hungers of a woman, but I'm no hedge-whore. I can hold my head up and look the world in the face without shame because even though I'm now a lone woman, I'm good-living. I don't go randying about with men, and for the sake of my own self-respect, I've no intention of doing so, now, or in the future.'

For the first time a trace of aggression sounded in the young man's tone, as he burst out indignantly, 'God's trewth! I only invited you to share a pot of ale wi' me, my wench. I didn't ask you to spread your legs, did I?'

Tildy was undeterred by his indignation as her own fiery spirit rose. 'And I'm only explaining to you why I won't share a pot of ale with you, Master Mogg. Thank you for the offer all the same, and now I'll say good day.' Suiting action to words she walked past him and headed for the entrance gate of the meadows.

Before she had gone many yards he had caught up with her and fallen into step by her side.

'Now don't be angered wi' me, Tildy,' he tried to mollify her. 'I'm sorry if I spoke a bit hasty . . . I'm a rough sort o' chap, and I arn't got lah di dah manners, I know. But I meant no offence to you. In fact, I admires you for being such a good-livin' 'ooman, and that's straight.'

Tildy could not resist indulging her vanity a little, pleased despite herself that an attractive man should chase after her in this way. To torment him a little further she merely answered coolly, 'I've taken no offence, Master Mogg,' without even glancing at him.

Their path took them closer to the forge mills, and as they neared them Tildy saw a man dressed like a pointer suddenly run from a low-lintelled doorway in the taller, easternmost building and cross to the front of the second building. There he halted and grabbed a rope which dangled from a big brass bell fixed high on the wall. The bell pealed loudly, its janglings scattering a flock of roosting pigeons from the ridge-tiles of the roof.

Harry Mogg came to an abrupt halt. 'Dear Christ, what's amiss?' he ejaculated, and Tildy halted also and swung to face him.

'What's the matter?'

'It's the bell,' he told her quickly. 'When it's rung at this time o' day it can only mean that there's bin a bad accident in the mill. Some poor bugger has bin sore hurt wi'out a doubt. I'll needs get over theer and see if I can help.' With that he broke into a pounding run.

Tildy stood for some seconds, then impelled by irresistible impulse she went after him towards that jangling bell.

At first she ran, but little Davy protested loudly at the jerky shaking it inflicted upon him, and Tildy was forced to merely walk as quickly as possible. When she came to the gravelled forecourt of the mill a group of men issued from the low-lintelled doorway carrying a limp figure between them. They laid the figure down on the gravel and stood silently around its sprawled arms and legs.

Tildy saw that it was a man, his face a smashed wreckage of blood and bone. From the cottages further along the stream other women came hurrying, their faces haggard with dread. Tildy slowed and came to a standstill some yards from the silent men, and one by one the other women joined her until fully a dozen of them were ranged upon the forecourt's edges, breathing heavily, eyes staring, hands twisting and kneading at dresses and aprons.

From the western building a top-hatted man wearing a dark frock-coat came hastening, only to blanch and slow his pace when he saw the sprawled body.

'Has he gone?' he asked loudly.

'Like a snuffed candle,' a burly pointer answered. 'Ne'er knew what hit him.'

'Well, that's one blessing,' Frock-coat observed bluntly. He entered the group around the corpse and gave loud instructions. Two of the workmen re-entered the low doorway. When they reappeared one was carrying a ragged coat, the other a door, the long hinges of which swayed jauntily as he moved.

The limp body was placed on the door, the dangling limbs decently arranged and the ragged jacket wrapped around the blood-soaked head.

A woman at Tildy's side shouted, 'It's Billy Jenkins, arn't it?'

'It is,' Frock-coat replied shortly.

'God help his poor missus and kids this day,' the woman uttered, and a muted chorus of moaned Amens greeted her plea. One woman burst into tears, smothering her face with her lifted apron.

'You'd best take him home, lads,' Frock-coat ordered. 'Tell his missus I'll be up to see her shortly, and one o' you goo round to Doctor Taylor and ask if him or his son can come to meet me at the Jenkins' house. He'll need to sign the death bill . . . Wilkes, goo and knock the drive shafts out. We'll close the mill for the rest o' the day.' His lips quirked into a scowl. 'That's a whole bloody arternoon's production lost.'

'God should strike you for being such a hard-hearted bugger, George Chillingworth,' a strident-voiced woman bawled. 'A poor chap just struck down, and all you can think on is your bloody profits.'

Unabashed Chillingworth scowled at the woman. 'Iffen I didn't worry about my profits, Sadie Clegg, your own man 'ud have no bleedin' wages come Saturday, and what 'ud you call me then? Take him home, lads.'

The door was lifted on to strong shoulders and the bearers shuffled away towards the Pigeon Bridge with their pathetic burden. A small sad procession followed with bared heads behind the makeshift bier.

Tildy watched them pass, badly shaken by the suddenness with which cruel tragedy had shadowed her day of holiday. She experienced a poignant sadness at the thought of the man's wife and children so unsuspecting of what was coming back home to them. Her hands began to tremble violently and her eyes brimmed with scalding tears.

'Come Tildy, I'll walk you back. Let me carry the young 'un for you.'

Harry Mogg spoke softly in her ear, and wordlessly she let him take her child and lead her slowly in the wake of the mourning procession. She fought to control her emotions, and finally was able to ask, 'What happened? What killed the poor man?'

Harry Mogg's features were grim. 'His stone blew up. It happens often enough.' Seeing that she did not understand clearly, he explained, 'Our grindstones be turned very fast on their axles, and we has to bend over real close to 'um to point the needles. They spins round like lightning, and if there's a crack or some other weakness in them, then they'm liable to break to pieces all of a sudden. They bangs like a bloody cannon blast when they does that, and the pieces come flying out like grapeshot. Iffen one hits you, then it breaks your bones as easy as if they was eggshells.

'Billy Jenkins' stone blew up and a big piece smacked him right in the face. Caved the whole front of his yed in, so it did. Killed the poor bugger on the instant . . . ' He lapsed into moody silence, then after a while went on. 'I reckon in one way Billy Jenkins was lucky because that's an easy way to goo for a pointer lad. The ''rot'' is a cruel death for us. It takes us slow and hard, and we suffers all the torments the Devil can inflict while the ''rot'' is taking us. At least the blow-ups takes us quick, and we knows naught about it iffen we'em lucky.'

He hawked and spat, then added gloomily, 'Mind you, I'se known lads to get their yeds crushed in by the stone and still linger for bloody days . . . ' He gusted a heavy sigh. 'I dunno, it seems to me sometimes that a pointer can't never win, ne'er mind which way he goes. I reckon God must like us to die hard because he must think we'm such wicked, sinful buggers while we'em living.'

'But why do you work at the pointing, knowing what it does to you all?' Tildy thirsted for an answer that would bring her understanding and insight of these men.

Mogg's lean features twisted into a bitter grin. 'Because

57

it's the only way a chap like me knows to earn good wages. Most other labouring men never knows what a good spree is, no matter how hard or long they toils for their masters. But us pointer lads earns good wages. We'se always got money to jingle in our pockets when there's work to be had. Ahr, and gold money as well, not copper only. We lives on the fat o' the land, and drinks and wenches like lords, so we does . . . Leastways, as long as our health and strength keeps with us.'

'But your health and strength are very soon gone if you work at the pointing. You told me that yourself, and it's a well known fact that very few pointers live longer from ten years after they take to the trade,' Tildy protested.

He shook his head, and it seemed as if the doing so cast out all his gloomy thoughts, for when he answered her his piquant grin was mirrored in his dancing eyes. 'Like I also told you, my duck, we wants a short life, and a merry 'un . . . And by God, that's what we has.' His laughter rang out, and hearing it Tildy felt her own gloom lift and to her fanciful imaginings it seemed that the shadow had passed from the sun.

By the time the Chapel Green was reached Tildy was thoroughly enjoying the lighthearted company of her new-found friend, and to her own surprise she experienced a distinct sense of deprivation when she reached for her child, now asleep with his head comfortably pillowed on Harry Mogg's shoulder.

'I'll needs leave you here, Master Mogg.'

'Why must you? I can carry the young 'un to your lodging for you. I've got all the time in the world to spend, and I'm liking spending this bit on it wi' you, Tildy.'

She searched for words which would not hurt or offend him. 'And I've enjoyed your company also, Master Mogg, but I think it best if I leave you here.'

A teasing note crept into his voice. 'Oh, I see, you don't want the respectable people of the town to see you keeping company wi' one o' them wicked pointer lads. That's so, arn't it?'

She began to feel flustered. 'No! No, it's not that at all.

I'll keep company with anyone I choose, and I pay no heed to what folks say. I follow the beat of my own drummer. But . . . '

'But nothing!' he cut her short. 'I'll carry the babby a little bit further for you. It 'ud be a cruel shame to wake the little cratur when he's sleeping so peaceful.'

She accepted defeat rather than create friction between them. 'Very well then, carry him as far as the new lock-up. But there we'll part.'

The new lock-up, or town jail, stood a couple of hundred yards from the chapel on the point of the road fork. The right-hand road being the street where the Red Lion Inn was situated, while the left-hand road went curving eastwards to pass the town's big pool some distance further on, the large pond which was the water supply for the buildings around it. It was also the receptacle for slops, offal, sewage, dead animals, and whatever else people cared to throw into its filthy, stagnant, stinking depths.

The grey sandstone lock-up resembled a squat church tower with a castellated parapet and a great gothic arched doorway. When they reached its forbidding mass Harry Mogg chuckled and jerked his head towards it.

'I'se had lodging in theer a few times. They had to build it because the lively lads used to break out on the coal-hole under the free school too many times.'

The building had two storeys. Arched windows let in light and air to the top storey, but at ground level only arrow slits penetrated the thick walls.

Harry Mogg handed the sleeping child to Tildy, then stretched on tiptoe to shout into one of the slits, 'I hopes youm all repenting of your wicked ways, you miserable sinners! May God have mercy upon your souls! Repent ye! Repent ye! The day of doom is acoming!'

Half-amused, half-embarrassed, Tildy begged him to be quiet. 'Folks are staring at us.'

'Let 'um stare.' He grinned infectiously, and from inside the jail a sepulchral voice intoned, 'As I am now, so you shall be, Harry Mogg . . . And wheer's that five shillings you owes me, you robbing bleeder?'

Harry Mogg laughed delightedly. 'It's Ritchie Bint,' he exclaimed. 'Good old Rich!' Again he stretched up to shout into the slit. 'How goes it, Rich? Come nightfall I'll try and slip you a drop o' summat to keep the vapours away.'

Tildy, uncomfortably aware of the attention he was attracting from passers-by, told him, 'You're making a show of us. I'm leaving you right now.'

He stared at her retreating back and his laughter rang out, then he shouted, 'We'll meet agen, sweet Tildy, don't doubt that. Take care 'til then, my honey.'

Two severe-looking, well-dressed women stared at her with censorious glares as she passed them, and a hot flush heated her throat and cheeks. Thankfully she reached the Red Lion archway and ducked through it into Silver Street. But even though he had caused her embarrassment she still thought pleasurably of Harry Mogg.

'He's a scapegrace without a doubt, but I can't help liking him,' she decided. Then the memory of the dead man came back and she felt troubled. 'Am I really become so callous-hearted?' she asked herself with a twinge of self-disgust. 'To have seen such a sight and yet a scant time later to be laughing with a man and enjoying his company.'

As she stepped carefully along the Silver Street, trying to avoid the worst of the filth underfoot, she pondered this question of her own apparent callousness. From birth onwards death was an ever-present companion to life, the living constantly seeing their fellows taken from them by accident and disease. The poor were even forced to share their cramped living spaces with the dead until the day of burial and were above all others accustomed to death's presence and its multitude of manifestations.

'No,' Tildy decided, 'I'm not really callous-hearted. It's just that I'm so well used to death, that apart from the first moments of pity in face of such tragedy as happened today, how can I expect to remain saddened by it? The man was unknown to me, after all.'

The visual recollection of the bloody head came sharply to her, but she knew that apart from the initial horrified shock she could accept that awful spectacle also without undue squeamishness. After all, terrible physical afflictions and deformities abounded in her world. A walk down any slum street could produce sights and smells to sicken and disgust the sensitive observer. But even the sensitive observer eventually became accustomed and accepting of such sights and smells.

'It's a cruel hard life we have here on earth,' Tildy knew only too well. 'But there's no use crying and wailing about it. We must needs do what we can to help what can be helped, and accept without whining that which cannot be helped.'

Mother Readman met Tildy at the door of the lodging house.

'My oath, but you'se took the sun, my wench, your face is all red wi' it. Wheer's you bin?'

'I went walking in the Abbey Meadows,' Tildy told her, and added, 'There was a sad accident at the forge mill there.'

The fat old harridan nodded her several chins. 'Ahr, I'se heard about it. Mind you, Billy Jenkins died easy at all events, God rest his soul.'

Amazement caused Tildy's eyes to widen, and the older woman chuckled.

'How does I know so quick, you wonders. Well, news travels fast hereabouts, my duck, and I allus gets to know what's happening in this town afore anybody else hears on it . . . Anyway, you'll no doubt he pleased to hear that Marmaduke Montmorency has ate four bowls o' my stew today, and now he's bawling for another to ate wi' his bottle o' porter.'

Tildy smiled. 'I'm glad to hear that he's thriving so well.'

The chuckle rumbled once more deep in Mother Readman's throat. 'Well, iffen I was you, girl, I'd not be that pleased. He's bloody ateing and drinking your money down so fast that you'll soon have naught left.'

'Well, to speak frankly, Mrs Readman, I could wish that he'll soon be well enough to earn his own bread. But I can't

61

find it in my heart to abandon him before he's fully recovered.'

Tildy inwardly prayed that Marmaduke Montmorency would be fully recovered very quickly. It was now more than a week since he had collapsed, and his voracious appetite for food and drink, especially the latter, was costing her more than she could well afford because she had not yet been successful in her search for work. She had called repeatedly at the homes of the local doctors to offer herself as a sick-nurse, but had not even been able to speak with the doctors in person. Servants had taken her messages and returned with brusque refusals of her offered services.

It was this that had impelled her that morning to buy the medical books to aid her in furthering a plan that had been formulating in her mind for some days past. She knew that only the better paid artisans, shopkeepers, tradesmen and, of course, the rich farmers and gentry could afford to pay the high fees the doctors demanded. Only those paupers who could get a charity ticket from the vestry, or were actual inmates of the poorhouse, could ever obtain treatment from a qualified medical man. The labouring masses and the poor, unable or unwilling to pay the high fees, turned instead during times of illness to the local wise-women, cunning men, white witches and travelling quacks, or they dosed themselves with varied patent cure-alls such as 'Cordial Balm of Gilead', 'Arnold's Pectoral Balsam of Coltsfoot', 'Marshall's Universal Cerate', 'Mr Lignum's Antiscorbutic Drops', 'Dr Freeman's Ointment for the Itch', 'Carrington's Vegetable Life Pill', and other such miraculous products guaranteed by their makers to cure each and every ailment and affliction that the human body was heir to.

Knowing this state of affairs, Tildy could see no good reason why she herself could not become a 'healing woman', and earn sufficient for herself and her child's needs by that means. She knew that compared to most of the people around her she was highly intelligent, even if uneducated, and although the complex of inferiority to the gentry and the rich that had been so deeply ingrained in her by upbringing could still exert its influence upon her, yet for the most part she was able to recognize the fallacy of that early-instilled complex. She had by this stage in her life come into contact with enough of her social 'betters' to realize that the majority of them, despite all their material advantages over her, could not match her in either native intelligence, or physical and moral courage.

Now, eager to begin her studies, she hurried up the rackety stairs to her attic room.

'Is it your good self, Matilda?' Marmaduke Montmorency called as she passed his room. 'Come in, I want to speak with you.'

'In a little while, Master Montmorency. I've the baby to see to first.'

In her own room, which she had scrubbed and cleaned until it was a haven of freshness in the reek of the house, she laid little Davy on the bed and busied herself in preparing a bowl of bread and milk sprinkled with a crumbling of cone-sugar. Even as she did this her eyes kept turning to the parcel of books and she experienced a fierce hunger to feast herself on the knowledge contained within that brown wrapping.

The baby awoke crying for food, and lifting him onto her lap Tildy carefully spooned the pap between his eager lips. When satisfied he burped and drowsily closed his eyes, then she settled him to sleep and went next door.

Rest, food and care had wrought an almost miraculous alteration in Marmaduke Montmorency's appearance. His pale skin was lucent with cleanliness, his long hair, now washed and brushed, hung like a soft grey cloud about his shoulders. His cadaverous features and body had plumped and smoothed a little, and the gentle eyes were no longer bloodshot, or glittering with fever in blue-black sockets.

Despite his protests Tildy had daily stripped and bathed his wasted body, sponging away the encrusted dirt, and scrubbing hard with vinegar to rid his armpits and groin of the lice and crabs which infested him. His filthy ragged clothing she had also disposed of, and had bought other clothes for him from the Jewish old-clothes dealer who patronized the lodging house during his perambulations of the district.

When Tildy came into the room the actor was sitting up in bed wearing one of Tildy's cotton shifts to cover his scrawny body. He held his fingers to his lips.

'Shhh! Listen, Matilda. They're ringing the ''Nine Tailors'' on the chapel bell.'

She did as he bade and heard the distant mournful tolling.

Nine strokes to denote that it was a man who had died. For a woman it would be six strokes of the bell, for a child, three strokes, followed by one for each year of the deceasèd's life.

'I hear it,' she told him. 'It'll be for Billy Jenkins, I expect.'

'Billy Jenkins?' Montmorency exclaimed in shock. 'I knew him well. A roaring, roistering blade he was too. How did he die?'

'He was killed this afternoon. His grinding-stone blew up in his face and a piece caught him straight on.'

'Ah well, it only goes to show, that when the good Lord desires your company, he'll use any means at hand to gain it.' The thin face twisted into a rueful smile. 'And if it were not for your kindness, Matilda, I'd even now be supping with the Devil. You saved my life, and I'll be eternally grateful to you for that.'

Tildy felt uncomfortable in the face of his gratitude, uneasily aware that she was by now beginning to regard him as a burden which she increasingly wished to lay aside.

Almost as if he could read her thoughts, he smiled sardonically and announced, 'But from this moment on, I'll no longer be a burden to you, Matilda.' He gestured theatrically with both hands. 'I shall rise from my bed of suffering and go forth to gain my fortune. I am a new man, Matilda. A phoenix risen from the ashes of his worthless past. Purged of all dross in the crucible of my sufferings, I shall rise to heights that I have never before attained, and I shall set forth this very day on the road to my destiny.'

Tildy was bemused by his outpourings. 'What road, Mr Montmorency?'

'Why the road to London, of course, my dear Matilda. I have dreamed a dream . . . a dream of fame awaiting me upon the stages of that mighty city. A dream of the acclaim of multitudes. A dream of cornucopias of wealth.'

'But how will you reach there?'

Paradoxically, now that her burden was intending to leave her, Tildy felt torn by guilt that she should ever have wished to lay it aside.

'I shall do as Dick Whittington did, my dear young lady. I shall walk, although I lack a cat to accompany me . . . And I know that, like noble Dick, I shall also find the streets of London to be paved with gold.'

'But you've no money to travel with.' Tildy could not help trying to bring him down to earth.

He snapped his long fingers above his head. 'Pshaw! What care I for such an insignificant problem as a lack of the ready. The good Lord will provide, my dear . . . the Lord will provide.'

She bit her full lower lip. 'Are you determined on going this very day, Master Montmorency?'

His eyes flashed dramatically. 'Nothing shall hinder me from that object, Matilda. Not fire, flood or storm. Come hell or high water, I shall leave for London this very day.' Dazzled by his own eloquence, he added, 'In fact, I shall leave this very hour.'

Suiting action to words he jumped from the bed and quickly dressed himself in the clothes Tildy had bought for him. He looked down at his rig-out: a checkered shirt, nautical reefer jacket, cord knee breeches, stockings and clogs.

'A trifle sailor-like perhaps, but they will serve until I can engage a suitable tailor.'

He struck a pose, one hand on his heart the other held aloft. 'And now I set forth, Matilda . . . "Alone alone, all, all alone. Alone on a wide, wide sea".' He winked at her. ' "The Ancient Mariner" by Samuel Taylor Coleridge.'

His droll manner brought laughter to her lips, and a

wave of fondness for the likeable reprobate coursed through her. She reached into her bodice and took three guineas from the now sadly depleted pouch between her breasts. 'Here, take these and when you have made your fortune, send them back to me.'

He stared down at the small golden discs in his hand, and his protruberant Adam's apple went up and down several times in rapid succession. When he looked at her his eyes were wet with tears and his voice was husky.

'God bless you, me dear. Someday I'll repay your kindness. I swear to that.'

He softly kissed her cheek and left her in the narrow room. The thumping of his descending feet grew fainter and died away and Tildy gulped hard, her eyes filling with tears as familiar loneliness enfolded its bleakness around her.

'Why must all those I like go from me?' she whispered. 'Does God intend me to be always friendless?'

For a full half hour she remained by the side of the narrow bed, remembering the times that Marmaduke Montmorency had made her laugh. Then slowly she returned to her own room. Little Davy rested peacefully, and gazing lovingly at him, she murmured, 'How I wish you were old enough to talk with me, Davy.'

Her eyes moved to the parcel of books, and with a sadness in her heart she quickly stripped the brown wrapping from them.

'You shall be my company and my friends.' She spoke aloud, and her heart eased. 'And mayhap my fortune also . . . '

Chapter Eight

The September sky was overcast with lowering clouds and the land was sodden with the rain that had fallen constantly for days and nights past.

The stonemason laid down his round-headed mallet and steel claw on the block of stone and straightened his back, grimacing as strained muscles painfully shortened.

'This fuckin' weather 'ull cripple me,' he grumbled aloud, and looked about him.

Some two and a half miles to the south-east he could see the hilly streets of Redditch, and for a moment he thought longingly of its alehouses. Raindrops spattered down as the clouds shed their loads, and the spattering became a hissing downpour.

'Oh, fuck it!' The mason moved into the shelter of the half-roofed cottage behind him and stood in its doorway miserably aware of the rheumaticky aches his chill damp clothes were causing him. The cottage he was working on was to serve as a lodge for the manor house known as Bordesley Hall, a mile to the north up the track leading from the turnpike road which the cottage fronted.

Along that track from the direction of the big house a woman came trudging through the rain carrying a cloth-wrapped bundle slung over her shoulder. The mason recognized her and shouted,

'Hey, Betsy, cummon in here. You'll get drenched to the bleedin' skin else.'

Her clogs squelched through the mud as she came to join him in the doorway. 'Better be bloody soaked to the skin than stay here.' Her broad red face was streaming wet, and her mob-cap plastered to her head by the rain.

'What's upset you then? 'As Dugdale bin bawling at you agen?'

'That bastard!' the woman mouthed vicously, and spat upon the ground. 'God's curse on him, that's what I wishes. He's a bloody madman, so he is, a bloody loony. You mark my words, he'll end by killing some poor body afore he's done. Ranting and raving and carrying on all the time like he does. Nothing suits the bleeder.' She paused to draw a deep breath. ''Tis his poor missus I feels sorry for. No wonder the poor cratur's out of her mind, the way he treats her . . . Anyway, I'm well out on it . . . I'll not step foot in that house ever agen, no, nor even on the bloody land he owns neither.'

'Youm leaving then.' It was more statement than question.

She nodded so vigorously that drops of rain sprayed from her soaked headgear. 'I am that! I'se had enough on it. Besides, I see'd a bat fly thrice around the house yester dusk, and that makes three times on the trot I seen it.' A note of fear crept into her voice and her eyes mirrored that fear. 'Thrice round the house it flew, and that's a sure sign o' death coming theer, so it is. A sure sign.'

Her fear communicated itself to the superstitious mason.

'A sure sign, is it?' he asked in low tones.

Again a vigorous nodding of the head. 'Certain sure, my buck, certain sure. I'se sin the same thing afore, yes, and me mam, and her mam afore her as well. It's a certain sure sign so it is.' She paused to give dramatic emphasis. 'Death's acoming to take someone from that house, and coming soon. You mark my words well. Death's acoming soon.' She shook her head. 'But it wun't be me that it catches theer. I'm off out on it, right now.'

With that, she stepped out into the hissing downpour once more and was gone, leaving a discomfited man behind her.

Time wore slowly on, minutes becoming tens of minutes, tens of minutes lengthening to hours and still the rain lashed down until great sheets of water collected in the hollows and carpeted the low-lying tracts of the sodden earth.

The stonemason rummaged in his toolsack and brought out a small rag-wrapped bundle containing a chunk of stale brown bread, a lump of hard yellow cheese and a large onion. Seating himself on a pile of dressed stones in the front room of the cottage he began to eat, stolidly munching his frugal fare and wishing that he was sitting before the cheerful fire of an alehouse with a hot rum toddy before him, instead of being here in this doleful place made dank and cold by the rain trickling through the unfinished roof and down the unplastered walls.

He heard the sucking squelch of footsteps but made no effort to rise, only shouted, 'Be that you, Betsy? Changed your mind about leaving, 'as you?'

'What in hell's name do you think you are about?' The man's voice shook with suppressed anger, and the mason gulped his half-chewed mouthful and jumped to his feet.

'I'm just ateing me bit o' snap while the weather's so bad, Master Dugdale,' he stammered, and stared with anxious eyes at the man standing in the doorway.

Henry Geast Dugdale was tall and strongly built, with long lean swarthy features and deep-set eyes which now glowed with a mad fury. He wore a narrow-brimmed top hat and a voluminous riding cloak saturated to blackness by the rain water which dripped from its folds on to his hessian boots.

'I do not pay good money for you to sit taking your ease like some fat-arsed bishop.' He grated the words. 'Go from here and do not return.'

A spark of resentment flared in the mason's mind. 'Now hold hard a minute, Master . . . ' he began to argue.

'Goddamn your impudence!' Dugdale bellowed, and his swarthy complexion darkened as the blood rushed to his head. In two strides he reached the mason and grabbing the man's coat collar he bodily heaved him through the doorway, sending him sprawling on to the muddy-puddled ground outside. The mason came up on to his knees, clawing at the dripping mud plastered across his face and his own temper alight. He then gulped with shocked horror as he saw the dark round hole of a pistol's muzzle only inches from his eyes.

'One word more of your impudence and I'll blow your scabby head from your shoulders,' Dugdale hissed. 'Now get your stinking carcass from here.'

The hammer clicked back and the long finger tightened on the trigger.

The mason vented a cry of fright and rocked backwards on to his heels to stand erect, slipping and staggering for balance on the greasy mud. The pistol exploded, and with a wail of terror the mason ran, his clogs splashing in the puddled ruts of the road that led back to Redditch.

Chapter Nine

Late that same evening Hugh Taylor and John Clayton were engrossed in their game of chess when the elder Taylor entered the spacious drawing-room of the house he shared with his son. Hugh Taylor looked up from the board and seeing the expression on his father's face, asked,

'Why such a look of thunder, Father?'

Charles Taylor's scowl deepened. 'That damned Dugdale! The man is becoming impossible!'

'What has he been up to now, Sir?' John Clayton enquired.

'Why, he's driven Betsy Marsden from his house, and frightened one of Moses Collins's workmen half to death. Firing a pistol at the man, no less. I've had Collins belabouring my right ear with the story for half the evening and Betsy Marsden belabouring my left ear half the afternoon.

'People seem to think that because we are related to the man by marriage we are responsible for his actions. I packed them both off with fleas in their ears, I can tell you.'

The two younger men exchanged amused glances. Henry Geast Dugdale's temper was notorious in the district. On one occasion he had even flung the Earl of Plymouth into a convenient horse-trough during a dispute about the Earl's huntsmen trespassing on Dugdale's land.

Charles Taylor directed his scowl at his son. 'It's not a matter for amusement, Hugh. Have you given thought yet as to where we are to find another nursing-woman for cousin Sybil?'

Hugh Taylor's amused smile was replaced by an impatient frown. 'Do you not think that Henry Dugdale would be best left to find his own nurse for his wife, Father?'

'Do you forget that Sybil Dugdale is your first cousin and your late mother's sister's daughter?'

'No Father, of course I do not forget that she is our kinswoman. But as Dugdale's wife she is his responsibility and not ours.'

'She is also one of our patients,' the old man snapped irascibly, 'and as such is also our responsibility.'

Hugh Taylor's handsome features became petulant. 'Very well, Father. If you insist, then I suppose we must look about for another nursing-woman. Though God alone knows where we are to find someone suitable. Every decent goodwife in the district refuses to stay under the same roof as Dugdale and that damned servant of his.'

'Nonetheless, we must do so,' the old man growled, 'and quickly too.' From his pocket he took a folded sheet of notepaper and handed it to his son. 'Read this.'

Hugh Taylor scanned the paper and chuckled grimly. 'By God, but the man has a hard neck.' He turned to John Clayton and explained. 'He states here that he leaves for Birmingham early tomorrow morning and does not know how long he may be gone. Therefore, would we be good enough to send another nurse-woman to the hall tomorrow to care for his wife.' He paused and whistled between his teeth, 'Now there's a thing!' He grinned happily. 'Was it not you, John, who first told me about a newcomer who wishes to work as a sick-nurse? That Crawford woman? Apparently she's called here at the house several times seeking for such work, or so the servants tell me. Would she do for the hall, d'you think?'

John Clayton looked doubtful. 'Mayhap she would do, Hugh. But is such a situation suitable for a young girl like Crawford? Apart from Dugdale's own violent temper, does not his servant also possess an unsavoury character?'

Charles Taylor, eager to grasp at a solution to his problem airily brushed aside Clayton's doubts.

'Nonsense, John, nonsense! She'll come to no harm at Bordesley Hall. You'll send for the Crawford woman in the morning, Hugh, and if you find her suitable, then engage her for the work . . .'

Chapter Ten

It was dawn when Tildy awoke, and at her side little Davy played with her long plait of hair, chuckling to himself in his pleasure with his new-found toy. She kissed his soft cheeks and tickled his lithe squirming body until he squealed with delight.

'Do you know what day it is today, my honey-lamb?' she whispered into his pink ear. 'It's the twenty-eighth day of September in the year of Our Lord, eighteen hundred and twenty-one, and your Mammy becomes twenty years old on this day.' She gently puffed soft breaths against his ear, and he giggled and wriggled away from her teasing lips.

Smiling she turned on to her back and lay looking at the underside of the roof tiles which was her ceiling.

'My birthday,' she thought with a tinge of sadness, 'and there's not one soul about me who knows, or cares a jot for it. I'll not get a single wishing of a "happy return".'

Her hands moved down her shift, feeling the warm firm flesh pulsing with life beneath the thin cotton material. A sudden fierce desire for the touch, caress, greedy seeking and claiming of a man's hands caused her to catch her breath, and her fingers sought and found the yielding, hungry moistness between her thighs. Driven by all-consuming needs, she gave herself release and writhed sensuously as that release shivered exquisitely through her body. Immediately afterwards she felt ashamed that she should have done this thing with her innocent child lying beside her.

'I'm no better than a whore, behaving so shameless . . .' But even as she berated herself it seemed that a tiny voice whispered in her mind, 'No Tildy, there's no shame in easing your hungers in that way. It's far better to do that, than to lie with men you have no love for, for sake of bodily pleasures . . . ' Thrusting the disturbing clash of thoughts from her mind she got out of bed and washed her hands and face in the wooden bucket of water she had drawn from the pump the previous night. Afterwards, with the same water, she bathed little Davy, changed him and washed the soiled clout before hanging it up to dry on a nail in the roof tiles.

Dressing herself was quickly done. She merely pulled her shabby grey gown down over her shift, rolled her white cotton stockings onto her slender legs, slipped her feet into her clogs and flung her shawl around her shoulders as protection against the chill air of the morning.

She carefully tucked Davy into the bed. 'Now lay quiet for a little time, my honey-lamb, and Mammy shall bring you some breakfast.'

With a farewell smile she took the bucket of dirty water and went downstairs.

After the comparative freshness of her own room, the foul air of the kitchen, thick with the night-time exhalations of a score of people, seemed to clog in Tildy's nostrils. But she had been above a month in the lodging house, and was now accustomed to its many and varied stenches. She threaded her way quietly through the humped, sprawling, snoring, sleep-muttering bodies which lay across the table, on benches and on the floor itself, and passed into the back yard.

She emptied her bucket's contents on to the midden heap, and then spent some time at the pump, scouring and swilling her utensil until it was white with cleanliness.

'Shift yourselves! Rouse up! Rouse up, you lazy bleeders! Shift and rouse! Shift and rouse!' From inside the kitchen a youthful strident voice shattered the uneasy peace. 'Shift and rouse, I told you, you lazy bleeders! Shift yourselves!' And a groaning, grumbling, farting, scratching, belching, cursing, grunting awakening began.

The owner of the voice came through into the backyard, and Tildy bade good morning to Mother Readman's maid of all work and general deputy – a parish bastard with the grandiose name of Apollonia – a tiny, skinny, birdlike creature, her hair a matted halo around her dirty face. She was aged fourteen, but looked nearer forty – at first sight a pitiful creature, but Tildy knew that Mother Readman treated the waif kindly, albeit with the absent-minded kindness given to a stray kitten. In one respect Apollonia was more fortunate that most of the parish bastards Tildy had known; she lived under the protection of Mother Readman's fearsome reputation and no one in the Silver Square or Street would ever dare to bully or physically assault her.

Tildy smiled at the urchin and gently teased, 'Come here, Apollonia and I'll work the handle while you wash yourself.'

The old eyes in the young face were as bright and beady as any bird's. 'Gerrout on it, Tildy, has you sin what water does to iron pans? It bleedin' well rusts the buggers. I arn't about to get my fuckin' face and hands rusty.'

Tugging up her skirt she squatted and relieved herself, watching with evident satisfaction the urine forming a snake of liquid writhing from her filthy bare feet.

This crudity evoked no disgust in Tildy. It was the way of the slums, and she had long since learned to accept certain aspects of slum behaviour without rancour or offence, even though it might be behaviour that she would never practise herself, or allow her own child to.

Letting her skirts fall, the child skipped to Tildy's side and announced proudly, 'I gained a few bob last night, Tildy, look at this.'

From a hiding place in her rags Apollonia produced a handful of silver and copper coins.

Tildy mentally calculated the total and said wonderingly,

'There's nigh on half a crown's worth there, child. How did you gain so much?'

One beady eye winked salaciously. 'How does you think I gained it? Them Taffy drovers who come in drunk last night was panting for a bit. Real randy bleeders they was, near rode the arse off me, so they did. I'm feeling a bit sore today, I'll tell you.'

Intense pity struck Tildy to the heart. 'Dear God, child, you shouldn't do such things. You'll end up pregnant or diseased.'

An expression of scornful knowingness greeted her words.

'Fuck me blind, Tildy, does you take me for a bleedin' mawkin'? A fuckin' chawbacon who knows naught? I'll not catch for a babby. I knows too much to get copped like that. Besides, even if I did fall for one, I'd soon get rid o' the little fucker.'

'How would you?' Tildy was becoming angry with the girl because she hated to see the child place herself in such jeopardy.

'Why, I'd soon goo down and see old Esther Smith, the cunning-woman. She'd soon sell me a dose o' summat to shift the little bugger. I knows lots o' wenches that she's done it for.'

Tildy, despite realizing the hopelessness of it, felt driven to try and make the girl see sense. 'Listen Apollonia, I can guess what sort of poisons Esther Smith pumps into the wombs of the girls who go to her. And when I was in the poorhouse at Webheath I saw what became of some of those girls who tried such things. They ended in their coffins.

'You take your life in your hands, child, when you use such poisons to try and get rid of a baby. And it's even more dangerous when the cunning-women use instruments inside you. And when you go with strange men for money you risk disease and bad usage, perhaps even a cut throat . . . Can't you see that?'

The small dirty face screwed into a furious scowl and the girl shouted stridently, 'It makes no odds to me what you

77

says, Tildy Crawford, so spare me your fuckin' sermons. Iffen I wants to pleasure meself and gain a few bob while doing it, then I'll fuckin' well do just that. So you just mind your own fuckin' business.'

Tildy shook her head in sad despair. 'All right Apollonia, all right,' she murmured quietly. 'I'll not quarrel with you . . . but remember, if you do ever find yourself in trouble, then I'll always stand ready to try and help you.'

She filled her bucket with musty-smelling pump-water and went back to her attic.

The baby greeted her with waving arms, wriggling his whole body and smiling his happiness at seeing her return, and Tildy's despair became a sensation of loving joy that she had such a precious possession as this, her child. Crooning softly she lifted and gently rocked him in her arms, surrendering herself to the deep contentment of these moments. But the magic time ended all too soon as worry pressed into her mind.

'I'm becoming short of money, there's but little of it left and still no sign of work for me hereabouts. Dear God don't let me be forced back into the poorhouse. I'll do anything rather than live there and see my baby raised as a parish child . . . parish bastards, as everyone calls the poor little souls whether they've been born in wedlock or out of it.'

Her gaze fell upon her treasured books and she drew comfort from knowing how much she had already learned from their pages. Every moment that she could spare from searching for work or caring for her child, Tildy devoted to studying her 'Buchan's Domestic Medicine' and the 'Dispensatory'

'I'm sure I could treat some diseases as well as any doctor, and better than most of the goodwives,' she thought, and experienced a surge of pride and confidence. 'I've learned well what Buchan can tell me,' she realized. 'I could recite parts of it by heart.'

Anxious to immerse herself once more in study, she bustled to prepare gruel and take it down to the kitchen fire to cook it. She and Davy shared the wooden bowl of the rough-grained, greyish mess, and then with a pleasing sense of anticipation Tildy settled to her books. It was just over an hour later that Doctor Charles Taylor's manservant came to the lodging house in search of her.

Hugh Taylor had an eye for the ladies, and a considerable appetite for them also, and he pleasurably studied Tildy's full-breasted, slender-waisted body as his father talked to the young woman in their drawing-room.

'. . . as far as I can ascertain, Crawford, there is nothing known by the constable to your detriment, and you appear to be of good character. Therefore I am, with reservations, prepared to accept your own assurances as to your previous antecedents. The Reverend Clayton has vouchsafed that you cared well for Mrs Coldericke, and also for the sick in the poorhouse.' The old man coughed suddenly and flourished a large handkerchief before burying his face in its folds and blowing his nose noisily. He returned the handkerchief to the laced cuff of his shirt. 'Damned colds!' he grumbled, as if to himself. 'Damned martyr to the damned things.' Then he told Tildy. 'You will be ready to leave for Bordesley Hall at two of the clock, Crawford. Be here at the house five minutes before that hour. I, or my son, will take you to the Hall and present you to Mrs Dugdale.'

When the young woman made no reply, but only stared at him with dark, questioning eyes the old doctor snapped irritably, 'Well, young woman, do you say aye or nay?'

Tildy quelled the tremors of nervousness that threatened to constrict her throat, and spoke out firmly. 'If you please, Sir, how can I give you aye or nay when I know nothing of what is being offered to me?

'Your manservant told me that you wished to see me. I come here and you question me about my previous life, then tell me to be here at two o'clock, and to be ready to go with you to somewhere named Bordesley Hall. With all respect, Sir, I would like to know more of what it is you want of me.'

She relapsed into silence, bright spots of colour in her cheeks engendered by her own temerity in speaking out so boldly to a gentleman.

Hugh Taylor chuckled and inwardly acknowledged the truth of John Clayton's observations concerning this girl. She was indeed a deal too forward and independent in her manners towards her betters. But enjoying pretty women as he did, Hugh Taylor was quite charmed with Matilda Crawford's independent air.

His father was not. Charles Taylor scowled and his first impulse was to berate the girl for her insolence and to send her packing. Then he reflected on his pressing need for a nursing-woman and the difficulty of finding one for this particular post. 'Bordesley Hall lies to the north of this town some two miles towards Alvechurch village,' he explained with a bad grace. 'The lady of the hall, Mistress Sybil Dugdale, is ailing and needs the constant attendance of a competent nursing-woman. You will receive very generous wages of one shilling per diem, plus bed and board, and an allowance of cider or porter, not to exceed two quarts daily. It may also be that the term of the position could be extended indefinitely if you give satisfaction to your employer.'

'But who is to be my employer, Sir?' Tildy asked curiously. 'Yourself, or Mistress Dugdale?'

Again Charles Taylor's gorge rose at her forwardness, but again he swallowed hard and controlled himself. 'Your employer, Crawford, will be the Master of Bordesley Hall, Mr Henry Geast Dugdale. At present he is absent from the hall, therefore I am acting as his agent in this matter. Mistress Dugdale is kin to me, so I have a personal interest in her welfare also. Now,' he frowned sternly at her, 'I trust that will satisfy your thirst for knowledge, Crawford?'

Steeling herself against his displeasure, Tildy said apologetically, 'There is one thing more, Sir. I have a child, an infant. Can I bring him with me to the hall? I have no kin or friends to care for him.'

Hugh Taylor smothered the desire to laugh aloud at his

father's incredulous expression, and to forestall the by now inevitable outburst, he quickly intervened.

'Unfortunately Crawford, that cannot be.' He smiled gently at her troubled face. 'We never allow a nursing-woman or goodwife to introduce members of her own family into the homes of our patients. Indeed, no doctor of repute would ever countenance such an irregular practice.

'You'll needs place your child into the care of someone, but I will personally request of Master Dugdale that you have time allowed to visit your child occasionally. That is if you should remain at the hall for any lengthy period of time.'

He saw the doubt and uncertainty in her, and went on in soothing tones. 'There are several women hereabouts who take in children, Crawford, and they are cheap enough. I think sixpence a day to be the usual charge.'

Tildy remained silent as she fought to come to a decision. She desperately needed the work, her money was all but exhausted, but to leave her child in the care of strangers? She could hear Hugh Taylor's pleasant timbred voice in her ears.

' . . . this could prove a great opportunity for you to better your position in life, Crawford. If you should render satisfaction in this post, then without doubt we shall be able to use your services in the future. Also you will be able to refer any prospective employer to us for your character reference, and without wishing to appear immodest, our name carries much influence in this district. This could be the making of you, Crawford. It might well lead to a financial security for your child in years to come.'

Through all her objections and misgivings one ines-capable thought kept clamouring with ever-increasing strength. 'Beggars can't be choosers, Tildy . . . beggars can never be choosers.'

Inevitably she was at last forced to surrender to what she perceived as the lesser of two evils. If she did not take this work, then in a very short while she would be forced to apply to the parish vestry for poor relief. In her own case that would mean a return to the poorhouse, perhaps never to escape from it again. At least if she took this work she would avoid that dread prospect for the time being. Her child would not grow up wearing the pauper's badge of shame and have to live with the stigma until it became indelibly etched on his very soul. Hesitantly she nodded acceptance.

'Very well, Sir, I'll come here at two o' the clock.'

The manservant ushered her from the room and back into the street, and still troubled by doubts she made her way back to the Silver Square.

'God dammee, but she's a proud-stomached, ungrateful bitch, that one!' Charles Taylor's face was mottled with an ugly flush of resentment. 'Not a word of thanks or gratitude for our kindness in finding employment for her did she deign to offer us. Damned slum bitch!'

Hugh Taylor did not share his parent's resentment.

'If you were a loving mother, would you give thanks to those who made you leave your child to the tender mercies of a baby-farmer?' he asked softly. 'I know well that I'd not do so . . . I'd be more inclined to offer them only curses . . . '

'It is her own choice,' his father spluttered. 'We did not force her to make it.'

'We did not need to force her, Father,' the young man stated firmly. 'You know as well as I that empty bellies do all the forcing for us . . . '

At the lodging house there was a visitor waiting to see Tildy.

'Now then, pretty girl, how bist?' Harry Mogg's gap-toothed grin greeted her. Then the grin vanished as he saw her face. 'Why be you looking so glum, Tildy? What's upset you?'

Briefly she told him what had transpired at the Taylor house. ' . . . and now I've got to look about quick and find a woman to take and care for my Davy,' she finished sadly, and her eyes glistened with unshed tears.

They were standing in the entrance to the lodging house, and Mother Readman's formidable bulk came waddling across the Square to join them. She also questioned Tildy and having heard the replies sniffed expressively.

'Well, girl, what can't be cured must be endured. It arn't as if youm sending the babby to bleedin' Van Diemen's Land, is it? You'll only be a few miles distant from him, and you'll be able to see him now and agen. God's trewth, Tildy, the job wun't last for ever, 'ull it? Look on the bright side o' things, girl,' she admonished. 'Leastways youm agoing to be earning a few bob, and what's more you'll be getting your fingers into the gentry pie, wun't you? Who knows wheer it might lead. You might end by making your fortune from it.'

'That's right enough, Tildy,' Harry Mogg added his optimism. 'Youm agoing to be living cheek by jowl wi' the gentry now. You'll meet all manner o' people up at Bordesley Hall, I shouldn't wonder. They'll be offering you work right, left and centre.'

Tildy made an effort to look on the brighter side. 'Yes, it might well turn out so.' She forced a smile. 'But now I must also look about quick for a place for Davy.'

Mother Readman sighed regretfully. ''Tis no use me offering to keep him here, Tildy. It arn't too healthy a spot for babbies, and besides, I've too much on me plate as it is. I'd not have time to care for him proper.'

'I know that, Mrs Readman,' Tildy told her. 'But can you recommend me anybody?'

The lips pursed in the vast tallowy face. 'Let's see now . . . theer's Mrs Tupman down Silver Street theer, but I'd not leave a mangy dog wi' her. She ought to have coffins, not cradles in her place. The babbies dies like flies theer . . . Old Mother Tanner down Easemore Lane? Nooo! She's always drunk out on her bloody mind . . . The Widow Harris, her's strict teetotal. She's in Paoli's Row next to the big pool. She might suit.'

Tildy thought of the noisome big pool from which Paoli's Row water supply was drawn. 'That's a very unhealthy spot, is it not, Mrs Readman?' she objected.

The older woman shrugged her massive shoulders. 'Well, it arn't the Garden of Eden, that's for sure, my wench. There's allus a powerful amount o' fever down round theer, and a lot of Widow Harris's kids does take sickly, and some dies.' Again she shrugged her shoulders. 'But then, any amount o' kids takes sickly and dies wherever they be, don't they?'

Harry Mogg struck the side of his head with his open hand. 'Christ, but I'm dull today! I'se just thought on the very thing. I knows a woman who takes in kids up at Boney's Point.' Satisfaction purred in his voice. 'And it's a rare healthy spot up along theer. Nobody can deny that.'

Mother Readman agreed with him. 'That's true, that is. Boney's Point is reckoned the most bracing air in the district. Mind you, there's a few real bad 'uns living thereabouts these days.'

The needle pointer reacted with scorn to this remark.

'Don't talk so sarft, 'ooman. There's plenty o' bad 'uns lives down along here as well, arn't there? You can find bad 'uns wheresomever you cares to look for 'um in this bleedin' town. No, little Davy 'ull do well enough up at the Point.'

'Who's the 'ooman?' Mother Readman wanted to know.

'It's the Widow Fairfax,' Harry Mogg informed her. 'Her's a good-hearted old soul as well.'

Mother Readman clucked her tongue loudly and shook her head. 'That'll be Ben Fairfax's old Mam, wun't it?'

'So what?' the pointer challenged.

'Well, he's one o' the Rippling Boys, arn't he?'

'So, what if he is, and that 'ud have to be proven.'

'So, he's into all sorts o' devilment. Him and that bleedin' Jonas Crowther. You knows that as well as I does.'

The argument was becoming heated.

'What bloody difference does that make to his mam afarming babbies? He's married now, arn't he, to Mary Crowther as was. He don't live wi' his mam any more.'

'That's as maybe, but her's still aliving in one of his boss's bloody tenements, arn't her? Her's living in bloody Crowther's Row.'

'And so be a hundred other buggers living in Crowther's Row,' Mogg shouted angrily. 'They aren't all bleedin'

Rippling Boys, bist they?' He paused to draw a deep breath, and then challenged, 'You tell me then of anything bad that Widow Fairfax is supposed to ha' done? Her's got the name of being a good-living woman, and that you can't deny.'

Grudgingly Mother Readman conceded the point. 'No, I'll not deny that. The 'ooman's got the name of a good-living soul, despite having such a black-hearted bastard for son.'

Scenting victory Harry Mogg pressed home his attack. 'And you tell me of an 'ealthier spot in this town wi' cleaner air than Boney's Point?'

Again Mother Readman grudgingly gave ground. 'No, I'll gi' you that. It's got the name for 'ealthy air.'

Harry Mogg launched his final grand assault. 'And you tell me of any babby-farmer in this town that you could put hand on heart and swear to that she was a fitter 'ooman to care for babbies than Widow Fairfax.'

Mother Readman was routed. 'Oh, bollocks to you!' she growled, and Harry Mogg crowed in triumph.

'That's settled it then. Tildy shall leave her babby at Widow Fairfax's. And I'll carry the little mite up theer for her. What say you, Tildy?'

Still weighed down by the gloomy sadness of her coming parting from her child. Tildy wearily acquiesced. 'All right then.' She almost whispered the words. 'We'll go up and see the Widow Fairfax.'

Chapter Eleven

From the hamlet of Headless Cross the turnpike road ran south along the high ridgeway, bordered on both sides of its narrow breadth by thick ancient woodlands. A mile south from Headless Cross was the hamlet of Crabbs Cross. Here the road split, the western fork continuing along the ridge towards the town of Evesham, the eastern fork plunging down the Slough Hill crossing the boundary between Worcestershire and Warwickshire, and into the valley of the Arrow River through the village of Studley and on to Alcester and Stratford-upon-Avon.

Crabbs Cross bore an unsavoury reputation in the needle district and was known as Boney's Point. That reputation owed itself to the fact that Jonas Crowther and certain of his Rippling Boys made their homes there.

Crowther's Row named for its owner, Jonas Crowther, was a long shallow-curved terrace of cottages at the side of the road leading into Crabbs Cross. Many of the Row's tenantry were well known to the local constables and magistrates, and the more timid of the respectable inhabitants of the area would hasten their pace as they passed the tumbledown buildings, reluctant to attract the attention of their rough occupants. Jonas Crowther himself lived in a large rambling house surrounded by yew trees and dark shrubbery a little distance further on into the hamlet on the same western side of the turnpike road.

The Widow Fairfax lived at one end of the long row, her

cottage from the outside looking to be in better repair than her neighbours' dwellings; at least, the leaded windows were unbroken and there were no tiles missing from the roof. Some of Tildy's misgivings left her when she met the old woman herself. Widow Fairfax was small and plump-bodied with a rosy wrinkled face and a comfortable, motherly manner, her blue linsey-wool gown, capacious white mob-cap and apron were clean and neat. On first entering the cottage Tildy was irresistibly reminded of the ancient nursery rhyme about the old woman who lived in a shoe. There were children everywhere, toddlers and tiny babies, all sleeping in individual wooden boxes ranged around the room.

The old woman listened intently to Harry Mogg's explanation of Tildy's need, and smiled reassuringly at the girl.

'Your bairn 'ull be all right wi' me, young 'ooman. A tanner the day is what I charges, no more, no less. And for that they gets well fed and lies warm. You take a look at these little morsels. Don't they all look clane and bonny?'

Tildy stared around her and accepted the truth of the statement. The children and their boxes appeared clean, as did their coverings, and none looked emaciated or ill. Yet disquiet tugged at her. They were all sleeping so deeply, and except for the occasional twitching of an arm or leg, they lay without movement.

'Do you dose them with any of the poppy syrups, Widow Fairfax?' she asked, and the old woman nodded vigorously.

'But o' course I does, young 'ooman. Like I said, I cares well for 'um. Babbies must have their sleep, and some I got at present be teething strong, and it's making 'um real fretful. Iffen I didn't give the poor little morsels a soothing drop, why none on 'um 'ud get a minute's rest or sleep, and then wheer 'ud we be?' She smiled proudly. 'And you'll note summat else, I trust, young 'ooman. You'll note that I arn't one of them old-fashioned biddies who swaddles the babbies so that they canna move a limb. No, I'm bang up to date, I am. They gets only a clout on 'um, and I keeps a warm room so they arn't chilled, and then they can kick their arms and legs to their 'eart's content, and make their bodies strong and lithesome.'

Tildy was impressed with such modernity of ideas coming from such an elderly woman. Her admired Doctor Buchan strongly advocated the very same thing in his chapters on the care of children.

Again she studied the room. A cheerful fire burned in the small grate and a burnished kettle sang merrily on the hob. For lack of space there was little furniture apart from the children's boxes, but what few articles there were looked scrubbed and clean, and the air itself smelled pleasantly of dried herbs, clean baby flesh and burning applewood.

Feeling easier and less anxious about Davy's welfare with this woman, Tildy steeled herself, and with a final kiss and cuddle gave her baby into Widow Fairfax's arms. He gurgled happily as her wrinkled face smiled down at him and her toothless mouth clucked a fascinating array of different sounds. 'Yes, you likes that don't you, my lamb?' Again she sucked and clucked and the baby wriggled, chortling with glee and reaching out to pluck the moving lips of the old woman.

Tildy felt a sharp pang of hurt as she watched. 'He doesn't care that she's a stranger.' Then she sharply told herself not to be so silly and childish. 'It's good that he should accept her so readily. Would you sooner have him bawling with fear and upset?'

She placed seven shillings on the mantelshelf above the fire. 'There's a fortnight's charges, Widow Fairfax. But I'll be up to see Davy long before that's done. There's naught ailing him . . . ' She started to detail how she fed him, and his likes and dislikes.

Widow Fairfax chuckled with indulgent laughter. 'God's trewth girl, bist you atrying to teach an old granny like me how to suck eggs?' she mock scolded. 'Now be off wi' you, and let me get on wi' seeing to this babby, and agetting him settled nice and comfortable. Don't you be fretting yourself about him, he'll thrive wi' me, and you come and see him any time you'se a mind to.'

Tildy took a last lingering look at her baby, then not

wishing to burst into tears in front of her companions, she hurried outside.

Harry Mogg came running after her, but she waved him away.

'Please Harry, leave me be for now. I'm very grateful to you, and I thank you for your kind help, but right now I'm better left on my own.'

He possessed sufficient sensitivity to understand and accede to her wishes. 'All right Tildy, I'll leave you to be by yourself,' he told her gently, 'and I'll come up to Bordesley Hall when you'se had a chance to settle and let you know how your babby is agoing on.'

'Yes, please do that. Please come and see me at the hall.' She forced a tremulous smile of thanks, and then waved him farewell and hurried away from Crowther's Row, smothering her sobs in her shawl.

At any other time Tildy would have taken pleasure in her journey to Bordesley Hall. The novelty of her first ride in a smart horse and chaise sitting beside such a handsome escort as Hugh Taylor would have been an event to relish. But all she could do was to sit in a glum silence and worry about her baby.

Hugh Taylor read her mood correctly and told her kindly,

'Do not concern yourself unduly about your child's welfare, Crawford. Widow Fairfax is of good repute for her care of the children in her charge.'

'Yes, Sir,' Tildy nodded, inwardly acknowledging that she was in certain aspects giving way to an exaggerated degree of self pity. 'Yes, Sir, I'll try not to worry.'

'That's better,' the young man answered heartily. 'And now let me see a smile on those pretty lips, young woman. The first precept when caring for the sick is to always display a cheerful countenance. The poor afflicted souls carry enough of their own gloom and doom, Crawford. It don't serve for the doctor or nurse to be glum-faced also.'

'No, Sir,' Tildy agreed, and then told herself forcefully,

'Look, Davy will be well cared for, and you are only scant miles distant from him. You were in desperate need of work, and by the grace of God you now have work, so stop being so self-pitying and try and be a little more cheerful about your good fortune in finding this position.'

Her forceful self-stricture did seem to have an effect, for she very soon felt a lifting of her spirits, and she began to take some pleasure from the ride.

'Have you ever encountered Mr Henry Geast Dugdale?' Taylor asked.

'No, Sir, I never have.'

'Have you ever heard talk about him?'

'No, Sir, never.'

'I see . . . ' The young medical man lapsed into a musing reverie and Tildy did not like to press him for more information about her new employer.

After a while Taylor pointed ahead with his long-handled whip. 'There is the approach lane by that unfinished building there. The hall lies just beyond the rising ground over yonder.'

A man wearing a moleskin cap, full-skirted coat and canvas-gaitered breeches was standing outside the lodge entrance. He turned to watch the newcomers' approach and Hugh Taylor recognized him as Dugdale's servant and gamekeeper, William White, a surly-tempered, brutal-featured man who bore an unsavoury reputation. Some years previously a young woman had been savagely raped by a hooded man in the Brockhill woods, and William White had been under strong suspicion, but nothing could be proven against him. Nevertheless general opinion in the district still held that he had been the attacker.

Hugh Taylor glanced sideways at the pretty girl with him, and experienced strong misgivings about what he was doing.

'Am I acting properly in placing this young woman in a situation where she could be virtually at the mercy of William White?' For a fleeting instant he felt an impulse to turn the horse's head around and carry Tildy Crawford back to Redditch, but that instant passed, and mentally he

90

shrugged. 'God dammee, I'm vapouring like some cretinous old maid. White could well be as innocent as a new-born lamb. Besides, he'll never dare to interfere with a sick-nurse that I have brought here. He knows well what would happen to him if he did.'

He reined back the horse in the lane's entrance and asked the keeper, 'Are the dogs running free, White?'

The man's heavy-lidded eyes measured Tildy, and she felt uneasy as she met their reptilian coldness. Then, still staring at her, White answered, 'That's so, Doctor Taylor. I'll needs come up to the house wi' you.' He lifted his long-barrelled gun from the wall it leant against and walked on up the lane, and the doctor urged the horse into a slow amble behind him.

As the chaise breasted the high ground Tildy saw below her the gables and chimneys of the rambling, half-timbered hall. The house was surrounded by thick woodlands and as the carriage descended the trees and bushes closed about it, cutting off all view of the hall and shrouding the narrow twisting lane in sombre shadow.

Tildy fought to keep her sinking spirits up. 'If I don't like it here I need not stay,' she told herself repeatedly. 'I can leave at any time I choose.'

Abruptly the woodland ended and Tildy saw what the close-set trees and bushes had previously hidden – the high brick wall that closely encompassed the house. The lane ran up to the massive, spike-topped gates and Tildy noted that the top of the wall also was thick with wickedly curved iron spikes.

'Dear Lord, it's like a prison!' she uttered aloud, and Hugh Taylor smiled at her shocked expression.

'You should draw comfort from such fearsome defences, Crawford,' he joked. 'You can lie secure and peaceful in your bed at nights, knowing that no rogues or vagabonds could scale those walls.'

As the chaise halted outside the gates a frenzied snarling and a scrabbling of many paws against gravel erupted from inside the walls and Hugh Taylor chuckled wryly.

'I'll take oath it sounds as if all the hounds of hell were

91

pent up within there, does it not, Crawford?' Again he smiled at her apprehensive expression. 'Don't be alarmed, girl, they're only Mr Dugdale's guard dogs. They'll not harm you once they become accustomed to your scent. William White has them well disciplined. They obey him like soldiers obey their drill sergeant.'

'Quiet, you bastards! I'll break your bleedin' yeds for you else,' the gamekeeper bellowed fiercely, as he produced a ringed bunch of keys and selected one to unlock the big padlock securing the crossbar of the gate. The frenzied snarls and barking muted to a low growling and the massive gates creaked open.

Tildy vented an involuntary gasp of nervousness when she saw the dogs. There were five of them, big, powerful-bodied animals with large flat heads, blunted muzzles and small pendulous ears.

Now those blunt muzzles lifted and the flattened heads weaved like serpents, questing for the scents of the newcomers. A deep-throated menacing growling accompanied their restless pacings backwards and forwards, but they never crossed the line of the gates; it was as if some invisible barrier prevented them from doing so.

'They are called mastiffs,' Hugh Taylor informed Tildy. 'Supposedly first bred by crossing our own English bulldog with the Irish greyhound – a mixture guaranteed to produce a ferocious beast, is it not?'

Tildy paid little heed to his words. The dogs frightened her and held her gaze. She wanted to turn back and leave this house, and was on the verge of asking the doctor to do just that, when at a shouted command from William White, the dogs loped away and the chaise jolted forward through the gates. William White swung them closed behind the chaise and then crunched across the gravelled foreground to the flight of balustraded stone steps which rose in an elegant sweep to the front entrance of the house. As the two passengers alighted from the chaise the game-keeper again selected a key from his bunch, unlocked the front door, then clumsily bowed and invited,

'Please to step inside, Doctor Taylor.'

Hugh Taylor entered the gloomy doorway, and Tildy drew a deep breath and followed, keeping her eyes averted from William White's reptilian stare.

The hallway smelled of musty decay, and their heels thumped hollowly on the dusty bare floorboards. There were no wall-hangings, no pictures on the dirty, damp-mottled walls, and not even a hatstand for furnishings. A flight of stairs led to the upper floors and closed doors were spaced along the hall.

William White pointed at a door beyond the stairs at the far end of the hallway.

'The kitchen is through theer, young 'ooman. You goo in theer and wait till I comes for you.'

Tildy stared questioningly at Hugh Taylor and he smiled reassuringly. 'Yes, Crawford, do as White bids you. He will command household affairs until the return of Mr Dugdale, but you will, of course, be responsible for the care of Mrs Dugdale.'

As the two men mounted the stairs Tildy opened the door to find it led into a long narrow unlighted passage. Traversing this she came to and opened a further door to find herself in the large stone-flagged kitchen. It was cold, gloomy and cheerless. No fire burned in the great rusted iron cooking range, and every surface and visible utensil was coated with stale grease and dirt and mouldy scraps of food. When she breathed in she could taste the cold stench of the room on her tongue and throat.

'Dear God,' she murmured, 'what have I come to here?'

She became aware of a scurry of movement in the vast stone sink beneath the solitary window and stepped towards it, only to recoil in shock and disgust as she saw the large wet-furred rat scavenging among the used platters, pots and pans that the sink was filled with. The rat lifted its head and its nose twitched as it calmly regarded her. Tildy's shock receded and she experienced a fast-mounting angry revulsion. Snatching up a billet of wood from the fuel box at the cooking range, she advanced upon the sink.

'Scat! Go on, scat!' she shouted suddenly, and darted forwards to swing her improvised weapon in a wildly-aimed blow. The wet-furred body exploded into movement and she felt it thump heavily against her thigh, then it was gone.

'Don't come back, because I'll not share a kitchen with you,' she shouted after the vanished rodent, and then realized to her own acute surprise that she had already mentally committed herself to remain in this house.

Searching for a relatively clean spot she laid her bundle upon the big table and started to move around the room, taking a mental inventory of its contents. She became so engrossed in this that the entry of William White took her unawares, and she flushed when she suddenly noticed him standing in the doorway.

'You startled me!'

'Youm to come wi' me, young 'ooman,' he told her, unsmiling, and she went to pick up her bundle.

'Leave it lay,' the man instructed. 'These 'ull be your quarters so you can leave your belongings here.'

'And where will I sleep?' Tildy asked.

'Wi' the mistress.' He ran his yellow-furred tongue over his thick lower lip. 'But if at times you fancies a change o' bedmate, then I'll be available.'

There was no humour in his voice or his expression, merely a flat statement, and again an uneasy tremor of nervousness ran through Tildy. She took care not to betray any of that nervousness when she answered him however, but presented a bold front.

'Let's be clear about things, Master White. I don't share any man's bed, and I don't enjoy loose talk. If you speak with me, then speak decently and properly, or I'll very quickly tell Doctor Taylor that you're insulting me.'

Again the furred tongue slowly licked across the thick lower lip leaving a glistening slime of saliva, but he made no answer, only jerked his head for her to follow, and went back along the dark narrow passageway.

Hugh Tayloe was waiting in the hallway. 'I've informed Mrs Dugdale that you are here, Crawford. White will take you to her.'

'Very well, Sir,' Tildy acquiesced, 'but will you give me

the full instructions as to Mrs Dugdale's treatments and regimen before you leave?'

She saw the gleam of annoyance in the young man's eyes.

'For God's sake, Crawford, do you think yourself a doctor? What need is there for you to worry your head about treatment and regimen? You are here only to see to the lady's bodily needs and to keep her company.'

Steeling herself against his patent displeasure, she persisted doggedly. 'But Sir, surely there will be tonics and medicines that Mrs Dugdale will need to take?'

'God dammee, Crawford!' he burst out impatiently. 'You are not here to treat the lady's afflictions, but merely to act as her nurse. She is suffering from hysteric affections and as always they display a variety of symptoms at different times. Headaches of bilious or hysteric nature, and the melancholia, for example. You are only here to ensure that she does no harm to herself during any of these attacks. Do not try and go beyond your station by concerning yourself with treatments.'

Tildy bit her lips and accepted the scathing rebuff without attempting any defence.

Hugh Taylor remained staring at her with a mingled incredulity and irritation. He had brought Tildy here to soothe the family conscience concerning their kinswoman. He personally had little interest in the woman or desire to treat her for anything other than pecuniary reasons. He was a doctor because that was his way of earning a comfortable living, not because it was his vocation.

'If you have need of me then come to my house, or send word by messenger,' he snapped at Tildy, and then ignored her completely, turning instead to the gamekeeper. 'Keep those damned hell hounds away, White, while I drive out.'

'Ahr, Sir, I'll do that.'

The two men went outside and Tildy remained standing in the gloomy hallway, hearing the chaise depart and experiencing a sense of lonely isolation as the great gates were closed, barred and padlocked.

William White re-entered the hallway and stood directly before her.

'Well now, young 'ooman, that just leaves me and thee here, doon't it?'

With an effort Tildy once again faced his cold reptilian eyes with a bold front. 'You're forgetting the mistress, are you not? She is here also, Master White.'

'Ahr, that's so, arn't it? I'm forgetting the mistress. But then, that's easy to do, for she hardly ever leaves her rooms.'

Unsmiling he pointed his spatulate hand through the doorway to the gravelled forecourt and the growling, restlessly pacing mastiffs. 'I'm forgetting my dogs as well, arn't I, young 'ooman? But doon't you ever be so foolish as to forget they'm out theer and go walking outside the house. They'd tear the throat from you in seconds.'

Tildy fought hard not to betray the fear that the dogs invoked in her. 'How am I to carry out my duties if I can't step outside without being savaged by those dogs?' she asked tartly.

'They'm barred off from the kitchen yard, and the brew'us and privvies, young 'ooman, so you'll be able to carry out your duties all right. And iffen anything else is needed outside, then I does it.'

Tildy frowned at his surly features. 'But that means I'm a prisoner in the house and kitchen yard,' she protested angrily, and for the first time a hint of a smile quirked his thick lips.

'Ahr, that's so, arn't it, young 'ooman? Youm like a prisoner here; and them buggers theer,' again he pointed to the dogs. 'Well, they'm kind of like the bloody turnkeys, arn't they?'

Tildy's fiery spirit ignited. 'Well Master White, I don't much like being kept within four walls as if I were a convict,' she declared.

His cold eyes mocked her. 'Iffen you doon't like it, young 'ooman, then you'll just have to fuckin' well lump it, wun't you?'

She realized that he was taking pleasure in baiting her,

and this fuelled her anger. 'Oh no!' she told herself, 'No, I'll not stay passive and let this man bully me. I've been bullied too much already in my life. I'll not submit to any more such treatment without giving battle.'

Summoning all her courage she held the man's eyes with her own and slowly shook her head from side to side, deliberately assuming an expression of contempt as she stated firmly,

'I'll not ''lump'' anything that does not suit me, Master White. You think me to be some friendless serving-wench that you can bully and put upon as you've a mind to. You're a fool for thinking that. A thick-skulled chaw-bacon.'

Savagery twisted his brutal features and he slowly moved towards her, fists bunching in threat.

Momentarily Tildy's heart quailed, but with an immense effort of will she stood her ground and kept the contemptuous look on her face. 'You just dare, White!' she challenged. 'You just dare to lift your fists to me, and you'll sorely rue the day you did.'

She saw the fractional wavering of uncertainty in him, and boldly stepped to meet him. 'I'm not afeared of you, and I've not come to this house to be bullied by you or by anybody else. My friends will not permit that to happen.'

White came to a halt and began to bluster. 'You 'eard what Doctor Taylor hisself said. That I was to command in house matters, and that you was to do as I says.'

Instinctively Tildy knew that for the moment at least, she had gained the upper hand. But her instinct also warned her not to press this man too hard, that there was a dark bestiality within his being that, once unleashed, would not be halted in its rampaging short of death. She carefully chose her words.

'I understood Doctor Taylor to mean that I was to come to you in matters concerning the management of the house, but that in anything concerning the care of Mrs Dugdale then it was my responsibility, and my charge only that was to be obeyed, and that you were not to gainsay me in such matters.'

He remained in sullen silence and Tildy sensed that the danger of any physical assault had passed for the meantime. 'I've no wish to quarrel with you, Master White,' she went on, relief from tension making her a little breathy as she spoke. 'But surely you can understand that it's a hard thing when I cannot even walk outside the house.'

''Tis not my doing.' The gamekeeper's voice held a placatory note. 'It's the master who will have the dogs running free behind the walls. He can't abide the thought o' burglars or suchlike.'

Tildy deliberately used her sexual appeal and smiled warmly at the man. 'Oh, I do not blame you for that, Master White, but it seems very hard that I cannot take a stroll and breathe fresh air occasionally.'

Twice White opened his mouth to reply and twice closed it without speaking. Tildy, inwardly despising herself for using such tactics, but at the same time realizing that they were the only weapons available to her, smiled again, and coquettishly tapped the gamekeeper on his arm.

'I'm sure that if you wanted to, then you could arrange it so that I could walk for a while each day in the woods. After all, Master White, you stand as the master of the hall while Mr Dugdale is away.'

He scowled and shuffled uncomfortably. 'I'll see what can be done, young 'ooman, but I'm promising naught,' he conceded grudgingly. 'And you must heed what I tell you now.'

'I will, Master White,' she promised submissively.

He stared at her keenly, then appearing satisfied with her present attitude, the scowl left his face. 'Youm only ever to goo into the rooms of Mrs Dugdale, and the kitchen and scullery. Youm not to poke and pry about the hall. Mr Dugdale is most particular on that. Youm to keep strictly to your own business.' Perhaps softened by Tildy's smiles, he added, 'There's rooms in the hall that even I arn't give entrance to, young 'ooman. The master's got some funny ways about him, and he's a man o' many secrets.'

'Do you live in the house?' Tildy interrupted curiously.

'No. I'se got a little cottage in the woods out back theer. But you'se got no call to worry about being two women alone in the house o' nights. The spikes and the dogs 'ud stop Old Nick hisself from getting in here.'

'Then are there no other servants at all?' Tildy was shocked. 'I mean, I know the kitchen looks neglected, but still I thought there would be some other servant here.'

The gamekeeper shook his head. 'Nobody! Like I said, the master's got some funny ways, and he don't like anybody poking about in the hall, nor even close to it either. His tenants on the farms 'ull not dare step within half a mile o' the house unless he's invited 'um special. Iffen the master was to catch any of 'um in the woods about the house, then he'd have 'um off the estate, bag and baggage within the hour.'

As she listened, Tildy could not help feeling a degree of wry amusement. 'It seems I'm always fated to end up with the weird ones,' she thought, and her lips quirked into a smile. 'I hope it's not a question of birds of a feather . . . '

'Come on, girl, I'll take you up to the mistress, and then I'm off, I'se got things to see to. You'll find food and drink in the kitchen cupboards when youm ready for 'um . . . Just remember though, doon't step outside the house, no matter what you might fancy breathing in the way o' fresh air. We'll sort out your walks tomorrow.'

The broad landing at the top of the stairs resembled the lower floor in its empty neglect, and from the landing a series of dark corridors stretched away from all sides. White slammed his hand against the panels of the door nearest to the stair-head and, opening it inwards, pushed Tildy through into the room.

'Here's your new nuss-'ooman, mistress,' he bellowed, and closed the door shut again as he shouted.

The room was in semi-darkness and Tildy stood for a couple of moments accustoming her eyes to the gloom. When she was able to dimly see the interior she looked about her. A round table dominated the centre of the room and ranged around it were four tall-backed, winged armchairs. On one of these chairs was seated the figure of a woman, and as Tildy strained her eyes to pierce the darkness she saw that the woman appeared to be heavily veiled.

'Why should she need a veil?' Tildy wondered, 'with the room already made so dark by drawn curtains? Is she mad, I wonder?' The thought sent a shiver of apprehension through her, but that apprehension was rapidly overtaken by annoyance. 'If she is then those fine gentlemen in Redditch have gulled me, sure enough – telling me that she was only suffering from hysteric affections when by the looks of this she could be stark raving mad.'

As quickly as the thought itself apprehension again gained dominance, and Tildy's eyes flicked about her, peering through the gloom for potential avenues of escape, or weapons of defence. Then her innate courage and stubbornness came to her aid.

'I'm behaving like a stupid, vapouring fool!' she thought scathingly. 'That's a poor sick creature on that chair, not some evil demon. God strike me for being such a pathetic sniveller.'

Slowly and deliberately she moved across to the tall windows and found the draw-cord of the thick, heavy drapes.

'I'm going to let some light into the room, Mrs Dugdale,' she informed the silent seated woman, and suited action to her words. Bright sunlight struck into her eyes blinding her for an instant and she squinted and blinked against it then turned to speak to the black-veiled, black-clad woman.

'You don't need the curtains drawn, Mrs Dugdale. It's better to have the sunlight. I'm come here to care for you. There's no need for you to be afeared of me. My name is Matilda Crawford, but most people just call me Tildy.' As she was speaking Tildy felt a sensation of surety burgeon within her. Now that the room was filled with sunny daylight she could take stock.

Like the rest of the house it smelled of damp and decay, and she saw that apart from the table and chairs there were only the fire-irons in the grate, two candlesticks on the table, and the threadbare carpet on the floor.

'And now, mistress, let me take a look at you.' Tildy was already deciding that no matter how she might feel inwardly, her outer manner would only ever radiate confidence and strength of purpose. Was that not what Doctor Buchan recommended?

She slowly lifted the heavy dark veil from the motionless head and laid it back across the black-clad shoulders.

'Dear God, but you are truly beautiful,' she murmured aloud in surprise. Having expected to find features ravaged with age or disease, instead of this pale translucent complexion, wide-spaced grey eyes and thick waves of chestnut hair framing an oval face.

Not a flicker of expression crossed the woman's features, and the grey eyes gazed stonily as if fixed on something beyond the confines of the room.

Tildy became conscious of the acrid smell of the woman's body. A smell interlaced with another heavier, more putrid odour. 'I'll need to bathe and change you, Mrs Dugdale,' she told the woman, but received no reaction from her. Frustration welled up in Tildy, and she desperately wished that there was someone here who could explain fully to her what exactly was wrong with Sybil Dugdale. Panic fluttered in her stomach and for a brief moment Tildy almost gave way to it, then she forced herself to think rationally. 'I've got my books here. They'll surely give me the answers I seek.'

The thought of the knowledge stored within her bundle down in the kitchen instilled fresh confidence in Tildy.

'But I must do things in the right order,' her own native commonsense intervened. 'It's warm and sunny at the moment, but soon the night will bring cold and darkness. So we'll need fires, and food and drink, and candles to give us light. Baths and medicine can wait till tomorrow, for now I've got all these other things to think on.'

She stood staring at her patient, and gently stroked the cold pale cheeks. 'You sit here, Mrs Dugdale, and I'll get matters in order,' Tildy whispered, and smiled happily as her spirits surged upwards in answer to the challenge.

The hours flew by as Tildy laboured, sweeping,

101

scrubbing, washing, scouring, coaxing damp wood to burn in the iron range, carrying coals and kindling to Sybil Dugdale's room and laying a fire there. She found food in the kitchen cupboards, and when the cleaning was done she prepared a meal of boiled eggs, toast and butter, cold sliced meats and pickles and a pot of tea, then carried the meal through the now dark house and upstairs.

Sybil Dugdale was still sitting in the winged armchair, but now when Tildy entered the room the wide-set grey eyes took note of her. The only light was that given out by the fire, but Tildy had found tallow candles in the kitchen, and now she set two of them into the candlesticks on the table and lit them with a flaring taper.

She was aware of Sybil Dugdale's regard, and she smiled at the silent woman. 'There now, Ma'am, the fire and candles make everything seem more cheery, don't they?' She arranged a knife, fork and spoon by the woman's hands and poured tea into a cup. 'There now, Ma'am, I've got your supper here for you.'

She placed the platter of shelled eggs before Mrs Dugdale and put the spoon into the flaccid hand. At the touch of the cold skin, Tildy exclaimed, 'You're so cold, Ma'am. Do you feel chilled?'

'Yes . . . yes, I am cold. I am always cold.' Sybil Dugdale's voice was low-pitched and hoarse as if from disuse.

Tildy experienced a rush of relief. 'I was getting feared that you'd never speak to me, Ma'am,' she burst out. 'Indeed, I feared that you didn't even know I was here.' She paused, and then went on quickly. 'You know that I'm here to look after you, don't you, Ma'am? I'm Matilda Crawford, your new nurse-woman, but everybody calls me Tildy.'

'You are Matilda Crawford.' Sybil Dugdale's face was curiously empty of expression and her voice likewise.

'Are you hungry, Ma'am?' Tildy indicated the platter of eggs and the buttered toast. 'If you eat something that will warm you, and eggs are good for you.'

'Eggs are good for me,' the woman repeated, and then

lifting the spoon she began to eat. Her movements were stiff and jerky and Tildy was irresistibly reminded of a puppet she had once seen when a child.

Looking towards the window she saw that the night was now very dark, so she went to draw the drapes. The window overlooked the tall spiked wall and the woodlands beyond. There was no moon, and in the faint glimmering of the starlight the woods were a black formless mass. Tildy drew the drape cords as she looked out over the woodlands, then abruptly her hand stilled. There was a flickering light moving among the trees. Tildy remained motionless, watching the light's erratic progress and wondering who or what it might be.

'It's probably William White,' she decided. 'Searching for poachers most like.' The thought of that sinister man wandering through the dark of the night caused a shiver to run up Tildy's spine, and she jerked hard on the cords to bring the drapes swishing violently together and shut off that disturbing vision.

Sybil Dugdale swallowed a few spoonfuls of eggs and then laid the spoon down.

'Will you not eat more?' Tildy asked. 'If not the eggs, then try a little of the meat and relish, Ma'am.'

'No, I want nothing else. I'll sleep now.' Still the woman's voice was flat and devoid of expression, and as Tildy watched Sybil Dugdale leaned back into the armchair and closed her eyes.

Made uncertain, Tildy said hesitantly, 'Which is your bedroom, Ma'am? I'll go and prepare the bed for you.'

Without opening her eyes Sybil Dugdale told her, 'I sleep here in my chair. Be quiet now, so that I may rest.'

Tildy stood still, absorbing this bizarre information, and her mistress added, still with eyes closed, 'You will sleep in the chair facing me. All my nurses sleep in that chair.'

'But to sleep in a chair will not rest you properly, Ma'am,' Tildy remonstrated.

The wide-set eyes opened and in the candlelight the whites of them seemed unnaturally large. 'I am mistress here, girl. You will do as I say.' One white hand lifted and pointed to the opposite chair. 'Sit there, girl, and make no further noise. I must not be disturbed.'

For a brief moment the urge to argue further caused Tildy to waver, then she mentally shrugged. 'What does it matter for this night where I sleep. I've known harder beds than that chair,' she thought with a trace of ironic amusement. 'If it makes the woman happy, then so be it. Tomorrow will be another day.'

Without further ado she took the chair allotted to her and settled herself as comfortably as she could within its capacious wings.

Sybil Dugdale's eyes closed again and within scant minutes the loud sawing of breath through her nostrils indicated that she slept.

Tildy gazed into the fire, her mind filled with a confusion of thoughts, feelings and mental images, of little Davy and William White, of the mastiffs and Widow Fairfax, of Mother Readman, and Harry Mogg's piquant, gap-toothed smile. Her head sank lower and lower and at last she drifted into sleep, shifting restlessly as from outside there sounded the howling of the guardians of the Hall, but not awakening.

The tallow candles burned low and spluttered out, and the leaping flames in the grate sank and died down. With soft cracklings the burning coals shifted and smouldered and subsided to a dull-glowing shapeless heap, and in the woods overlooked by the tall window of the room the mysterious light still bobbed erratically through the trees . . .

Chapter Twelve

Tildy awoke cold and stiff-jointed, and for a moment or two she stared bemusedly about her until recollection came with full wakefulness. Across the table Sybil Dugdale was also awake. But she sat staring blankly at the remnants of the previous night's supper, and when Tildy wished her a good morning she gave no sign of having heard.

Tildy sighed and rose from the chair to draw back the curtains. Memory of the mysterious light caused her to look keenly at the woodlands, but the great masses of yellowing dying leaves and shadowed undergrowths were still and peaceful.

Below the window a solitary mastiff sat on its haunches, burrowing for fleas in its short thick fur. From around the corner of the house the other dogs erupted into furious barkings and the mastiff instantly added its own deep-toned voice to the chorus and went loping away to join its fellows.

'Someone must be at the gates,' Tildy thought, and eager to see what might be a friendly face, she hastened to gather the supper dishes and take them downstairs to the kitchen, then ran to the front door and cautiously cracked it open. She could see no one, except the now silent pack of dogs clustered in the forecourt, and disappointed she closed the door and went back upstairs.

As she moved around Sybil Dugdale, Tildy was again

made aware of the woman's foul body odours and she said softly, 'You'll need to be bathed and changed today, Ma'am; and I wish you would tell me when you want to go to the privy.'

There was no reply, no change of expression, only the same blank stare.

'Poor soul,' Tildy murmured and patted the woman's slender shoulder. 'As soon as your husband returns I shall ask him to let me get some medicines for your affliction. I'm sure I'll be able to find a suitable treatment for you from my books . . . ' Again the foul stench filled Tildy's nostrils. 'But first, Ma'am, a bath is what's needed. There's no doubt on that, at any rate.'

Down in the kitchen again Tildy lit a fire in the cooking range and set a cauldron of water to heat. In the adjoining brewhouse she filled the great copper boiler and lit the fire beneath that also. Then from the scullery she carried the tin hip-bath out into the yard and scoured it beneath the pump. As she worked visions of little Davy continually filled her mind's eye, but she forced herself to thrust away all thoughts of her child.

''Tis no use my pining for my Davy,' she realized sadly. 'I'm here and he's at Crabb's Cross, and there's naught can be done about that at this time.'

As soon as her preparations were completed downstairs Tildy carried coals and kindling to Sybil Dugdale's room and laid a fire there also. She felt the woman's ice-cold hands and clucked her tongue in sympathy.

'Dear God, Ma'am, you're like ice again.'

'Yes, I'm cold. I'm always so very, very cold, so very cold.' Sybil Dugdale's voice was devoid of all inflection, and Tildy was yet again reminded of a puppet-doll.

From outside the dogs sent up a volley of excited barking and Tildy ran to the window, peering out, searching for what disturbed them, but could see only falling leaves being tossed and tumbled by a skittish wind. She became conscious of the stale taste of her own mouth, and the greasy feel of her body. 'I need a bath myself,' she acknowledged, and grinned mischievously. 'I can bathe in the copper before it gets too hot. The water will also do to wash Mrs Dugdale in. I can use the water from the range to rinse her down.'

Eager to feel clean and fresh again, Tildy made sure that her mistress was comfortably settled before the warming fire then hurried downstairs.

She rummaged in her bundle for a towel and a cake of hard yellow soap, and took them with her to the brew-house. As she crossed the few yards which separated the outhouses from the main building she heard the dogs barking excitedly yet again, but she paid no further heed to them. 'It'll be the leaves blowing about that's upsetting them,' she was sure.

'It was in the Mer-ry month of Mayyyy
In the Springtime of the year,
T''was down in yonder meadowland
That runs to the rivvvverrr clear . . . '

The sweet-toned singing reassured William White that he could not be heard as he edged his way towards the small window of the brewhouse. From its crack-panelled door wisps floated out, white on the crisp air, and the man guessed that Tildy Crawford was washing clothes or bedding. Yet still he crept stealthily, for that was his way, to skulk and hide and observe without being observed, relishing the sense of power it gave him to watch un-suspecting women, knowing that he had them at his mercy.

'Oh, see the little childrennnn,
How they do sport and playyyy,
From the morning to the evening,
When we are making hayyyyy . . . '

Happiness throbbed in Tildy's voice as she sang, physically lost in the sensual pleasure of hot water laving her body, cleansing away the staleness of the night.

The man reached the window and cautiously peered in through the cornermost pane. What he saw through the misted glass made him catch his breath. The girl was naked. Standing in profile to him beside the copper, washing her upper body.

White's bleary eyes greedily devoured the full shapely breasts, the slender waist, the plumply dimpled buttocks and the dark triangle that crowned her rounded thighs. His furred tongue ran across his lips and his mouth dried with lust. His first impulse was to kick open the door, to glory in her terror as she saw him come. To savour the terrified frantic turnings of her eyes as she sought for escape. And then to relentlessly ravage her lush body and brutalize her until she begged and prayed for mercy.

His heart thudded and his breathing quickened to panting. His hands went inside the waistband of his breeches and clutched and rubbed his hard-throbbing maleness, while in his mind conflicting demons battled for domination. 'Have her now, while no one's around. Fuck the arse off her. Do it now! . . . No! Wait! You were lucky last time. You nearly got caught by going arter that wench wi'out a plan . . . Wait, and plan this 'un careful. When you have her, make sure it canna be laid at your door. Don't go busting in there like a fool. Wait and plan it careful. Then you can do what you wants to the bitch, and spend all the time you wants adoing it . . . Oh, the sweet-bodied bitch. The dirty little whore . . . The dirty, cock-teasing bitch.' Even while the conflict raged within him, his spatulate hands kept on kneading and rubbing and pulling until with a gasping intake of breath he climaxed and his seed exploded from him . . .

'Up comes the jovial scytheman
To cut the grass all down.
With his good old leathern bottle,
And the ale in it so brownnnn . . . ' Tildy sang on as she lathered her tender skin with the coarse gritty soap, and washed and sluiced until she felt a deep-glowing cleanliness that brought with it a sense of well-being and contentment such as she had not experienced in many long weary months.

'There's many a stout strong labouring man,
Comes here his skill to tryyyyy.

108

      And he whets, he blows, he stoutly mows,
      And his grass cuts very dryyyyy . . . ' she sang
on, as the man crept silently away.

Cheeks flushed, eyes shining, Tildy came into the kitchen
still humming her song, and then halted abruptly, her body
tense.

'Master White, I never knew you was here.' She was
flustered and afraid of what could have happened had the
man come into the brewhouse while she was naked.

He loured dourly at her. 'I'se only this second come,
girl. Wheer's you bin?'

Relief coursed through her and she visibly relaxed. 'I'm
acting like a fool,' she scolded herself, ''imagining every
man is going to jump on me if he gets half a chance. I'm
worse than some vapouring old maid!'

Guilty about her initial reaction on seeing White in the
kitchen, Tildy talked to him in friendlier manner than
would have been her normal inclination. 'I've been
washing myself, Master White. I felt so stale and dirty, I
couldn't resist the chance of a good scrub-down . . . and
now I'm going to bathe the mistress. Would you know
where the linen-press is? I must have fresh clothes for the
mistress.'

White stared into her eyes, and inside his head he saw
her lying under him, beaten and defenceless, and his hands
twitched as if his fingers were even now cruelly mauling
and squeezing her firm breasts. Suddenly he realized that
she was looking at him now with uneasy eyes, as if she
sensed what was going on within his head, and he forced
himself to calm down.

'I'll need to box clever,' he told himself. 'It's no use me
getting her scared o' me now. That 'ull have to come later,
when I'se got her wheer I wants her.' Aloud he muttered,
'The press is two doors along the landing from the
mistress's room. Mind you don't goo poking about in the
other rooms. The master 'udden't like that.' He essayed a
grim smile. 'But I arn't moithered iffen you should happen

109

to goo into the other rooms by mistake like . . . They'm all locked anyways, and the master holds the keys.' The dogs began their deep-pitched barking once more, and White told her, 'I'd best goo and see to them. I'll see you later, girl.'

With a nod he left her, and Tildy sagged from her tenseness with a sigh of relief.

'I'm scared of him,' she admitted. 'There's something in him that affects me so, no matter how hard I try not to be fritted.' She smiled wryly. 'Still, like Mother Readman says, what can't be cured must be endured.'

She carried the tin hip-bath upstairs and placed it in front of the fire in Sybil Dugdale's room. The woman was sitting as Tildy had left her and she made no move even when Tildy inadvertently banged the bath loudly against the door jamb.

Tildy was pleasantly surprised to find in the various chests and hampers of the linen press a plentiful quantity of clean clothing and linen. She quickly selected white cotton petticoats and stockings, an undershift and a dark green, ruff-necked day gown. Mindful of the increasing chill of the weather she also laid aside a variety of shawls, merino-woollen ones among them. In one chest she found an assortment of stays, but rejected the idea of taking a pair for Mrs Dugdale. 'I'll not add to the poor soul's troubles by lacing her into these until she can't draw an easy breath.' Not for the first time Tildy was thankful for the slenderness of her own waist - which enabled her to do without the strictures of leather, whalebone and laces.

A pile of clean towels completed Tildy's selection and she triumphantly carried her armful back to the room. A wearying succession of trips up and down the stairs followed, but at the end of them the hip-bath was filled with steaming hot water and ready to receive its occupant.

Sybil Dugdale docilely allowed herself to be undressed. Unpleasant as the smell of the woman's self-soiled body was, Tildy was able to disregard it. Unpleasant smells had been a constant accompaniment throughout her life, after all. What she could not disregard however, were the

110

numerous bruises on the thin white body of her mistress. Sybil Dugdale's torso, arms and legs were mottled with both old and fresh bruises and abrasions, some yellowing and faint, some greenish, and some black-purple. On the soft skin of her inner thighs small round blotches of discoloured flesh brought an unhappy frown of recognition to Tildy's face. 'I've borne such bruises . . . ' It was a shaming, sickening memory, and unable to stop herself she asked, 'What caused these here, Ma'am?'

The woman blinked and looked uncomprehendingly at Tildy's pointing fingers, then the fearful look of a hunted creature entered the blank eyes, and the thin body trembled violently.

'He did it . . . Master Dugdale . . . It was his hands that marked me so . . . He hurts me . . . ' As quickly as it had come, the moment of recognition passed and the shivering ceased. Again the wide-set eyes became dulled and emptied of expression.

'Dear God, what sort of an animal is this man, to force himself on a woman who is sick in mind?' Tildy thought bitterly. 'And how many other men have I known who were equally bad? The tragedy is that most of we women are helpless to defend ourselves against them.'

Gently and slowly she led Sybil Dugdale to the hip-bath and guided her into its warm depths. Then she carefully sponged away the encrusted filth from the thin white hips and legs. As the bruises on the thighs again confronted her eyes Tildy was overcome by apprehension about Henry Geast Dugdale's return to Bordesley Hall. 'What might he not do to me, who is only a servant, if he serves his own wife so?' she pondered anxiously. 'Dear God, have I this time bitten off more than I can ever chew, I wonder . . . '

Chapter Thirteen

Just across the street from the new lock-up, in the middle of a huddle of buildings, was Professor Parr's barber shop. Today was Sunday, and while the godly made their way to worship, numbers of the ungodly gathered at the premises of Ebenezer Parr. He was a bespectacled, rotund, jolly man who favoured the powdered short-bobbed wig, and always wore a dull red-coloured coat and waistcoat beneath his bibless, pocketed chequered apron. The colour of his clothing was deliberately chosen for its practical nature, because in addition to cutting hair, shaving chins and renovating dilapidated perukes, Parr also pulled teeth, performed blood-letting, and treated cuts, bruises, sprains and dislocations. It was these latter accomplishments which had earned him the sobriquet of 'professor'.

When Harry Mogg came into the shop its benches were crowded with men and the air was thick with tobacco smoke and reeking breaths from the previous night's ales and ciders. Professor Parr was busily trimming the hair of a sheet-swathed young needle pointer, Seth Adams. Adams looked into the large wall-mirror before him and exclaimed,

'Bugger me, Harry, who gi' you the shiner?'

Mogg smiled ruefully and cautiously touched his hugely swollen and discoloured eye. 'Me and Pincher Cull had a falling out over the dominoes. He gi' me this afore I laid him out. He Judas-punched, the crafty bastard.'

After casual glances no one paid any further attention to the damaged eye. Injuries caused by violent brawls were so commonplace as to be regarded as part of normal physical appearance in the poorer quarters of the town.

Ebenezer Parr cast a professional eye at the contusion.

'Set yourself down, Harry, I'll deal wi' you directly I finish this bugger's mop o' wool.'

'Less o' the cheek, you saucy old sod,' Seth Adams mock-growled. 'I'se got nice hair, I 'as. All the girls likes to run their fingers through it.'

'It arn't the hair on your yed that you makes 'um run their fingers through, but the crop lower down, you randy little bleeder,' Parr chortled. 'I'se sin you and Billy Carter's youngest girl down the Abbey Meadows under the bushes.'

'Ahr, and if Billy Carter see's you under the bushes wi' her, you'll get two o' what Harry's sporting this morn,' another man interjected.

'Phew! I'd like to see him try and gi' me a hammering.' The rosy youthful features assumed an expression of exaggerated ferocity. 'I'm a regular hard-chaw, I am, Owen Buggins, and don't you be forgetting it. Konks 'um down like ninepins, I does, when me blood's up.'

The shop erupted with jeering laughter and catcalls, and Seth Adams joined in the laughter against himself.

Harry Mogg sat quietly, enjoying the rough banter and camaraderie. Most of the men present were pointers and they all bore the marks of their hard living and reckless pleasures. But Harry knew that despite their brutal manners, the majority were good-hearted enough.

'I hears tell that Annie Amor has bin before the justices to swear an order agen you, Seth,' an older, grey-headed man winked at his fellows.

The young pointer took the bait. 'Agen me? An order agen me? What for? A bastard, or what? Telling 'um I'm the father, is she?'

The room hushed expectantly as the older man deliberately prevaricated to bait Adams further.

'Come on, spit it out, badger-yed,' Adams pressed

impatiently. 'You'se made a statement, now let's hear the rest on it. What's she swearing an order agen me for?'

The older man grinned delightedly. 'Well it arn't for giving her a full belly, that's for sure, Seth my buck. No, from what I hears it's for just the opposite. Her reckons that you canna get it up at all, and she wants the justices to stiffen your prick for you.'

The young pointer's rosy cheeks flamed into a fiery red, and again a howl of jeering laughter filled the room. Unable to think of a suitable rejoinder because he had indeed failed with Annie Amor, Seth Adams subsided into sulky silence.

'Theer now, that 'ull do for you, my handsome.' Ebenezer Parr whipped away the protective sheet with a flourish. 'That's tuppence, and another tuppence for your shave.'

Seth Adams paid and then came to squeeze in beside Harry Mogg.

'I'se got a message for you, Harry, but it's private,' he whispered, and Mogg nodded.

'All right Seth, but let me get this eye seen to fust.'

On wall shelves each side of the mirror were ranged a variety of glass and stone jars of differing sizes, and Parr took down one of the larger vessels and removed its lid to display that it was filled with dark stained water. 'I got some beauties here lads, got 'um out o' Dunkerley's Hole yesterday.' He inserted his fingers into the jar and fished about for a couple of moments then brought out a thin sluglike grey-black leech to show it to the assembly. 'He's prime, arn't he? He's a little beauty, so he is.' Dropping the leech back into the jar, Parr deftly soaped and cleansed the skin of Harry Mogg's damaged eye, then laid the towel on the pointer's knees. His touch was so light that Harry hardly felt it.

'My oath, Ebenezer, iffen you touches your old woman so gentle as you touches me, then it's no wonder she looks so happy and contented all the time.'

Another outburst of laughter greeted Mogg's words. It

was well known in the town that Mrs Parr was an exceptionally sour-faced shrew of a woman.

Parr grinned and sharply nipped the swollen eye between his finger and thumb.

'Owww!' Harry Mogg ejaculated in pain, and Parr told him,

'That'll learn you not to be so saucy about the light of me life.'

Again he reached for the big jar, and this time fished out three leeches in succession, and held them against the blackened, swollen flesh until they bit in and took hold. Almost immediately their thin glistening bodies began to visibly expand as they voraciously sucked in blood.

The barber nodded in satisfaction. 'I'll leave 'um to take their fill, Harry. You got a big 'un theer, and it'll need a lot o' sucking to bring it down . . . Right then, who's next for shaving? Is it you, Jemmy?'

The suckings of the leeches were only a slight discomfort and Harry was able to ignore them completely. 'Now Seth?' he asked in a low tone. 'What's the message?'

The younger man put his lips close to Harry's ear. 'Well, it arn't a message as such, Harry. But I reckoned you oughter know what's agoing on. You oughter be told.'

'Told what?' Harry was only mildly interested. The ale and gin he had drunk in such huge quantities the previous night were causing him to feel weary and hungover.

'It's about your kid,' the whisper came into his ear again. 'Your Susan.'

Now Harry Mogg's interest quickened. 'What about her?'

Seth Adams glanced about him, then satisfied that no one was paying any attention to their conversation he went on, 'Her's in a bad state. You know her's got a cottage in the next row up from me in Bredon Hill. Well, I comes under Ipsley Parish, but her comes under Tardebigge, doon't her?'

'So?' Harry queried. 'What of that?'

'So, her applied to the Tardebigge vestry last Thursday

for relief and they turned her back. They said her 'ud have to apply to Ipsley, so her did, but them buggers turned her back as well.'

'Why?' Harry was becoming concerned. He and his older sister, Susan, had never been close, and during recent years had rarely seen or spoken to each other, yet still there was a sense of family loyalty in Harry, and he was always prepared to help his sister, even though the last time they had met they had quarrelled bitterly.

'Well, it's the fault o' that bloody man of her's, arn't it? It was him who had settlement in Tardebigge, not her. Her was Ipsley born. But two weeks since, the bugger ran off from her and the kids agen, and nobody's seen hide nor hair of him since, and her's bin left wi' no rightful settlement. Mind you, it's a good riddance, I'd say. He was battering her summat cruel lately.'

Harry cursed vilely. His sister had taken up with a worthless violent drunkard and had remained with him despite anything Harry could say or do. She was not married to the man and Harry could understand why the local vestries would try and foist responsibility for her and the children on to each other's poor rates.

'I should ha' buried that bastard she took up with long since,' Harry cursed angrily. 'But whenever I give him a taste of his own medicine, our Susan used to take his part and turn on me.' He spat disgustedly on to the floor and then told his friend, 'All right Seth, I'll goo down to Bredon and see her. Mind you, I'm near skint meself, there's little or no work around even for us pointers. Still, blood's blood, and kin's kin, when all's said and done. I'll have to do what I can for her, iffen only for the childer's sakes.'

Susan Mogg had once been a pretty girl, but now she was a raddled caricature of femininity. Her battered face bore a permanent expression of cowed resignation, and her only reply to Harry's questions was a mute shaking of her head.

'You arn't seen that bugger for a sennight past then? And you doon't know when he might be back?'

Now the doleful features crumpled and tears streamed down the grimy cheeks, but the woman made no attempt to wipe her eyes, only squatted on the three-legged stool beside the fireless grate and stared at her brother with hopeless despair. Her scabbed, rickety, stick-ribbed brood huddled about their mother, and they too more resembled bent-bodied old men and women rather than young children.

Harry's anger at his sister's man mounted as he looked around the cramped, earth-floored room with its sticks of broken furniture, foul stench and rag-stuffed window. 'Bugger me, he's a bloody brickie's labourer, he could at least have laid a brick floor and mended the bleedin' window . . . ' Aloud, he said, 'Listen Susan, I'll give you some money to get food and coals.'

'I canna take any money from you, Harry.' For the first time the woman answered with words instead of silent gestures. 'Not arter the things I said to you last time we met.'

Exasperation caused him to shout at her, 'Fuck me, girl! Bloody hunger and cold 'ull likely kill you if you doon't take me money. What's the matter wi' you anyway, be you too proud to take charity all on a sudden? You'se never bin too proud afore . . . ' The visible fearful flinching his raised voice generated in the woman and children caused Harry to feel a rush of guilt, so he forced himself to speak softly and gently to them. 'Look, I doon't mean no harm to you when I shouts, so doon't be afeared o' me.' He took some coins from his breeches pocket and clasping the woman's limp hand he closed her unresponsive fingers upon the money. 'You'll take this, Susan, and you'll get a bit o' grub for you and the kids at any rate, so there's an end to it. Now I'm going to see what can be done about the other things.'

Harry retraced his steps back towards the town centre and as he walked tried to formulate a logical course of action.

'The best thing for me to do fust is go and see if I can find out why she was refused relief,' he decided, and headed directly towards St Stephen's chapel to await the ending of the morning service. He knew that at least three of the select vestrymen would be at that service. Reverend John Clayton, William Smallwood and Josiah Cutler. Harry Mogg knew all the men personally. Cutler was the biggest coal dealer in the district and William Smallwood was a needle master and factor. Harry decided to approach the latter. He had at times pointed batches of needles for the man and had liked him well enough.

The young pointer reached the chapel yard just as the service ended, and he stood a little distance from the doors and watched the congregation as they left the building. Most were people of some substance in the district, top-hatted needle masters and merchants, soft-handed shop-keepers and clerks, red-faced leather-gaitered farmers and the like, with just a smattering of the respectably shabby poor. The women were well-fed and well-clad, ornately bonneted and gowned, and many of the young girls twirled parasols above their heads and exchanged flirtatious giggles and glances with the marriageable men.

The burly, mutton-chopped whiskered William Small-wood, flanked by his fat wife and skinny daughter stopped on the chapel steps to have a word with the surpliced, be-wigged John Clayton.

'What's this me womenfolk here bin telling me, Parson John?' he demanded with heavy joviality. 'Is it right that I'm to miss my arternoon nap because youm acoming to take tay wi' us?' Like most of the needle masters Smallwood was a self-made man who had risen from humble beginnings and possessed little or no formal education and culture. In a district renowned for blunt speech, he was notorious for calling a spade a spade.

The clergyman smiled, and Eurydice, Smallwood's plain-faced, bony-bodied daughter blushed deeply and simpered, for she nursed a strong infatuation for the attractively ugly clergyman.

'Indeed Master Smallwood, I've been honoured by your

118

good lady wife with a most kindly invitation to join your family for high tea.'

'Excellent! I'm glad that you've accepted,' William Smallwood said bluffly. 'And you'll find the fare is like me, plain, but good and wholesome, and there's plenty on it to fill your belly . . . '

'Yes, plenty on it! It's a pity that you can't spare some on it to fill me sister and her kids' bellies, Will Smallwood.'

All the group swung to stare at Harry Mogg. Unabashed by their challenging eyes he went on, 'Why did you turn our Susan back when her asked for relief, Will Smallwood? That's what I wants to know.'

'This arn't the time, nor the place to talk about such matters, Mogg,' Smallwood stated irritably. 'That's vestry business, that is, and if you seeks to meddle in vestry affairs, then come to the next meeting. Now, be off wi' you!'

The needle pointer grinned, but there were sparks of anger dancing in his reckless eyes. 'Don't you use that tone wi' me, Smallwood. I arn't one o' your beat-down paupers, so doon't try to chase me away like a bloody cur dog. I've come to seek an answer, and you'd best gi' me one and be civil wi' it, as well.'

'Why, you cheeky young bugger . . . ' the needle master began to bluster furiously, then John Clayton smoothly intervened by stepping between the pair, saying as he did so, 'I shall call on you this afternoon then, ladies, Master Smallwood . . . And please to step inside the chapel with me, Mogg. I was present at the meeting your sister made application to. I will fully explain the reasons for our refusal of relief to her.' With deceptive strength he took hold of Harry Mogg's upper arm and walked him through the wide doorway.

As soon as they were inside Harry shook off the restraining hand. 'Theer was no call for you to step atween me and Will Smallwood, Parson,' he said with his gap-toothed grin. 'I'd not ha' lifted me hand agen the old bugger. I likes him well enough even if he does get a bit aerated now and agen.'

John Clayton returned the grin. 'I accept what you tell me, Mogg, but on the Sabbath I make a point of smoothing ruffled feathers, no matter how slightly they may be ruffled. Now I shall speak very frankly about your sister. She was refused relief because she is living with a worthless drunken ne'er-do-well, and in my opinion the parish would be well rid of him.'

Harry Mogg's piquant grin never faltered. He casually nodded agreement with the clergyman's statement.

'That's very true, Parson, I accepts what you say about him. But why do you make Susan and the kids suffer so? They arn't done anything wrong.'

Clayton was momentarily discomfited by the question, but recovered himself almost instantly. 'I did make that very point to the vestry myself, Mogg, but in all fairness the vestry did offer to take the woman and her children into the poorhouse at Webheath.'

Harry was unimpressed. 'That arn't doing 'um any favours, is it, Parson? Why couldn't you allow her outdoor relief so that she might stay in her cottage?'

'You know as well as I do what happens when the vestry allows outdoor relief to the womenfolk of habitual drunkards.' Clayton was scathingly dismissive of Harry's argument. 'Her man would undoubtedly have taken the money intended for his family and drank it away in the nearest beer-ken.'

'That's as maybe, but you can't know it for certain,' Harry argued doggedly, and now the last traces of the grin did leave his face, and again the sparks of anger danced in his eyes. 'You say that he's a drunken ne'er-do-well. I'll not argue the truth on that score, but the bugger's bin gone for a sennight, and me sister's bin nigh on starving. You could have granted her relief.'

Clayton pursed his lips and took a considerable time before replying. 'It was a vestry decision, Mogg, and I stand by it. Your sister and her children can enter the poorhouse if she so wishes. If she chooses to refuse our offer, then she must make her own way. If you are so concerned about her, then you must help her yourself. You are a single man with no responsibilities and earn good wages at your trade. I see naught to prevent you doing so.'

Harry Mogg grimaced in disgust. 'Naught but a lack o' bloody work, so I could earn enough to help her, Parson. Still, I'll say no more except good day to you . . .'

Chapter Fourteen

The flames roared high and sparks flew as Nail Styler pitched fresh logs on to the taproom fire.

'Fucking hell, Nail, bist you trying to roast us?' a man near the fire bawled, and Nail Styler turned his broken-nosed face to the crowded room and roared laughingly.

'Heat makes sweat, and sweat makes thirst, and thirst makes me my pennies.'

A chorus of good-natured jeers and catcalls answered him as he pushed his way back to his place behind the tall narrow counter of the big room. A dozen hanging lamps cast their smoky yellowish-red glare over the flushed-sweaty heads and faces of the close-packed men and women who drank and shouted and laughed in a tumult of merry-making, and Styler beamed happily as he anticipated the profits he would make that night.

It was the weekly gathering of the drinking club known as the 'Grindstone and Coffin Friendly Burial Society', and the black humour of its title was peculiarly apt, for the club members were mostly needle pointers. Nail Styler had himself been a pointer until an unexpected legacy had enabled him to become the landlord of the White Hart Inn at Headless Cross. He was also a prize-fighter of local renown, and because of this his house attracted to it the local sportsmen and their hangers-on, including the whores and the criminal elements of the district.

'A song! Who'll gi' us a song?' The shout went up, and a young pointer stood up on his bench and bawled,

'I'll gi' thee one, but close your ears, girls, it might get you all lathered.'

'It takes more than a song to get us lathered, Cully.' A gaudy-bonneted, heavily-rouged young girl laughed raucously, and winked broadly at her companions, women as thickly painted as herself.

'Give us the song then, Milky.'

'Gerron wi' it!'

'Let's have some hush.'

Voices bellowed from all parts of the room, and Milky Bradman waved his arms for silence, and ordered lame Ben Mitchell the fiddler, 'Play up, Ben, you knows the tune to the "Millstream" doon't you?'

The white-haired, twisted-bodied old fiddler lifted his fingers in a lewd gesture. 'Bollocks to you, Milky!' he snarled with assumed ferocity. 'I were playing that fuckin' tune afore you was in your Mam's belly . . . O' course I knows the fuckin' thing.'

'Then play it, you bloody old mawkin!'

Milky Bradman lifted his fist in mock threat. 'Or I'll be giving you this in your bloody lughole.'

The crowd laughed and applauded and lame Ben Mitchell whipped his fiddle-bow across the head of a noisy man near to him. 'Shurrup 'ull you, and hark to me music.'

'Let's have order, ladies and gennulmen. Order please!' Nail Styler added his stentorian voice to the general hubbub, and mindful of the heavy weight of the landlord's fists, the crowd quietened.

The fiddle squealed and Milky Bradman's fine tenor voice filled the air.

'Oh, we was gathering nuts and may,
Nuts and may, nuts and may,
Down by the old mill streammmmmm,
But instead o' gathering nuts and may,
I got her in the family way,
Down by the old mill streammmmmmm.'

123

'All together nowwww,' Milky exhorted, and the room came bawling in with the chorus.

> 'No, you can't have it tonight,
> Because the moon is shining bright,
> And the stars are twinkling in the sky oi oi oi,
> Somebody's watching us,
> Watching you and I,
> So let's go round the corner,
> And 'ave a bit on the slyyyy . . . '

Milky waved his arms above his head, signalling the crowd to hush, and went on alone,

> 'Oh we were gathering paper, paper, paper,
> Down by the old mill stream.
> But instead o' gathering paper,
> I laid her down and raped her,
> Down by the old mill streammmmm.'

Another wave of his arms, and the chorus thundered out.

> 'No, you can't have it tonight,
> Because the moon is shining bright . . . '

Nail Styler's eyes roved the room continuously, and he saw the door open and a tough-looking face appear round the edge of it. Nail Styler recognized Ben Fairfax. Fairfax's eyes searched and found Nail Styler, and he jerked his head meaningly. The landlord gave a single nod in reply and Fairfax drew back and the door closed. The sequence had only taken seconds, and now Styler's gaze flicked round the room, until he was satisfied that no one had noticed the exchange. Then he told his serving man, 'Keep things aboiling in here for a minute, Jerry,' and left the taproom through a half-concealed door behind the counter.

Ben Fairfax was waiting in the kitchen at the rear of the inn, and with him was an older man – tall, sparse-framed and hard-featured, well-dressed in a white ruffled shirt and cravat, sombre dark brown coat and pantaloons and a low-crowned top hat – Jonas Crowther.

'Now then, Master Crowther, how bist?' Styler greeted.

'How bist yourself, Nail?' Crowther's thin lips parted and showed a gleam of ivory false teeth in a bleak smile. 'I knows youm busy tonight, Nail, so I'll not detain you for more than a moment.'

> 'And the stars are twinkling in the sky oi oi oi,
> Somebody's watching us,
> Watching you and I . . .'

The roaring chorus reverberated along the passageway, and Nail Styler chuckled with satisfaction.

'That's so, Master Crowther, I'm busy all right, but I can allus find time for you.'

The flattery visibly pleased Crowther and his false teeth gleamed again in the dull light of the hanging lamp. 'I takes that kindly, Nail, most kindly. But I only wants a morsel of your time tonight. Harry Mogg uses your taproom a lot, don't he?' he questioned.

Nail Styler's broken teeth bared as he burst into laughter. 'Uses my taproom a lot, does you ask, Master Crowther?' he spluttered as his laughter diminished. 'The bugger uses every taproom in the parish a lot when he's got money.'

A slight frown of impatience deepened the harsh lines between Crowther's eyebrows. 'I knows he's a roaring boy, Nail, but tell me, be you expecting him here tonight?'

The landlord, recognizing Crowther's impatience, sobered. 'I doubt he'll come tonight. I arn't seen him for a few days, not since he got laid off from his work.'

'No, he'll have no money to booze with, will he?' Satisfaction throbbed in Crowther's voice. 'So what I wants you to do, Nail, is to get him here tonight. I wants to have a word wi' him, but I don't want anybody to know that I has.' He winked. 'Get me?'

Nail Styler had carried out such tasks for Crowther before, and now he winked back. 'Nobody 'ull, Master Crowther. You stay and make yourself comfortable in here, I'll make sure youm not disturbed. Shall I bring you in a drop o' summat to pass the time wi' until I can get hold of Harry Mogg?'

Crowther arched an eyebrow at Ben Fairfax. 'What's your fancy, Ben?'

'Hollands 'ull do for me,' the younger man grunted.

'Then Hollands it is,' Crowther said graciously, and added as Nail Styler was leaving, 'Better make it a full bottle Nail, in case we has a long wait.'

In the event it was only a short one.

'Here you are, Harry,' Jonas Crowther beamed in welcome, and pushed a full tumbler of gin towards the newcomer. 'Get this down you, lad, there's plenty more where it come from.'

He studied the young man closely as the pointer pitched the spirits down his throat.

'My oath, Harry, it looks like you needed that,' he exclaimed genially, and refilled the tumbler, then said bluntly, 'I arn't agoing to beat around the bushes wi' you, Harry. I knows that youm having hard times, what wi' being laid off from your work and having to take care o' your sister and her kids as well. So, does you want to work for me?'

Harry Mogg grinned. 'Become one o' your Rippling Boys, does you mean, Master Crowther?'

The other man nodded. 'That's about it, Harry. I'se had me eye on you for a long time. I reckon you'se got the balls for the work.'

The young pointer's reckless eyes mirrored a flash of doubt, and in his mind he briefly debated with himself about the wisdom of accepting Crowther's invitation to become one of his gang.

'What's the sort of work you'se got in mind for me exactly?' he queried, and Crowther's genial smile spread across his hard features.

'Oh, a bit o' this and a bit o' that and a bit o' the other, Harry. You arn't a fussy cove, am you?'

Harry Mogg thought about his sister and her children. He thought about Tildy Crawford and her child. He thought about his own empty pockets, and the uncertainty of finding more work quickly, and his piquant grin was wry. 'No Master Crowther, I can't afford to be a fussy cove.'

He emptied his glass in two swallows and held it towards the other man. 'This is going down a treat . . . boss.'

Chapter Fifteen

'So, you are the new nursing-woman.' Henry Geast Dugdale's deep-set eyes regarded Tildy with an intensity that was so searching as to cause her to swallow uncomfortably before she answered.

'I am, Sir. My name is Matilda Crawford.'

Still wearing his tall hat and black travelling cloak he was a dominating, forbidding presence in the kitchen which he now scanned briefly.

'You have wrought something of a transformation here, Crawford.' There was a hint of grudging praise in his voice. 'The other nursing-women I have previously engaged to tend Mrs Dugdale never cleaned this room so well.'

The kitchen had indeed been made into a clean cheery room with a fire crackling in its now blackened and polished cooking range, the reflection of flames sparking from the neatly hung rows of burnished pots and pans, and the wooden fitments and furnishings all scrubbed to a whiteness.

Tildy kept her eyes downcast. The formidable physical presence of the man engendered an uneasiness within her, that even at this initial meeting with him she realized would take time and a conscious effort to dispel.

'Come Crawford, we will go upstairs to Mrs Dugdale.'

'Very well, Sir.' Tildy followed the man down the dark passageway and up the stairs.

Sybil Dugdale's room had also been subjected to Tildy's

onslaughts with brush, pail and water, and now presented a freshness of sight and smell, even if still austere and sparsely furnished.

Sybil Dugdale was sitting before the fire, dressed in the ruff-necked green gown, her thick hair parted neatly in the centre and tied loosely at the back of her neck, so that its brushed-shiny waves framed her thin white face, imparting a fragile beauty. Her wide-set eyes glanced up as her husband entered and a flickering of fear passed across them. Then she dropped her gaze to her entwined writhing hands.

Henry Dugdale took off his tall hat, displaying close-cropped dark hair thickly streaked with grey. His forehead was exceptionally high and deeply creased with heavy lines, creating a constant expression of grim dourness on his long lean features.

'Well Madam, have you no greeting for your husband?' he demanded harshly.

Tildy saw how Sybil Dugdale flinched at the sound of her husband's voice, and her heart flooded with pity for the sick woman.

'She's tired, Sir, she did not sleep well last night.' Tildy attempted to ease the palpable tension on the atmosphere, but Dugdale brutally cut her short.

'Hold your tongue, Crawford. When I want you to speak, I will so request you.' He turned again to his wife. 'Now Madam, rise up and greet your husband in the manner of a dutiful and loving wife,' he ordered harshly, and like some clumsily operated marionette Sybil Dugdale rose from her chair and moved jerkily and hesitantly towards him.

'That is better, Madam,' he snapped curtly, and leaning forwards, tall against her smallness, he briefly touched his lips to her cheek, then straightened, to exclaim with notice-able surprise, 'God strike me, you smell of lavender, instead of some damned midden-heap.'

A stirring of resentment burgeoned within Tildy on Sybil Dugdale's behalf. Although she had always been accustomed to men treating their social or physical inferiors

128

with arrogant contempt, yet she found it offensive that a gentleman should say such things to his wife in front of others, even if those others were merely servants. The next instant she blushed as she realized that Henry Dugdale was regarding her with such an expression of knowingness that it was as if he read her thoughts. His next words gave her the incredulous certainty that he truly was a mind-reader.

'You resent the manner of my speaking to Mrs Dugdale, do you not, Crawford. Well, before you become too irate, you had best recollect that I have been forced to endure the stench of her incontinence for some considerable passage of time. It makes a surprising change for me to return from one of my journeys and find her sweet-smelling.'

The hard thin line of his lips softened and it seemed to Tildy that a smile lurked in the deep-set eyes, but when he next spoke his voice was still harsh.

'You might well turn out to be an improvement on the previous sluts I've employed as nursing-women, slum-bred though you are.'

An angry retort trembled on Tildy's lips, but she bit it back. Then, in another display of prescience, Henry Dugdale told her,

'Come Crawford, spit it out. You are burning with the desire to give me a hard answer, are you not?'

For a moment her nervousness of the man held Tildy back, but her fiery spirit would not allow her to surrender so cravenly to her own timidity.

'Very well, Sir, since you so order me, I'll give you answer. I am not, nor never was a slut in any manner of speaking. I came here as a nurse-woman, and for the last four days and nights I've tended Mrs Dugdale the best way I can. If you are not satisfied with what I've done, or with my manners, then you may order me to leave your house and I'll do so without argument. But while I remain here, then I'll thank you not to talk to me as if I were a brute beast. I may be beneath you in my station in life, but I'm not beneath you in any other way, and I'll not stay here to be spoke to as if I were a hedge-whore or street drab . . . I deserve to be treated with respect . . . I deserve that!'

She faltered as scalding tears threatened to spill from her eyes. Angrily she rubbed the back of her hand across her face to clear her blurring sight, and with a mingling of defiance and apprehension awaited his reaction.

His face was dour and his eyes held the threat of fury. A nervous lump rose in Tildy's throat as the silence lengthened, and still he made no reply. But she swallowed hard, and forced herself to hold her head high and meet his menacing stare with bold eyes. Finally he jerked his chin towards the door.

'You doubtless have many duties to attend to, Crawford,' he said evenly. 'Go about them. I wish to be alone with my wife. When I require you, then I'll ring, so listen well, for I' do not like to be kept waiting by my servants.' He turned from her in dismissal.

For a moment Tildy was confused by this unexpected reaction. She had been steeling herself to withstand an outburst of fury, culminating in her dismissal from his employment. Now, she was totally confused. Automatically she bobbed a curtsy.

'Very well, Sir.' Her voice seemed to act independently of her will, and her thoughts awhirl, she did as he had instructed.

Later that afternoon William White came to the house. During the preceding days he had kept his contacts with Tildy to a minimum. Not wishing to make her afraid of him he had done his best to be pleasant and polite, and for her part, although still wary of him, Tildy had become a little easier in his company.

She was reaching out a fresh-baked loaf from the cooking range's small bread oven when White came through the rear door, and for a brief moment he let his eyes dwell on her rounded buttocks straining against the thin cloth of her gown as she bent to her task.

'Someday soon, little bitch,' White promised mentally. 'Some day soon I'll be enjoying that sweet arse o' yourn.'

Tildy straightened and turned to place the round

130

savoury-smelling loaf on the table. Her face was flushed by the heat of the fire and dark tendrils of glossy hair had escaped from beneath her mob-cap to fall about her cheeks. She looked very beautiful and for a second or two a softer emotion stirred in the man's mind, but then he saw in the opened neck of her bodice the deep cleavage of white swelling breasts and his lust consumed all other feelings. But he was careful to show nothing of it.

'That bread smells real good, Tildy,' he complimented gruffly. 'Youm a dab hand at the cooking, arn't you?'

She smiled briefly, pleased by his words. 'If you can wait till it cools I'll give you a piece of it, Master White.'

'Oh, I can wait all right, Tildy.' He could not help staring hungrily at her body. 'I can allus wait for summat good. A pretty woman allus tastes the sweeter arter you'se waited to have her.'

The smile left Tildy's lips and her mood darkened. 'Why do men always have to turn everything towards sex?' she wondered. 'Why can they never pass a remark without putting a double-meaning to it?' She corrected herself. 'Hold hard, Tildy, there are those who don't do so. I've known good and decent men, as well as this sort.'

'What time did the master get back?' White wanted to know.

'A couple of hours since. He's upstairs with Mrs Dugdale.'

White chuckled lewdly. 'Ahr, he's powerful fond of his missus. She'll not be sleeping in her chair this night, that's for sure. She'll be in his bed, but I doubt she'll get much sleep theer.'

'They're man and wife.' Tildy was unhappy with the turn of the conversation. ''Tis only natural they should share a bed. And anyway, it's no concern of ours. I've no wish to talk about it.' Inwardly she was appalled by the prospect. 'What if he makes her pregnant? What sort of a child will she bear? It's wicked of Henry Dugdale to have connection with the poor demented soul, it's wicked, so it is . . .'

Again William White broke into her thoughts. 'The

master wun't be pleased wi' what I'se got to tell him. Some bugger's bin springing our traps.'

'Traps?' Tildy queried. 'What sort of traps?'

White's furred tongue snaked over his lips and he grinned ferociously. 'Why, the sort you catches poachers with, my wench. Man-traps! Theer's a bloody spring-gun gone missing as well. Fuck me! The master 'ull go bloody mad when he hears about it. That gun cost a fair few bob so it did.'

Tildy made no reply. She knew all about man-traps and spring-guns, and knew also of men who had been maimed for life, even killed by those savage instruments.

'I didn't know you had a lot of poachers coming on to this estate,' she remarked, remembering the mysterious lights moving about the woods on her first night at the hall, and realizing that it must have been poachers.

The man pushed his moleskin cap back with his fingers and scratched hard among his gingery, greasy mop of hair. 'I'se got bloody pigs in me yed agen,' he grumbled. 'I'll ha' to shift 'um out, or I'll not get a minute's peace from 'um.' Then he told her, 'Up to now we arn't had too much trouble wi' poachers. The master's too well known in these parts for shooting fust and asking arterwards, and I acts in the same way . . . But times am bad agen, and there's a lot bin laid off from their work up in the town theer. Then the harvest was a poor 'un what wi' the bad weather, so there warn't a lot to be gleaned, and there warn't many extra hands took on by the farmers. There'll be short rations for a lot o' folk this winter, and that means the lively lads 'ull be paying us a few visits, I expect, to lift the master's game.' He paused, and stared hard at her. 'You arn't seen anything, has you Tildy? Any strangers in the woods, or anything like a light moving about of a night-time?'

It took only the briefest moment of reflection for Tildy to decide against telling him about the light. She knew from bitter experience how hunger could gnaw at both stomach and brain. If men were desperate enough to risk transportation or worse by poaching to fill their families' bellies, then good luck to them.

132

'How could I see anything, I've not been out from the house,' she answered tartly. 'If you remember, you were supposed to arrange it so that I could get a walk in the woods sometimes.'

His yellowed teeth grinned at her. 'I arn't forgot, girl, but I've bin real busy lately. I'll arrange summat for you.'

'When?' she challenged.

'Soon, girl, soon,' he told her. 'Now I reckon I'll not disturb the master at present. Let him enjoy his fust night back wi'out aggravation. I'll see you tomorrow, Tildy. In the meantimes you could take a peep out o' the upstairs windows now and agen, just in case you might see summat.'

Tildy nodded. 'I will, Master White . . . Here,' lifting a long-bladed knife she cut a thick golden-crusted chunk from the loaf and handed it to him. 'Have this with your supper.'

'I will, Tildy.' His tongue left a glistening slime of saliva on his thick lips. 'And I'll think on you while I'm chewing it, girl . . . '

It was getting dusk before Tildy heard the jangling summons of the bell. In the upstairs room Henry Dugdale and his wife were sitting in the winged armchairs opposite to each other across the table. The fire in the grate had died to ashes and the room was a darkening gloom. Tidly looked at Sybil Dugdale and saw that her head was downcast and that her entwined hands were on the table-top, fingers twisting and writhing together like a nest of serpents.

'My bedroom is the one opposite this, across the landing, Crawford.' Shadowed by the wings of the armchair Henry Dugdale's facial expression could not be seen clearly, but his voice was dulled as if by a great weariness of spirit. 'Prepare the bed, it will need warming. Then return here and make Mrs Dugdale ready for the night.'

'Do you wish supper, Sir? Mrs Dugdale has not eaten since her breakfast, and that was but a bowl of milksops.'

The man's tone became acid. 'Kindly do as you are told, Crawford. No more. No less.'

Tildy bit her lips, then bobbed a curtsy and went.

Henry Dugdale's bedroom was a resplendent contrast to the rest of the house, at least, the rest that Tildy had seen. A four-poster bed with richly brocaded velvet curtains stood massively against one wall. On the other walls gilt-framed pictures and tapestries hung in abundance. A thick carpet muffled the clattering of Tildy's clogs, and heavy, opulent furniture overcrowded the available space.

She lifted a long-handled brass warming pan from beneath the bed and took it downstairs to fill its capacious bowl with burning coals from the kitchen-range, then returned and slipping it between the sheets moved it slowly backwards and forwards until the bed was thoroughly heated. As she worked Tildy's mind filled with a growing distaste and resentment against Henry Dugdale.

'Fancy making his wife sleep on a chair while he keeps this bedroom locked. The man's cruel. Cruel and hard.'

She sighed heavily as her vivid imagination pictured what the coming night would bring to Sybil Dugdale. 'More pain, and more bruises. The poor soul! The poor demented soul, and she knows what is to come, which makes it even worse for her. No wonder her hands were clawing together so. She must be in mortal dread.'

Helpless frustration overwhelmed Tildy and anger flared against the man-made laws which made women virtual slaves to their husbands. Without protection. Without rights.

'It's so wrong!' she burst out. 'It's so wickedly wrong! Women are human beings too. We should not be treated so inferior to men. We should be their equals, not their slaves . . . And how will you change the state of things, Tildy?' a tiny voice whispered in her mind. 'I don't know,' she admitted, then added stubbornly, 'but there will come a day when I'll try to change things . . . I'll try . . .'

She replaced the warming pan beneath the bed where its heat could spread through the chill air, and returned to the other room.

'Do you wish me to light a fire in your bedroom, Sir?' she asked. 'The nights have been very cold of late.'

'No, that will not be necessary. But you may light the candles there,' Henry Dugdale told her. 'Now take Mrs Dugdale and put her to bed in my room, Crawford. Ensure that she is clean in her body before you leave her.' Abruptly he rose to his feet, a towering shadow of darkness in the gloom. 'I am going to open a room on the upper floor for you Crawford. That will serve as your quarters and you will sleep there from now on.'

He moved past Tildy and her nostrils caught the mingled scents of horses, leather and male sweat. Involuntarily she flinched back as he brushed past, and instantly he halted and snapped curtly,

'God strike me, Crawford, there is no call for you to shrink in fear when I come near to you. I'm not intending to lay hands on you, young woman.'

Tildy felt the hot rush of blood to her face, and was thankful for the darkness which hid her embarrassment. He walked on, and she heard the clump of his boots upon the bare floorboards of the landing, then the hollower clumping as he ascended the stairs leading to the upper floors.

Sybil Dugdale docilely allowed herself to be led across the landing, but at the bedroom door she jibbed back like a frightened colt. 'No, I do not like that place,' she whimpered. 'I won't go in there. I do not like it.'

'But Mr Dugdale has said that you must go to bed now, Ma'am.' Reluctantly Tildy coaxed the other woman. 'I've warmed the bed for you and it's real cosy. Come now, Ma'am, and I'll see to it that you are settled comfortably. Come now, there's a good girl.' With gentle pressure she half-pulled, half-pushed Sybil Dugdale through the doorway.

The room was dark and Tildy clucked her tongue in self-annoyance. 'There now, I've forgot to light the candles first. That's what's making you so nervous, Ma'am, isn't it? You stay here for a few moments, I'll be back directly.'

She ran downstairs and returned with a lighted taper.

When she lit the candles the room appeared even more richly opulent as the gilt frames and brocade and tapestries gleamed in the soft glow. 'There Ma'am, it's a lovely room, fit for a queen to sleep in.'

Tildy undressed the thin white body, trying to ignore the dark-shadowed, haunted eyes in the tense face. She checked that Sybil Dugdale was clean and then dressed her in a lacy silken nightdress and tied a flat, lace-edged night cap over the chestnut hair, tying the ribbons in a bow beneath the small peaked chin. 'There now, you're as clean and sweet as a pink.' She led the woman to the bedside and drew back the coverings.

Sybil Dugdale whimpered again, but more loudly now, and with pitiful distress she begged Tildy, 'Do not make me stay here. Do not make me. Please . . . Please.'

The fragile hands writhed and twisted, the thin fingers tugging and tearing at each other, and Tildy's stomach turned over as her resentment of Henry Dugdale boiled up in a maelstrom of emotion.

'But what else can I do, Ma'am?' she beseeched. 'How can I not leave you here? I'm only a nursing-woman.' She begged the woman to understand her powerlessness. 'I've no power to take you from this room and this house. If I had, then I would. Please believe me, Ma'am, that I would, I truly would.' She heard Henry Dugdale's boots on the landing and shook her head helplessly. 'I can do naught, Ma'am,' she whispered sadly. 'Naught, but leave you here.'

Dugdale came into the room and, not trusting her own capacity to control her rampaging emotions, Tildy bobbed a curtsy without even looking at him and hurried from the room with averted eyes and burning cheeks.

When she had finished her chores Tildy seated herself by the kitchen fire and gave her mind up to idle reveries. Foremost in her thoughts was little Davy, and as she visualized his face Tildy came close to tears. 'I miss you, my honey-lamb,' she whispered aloud. 'I miss you so much that sometimes I feel I can't bear being separated from you a moment longer. But I'll come and see you very soon. In

136

fact, I'll ask Henry Dugdale tomorrow for time to visit you.'

The notion of asking Henry Dugdale if she could bring her child to stay with her at the hall, also occurred to Tildy, but even as she thought of it, the certainty that Dugdale would not allow it crushed down upon her.

'You see, Davy,' she spoke to her child in her mind, 'the poor don't love their children, at least, that's what the gentry like to believe of us. They prefer to think that we are heartless, unthinking, unfeeling brute beasts, fit only to toil, and get drunk, and rut like animals.' Her common-sense stirred itself. 'Come now, Tildy, don't become so bitter that you exaggerate so badly. The gentry are like the rest of us. Some are good, some are bad, and most fall somewheres in between the two. You're becoming over-morbid and self-pitying, girl. 'Tis best that you go to your bed.'

Taking her candle she made her way up to her new bedroom.

'My God! Has he opened the wrong room for me?' Tildy held the candle above her head so that its weak light might reach further, and gazed open-mouthed at what she saw. By her standards the room was luxurious, with carpeting, wall-mirror and pictures, a chest of drawers, a tallboy, a linen-hamper, a marbled washstand with jug and bowl, and a canopied tester bed. True it smelled musty and the bed seemed a trifle damp to the touch, but in all her life Tildy had never had a room like this to call her own.

For a while she wandered about the room, then on impulse went back on to the landing and checked the other doors ranged along it. They were all locked.

'Then this room must really be meant for me,' she decided, and could not restrain a smile of pleasure. 'Once I've cleaned and aired it, it'll be like sleeping in a palace,' she thought happily. 'See, there's even a warming pan and a painted jerry pot with its own lid.'

It took only moments for her to run to the kitchen, collect her bundle and fill the warming pan with hot coals.

Later, lying in the canopied bed studying her books by

the candlelight Tildy was able to fully savour the peace and quietness that surrounded her. 'Why, if only Davy were with me, at this moment I'd be a truly happy woman,' she realized with a touch of surprise.

It was then that she became aware of voices – the low tones of Sybil Dugdale and the louder, harsher words of her husband. Tildy realized that she was in fact directly above the Dugdale's bedroom. Unable to still her curiosity she listened hard, trying to distinguish what was being said, but unable to. Then there came a series of long wailing cries as if someone was being hurt, and intermingled with those cries the angry exclamations of Henry Dugdale, and Tildy's happiness fled, leaving her feeling only a distressed disgust and anger.

'God save us! He's raping the poor soul. That's what that evil bastard is doing. He's raping her . . . '

The harrowing noises were soon ended, and Tildy thought that she could hear Sybil Dugdale weeping. Nausea swept over her. Nausea and helpless rage. 'He should be hung, that bastard should be hung.' The words reverberated through Tildy's mind. 'He's too bad to live, he should be hung.'

Slowly she calmed and tried to absorb herself in her books once more but her mind was still too full of alternating pity and rage for her to concentrate on the pages, and at last she abandoned her studies and, blowing out her candle, tried to compose herself to sleep. But sleep eluded her, and it seemed that she lay for endless hours, staring into darkness, wondering futilely how she could rescue the pathetic woman in the room below from such a cruel existence.

Then fresh sounds from the lower floor disturbed the stillness. Someone was sobbing yet again, but not softly, not with muted, muffled outcries. These choking, retching outbursts were loud and full-throated, the lamenting of a soul suffering all the torments of hell, and those torments went on, and on, and on until it seemed that the whole of the sleeping world must inevitably awaken and hear them.

'Dear God!' With a physical sense of shock Tildy recognized who it was that grieved so heart-wrenchingly. 'It's him! It's Henry Dugdale . . . '

Finally silence returned and again Tildy lay staring into the darkness, her thoughts troubled and her nerves on edge. Even when sleep at last came to her it was shallow and uneasy and when she awoke at dawn her head was aching and her body felt drained of energy.

As she went about her chores in the kitchen, Tildy attempted to come to terms with the events of the night.

'Can I stay here?' she asked herself over and over again. 'Can I stay in this house of torment?'

She experienced a curious sense of duality as though two separate entities were arguing inside her brain. 'Of course you must stay. You must earn some money . . . But how can I stand seeing and hearing Henry Dugdale misuse that poor creature? How does it concern you, girl? You're only a servant, a hired nursing-woman. You have only to obey Dugdale, and pay no attention to what is not your concern . . . But he misuses her! He has the right to do what he chooses with her. She is his wife . . . But she is suffering! The woman is mad! How can you say that she even knows what is being done to her. To her it might seem only a dream . . . I heard her weeping and shouting out in the night . . . And did you not hear Henry Dugdale also weeping in the night? Is he not suffering equally?'

The jangling of the bell echoed from above, and Tildy was grateful for the summons because it enabled her to temporarily still the discordant voices in her head.

She knocked on the bedroom door and Henry Dugdale's voice bade her enter. He was standing by the window staring out at the woodlands, dressed in a long plaid dressing gown which reached to the floor. Tildy's eyes went to the bed, but the curtains were closed and no sound came from within their brocaded folds.

The man turned to her, and Tildy was shocked to see how drawn and grey his face was, and the black shadows that ringed his eyes.

'Crawford, I wish you to prepare Mrs Dugdale for

outdoors. I am taking her to Henley-in-Arden, and you are to accompany her.'

'To Henley, Sir?' Tildy repeated in surprise, and Dugdale's complexion darkened as he shouted angrily,

'God blast your eyes, Crawford! Don't stand there parroting my words like a damned simpleton. Make haste and dress your mistress, blast you.'

Tildy saw that he was physically trembling, as if fighting to hold himself in control, and judging it wiser not to provoke him further she hurried to draw aside the curtains of the bed.

Sybil Dugdale was lying on her back, her eyes wide open and staring blankly at the canopy, her body as still as a corpse beneath the coverings. When Tildy pulled back those coverings she saw that the woman was naked, and saw also the raw, weeping lesions on the soft inner skin of her thighs. For a brief instant the urge to physically assault Henry Dugdale, to tear his flesh as he had torn his wife's tender skin, coursed through Tildy. But she knew, even as she inwardly raged, that she was powerless to do anything against the man.

'Come Ma'am, let me dress you,' she said, and with gentle hands lifted Sybil Dugdale's head and shoulders from the pillows.

'Be as quick as you can, Crawford,' Dugdale instructed as he went from the room. 'I wish to leave within the hour.'

Chapter Sixteen

Harry Mogg was whistling a jaunty tune as he walked up the track leading to Bordesley Hall. The morning was fine and the crisp air and bright sunlight gave an added fillip to his customary light-heartedness. Even the sight of the long gun, moleskin cap and canvas gaiters of the man waiting for him higher up the track did not dampen the pointer's high spirits.

'Now then, William, there's no call for you to pull such a long face at me. I arn't come to lift your game,' he bantered.

'Them youm the fust bloody pointer who arn't come here for that,' White rejoined sullenly. 'What does you want here then?'

By now Mogg had reached the other man and he stopped only a yard away from the gamekeeper. Although White topped him by inches and outweighed him by a score of pounds, Harry Mogg was confident that if it came to a fight, he could master the gamekeeper. So now he grinned and said easily, 'Why should you ask me that, William? Is your conscience bothering you about anything?'

'No, it fuckin' well arn't,' White growled. 'So iffen that's what you'se come here to ask, then you'se got your answer, and now you can fuck off back to wheer you'se come from.'

Harry's easy manner did not alter. Still grinning he replied, 'That's fair enough, White, and I'll gladly fuck off

141

when I've done what I come to do. And that's to go up to the hall and have a few words wi' Tildy Crawford.'

At mention of Tildy's name the gamekeeper's bloodshot eyes narrowed warily. 'She a friend o' yourn, is she? One o' your hedge-whores?'

'She's a friend.' Harry's grin left his face. 'And watch your mouth, White, because she arn't a hedge-whore.'

He went to move on, but the gamekeeper stepped to block the track, his long-barrelled gun swinging up to aim at the pointer's stomach.

Harry tensed. 'Iffen I was you, White, I'd step aside,' he advised quietly.

The gamekeeper's tongue ran across his thick lips. 'Be you threatening me, Mogg?'

Harry's breathing quickened as the adrenalin pumped through his tautly-muscled body. 'No White, I'm not threatening you, but I intends going up to the hall to see Tildy Crawford, and you arn't agoing to stop me.'

The round black hole of the gun muzzle swung in short arcs, and the pointer's teeth bared in a wolfish snarl.

'You'd best be ready to use that fuckin' gun, White, because if you keeps waving it at me, then I'm likely to shove it up your arse and pull the trigger.'

'Is that a fact?' White sneered openly, and Harry nodded grimly.

'It's a fact you'd best believe.'

For a few seconds both men were motionless, eyes and wills locked in a silent combat. Then imperceptibly Harry moved his feet and balanced his body, readying himself to spring, nerving himself to act. But just as he reached the moment of commitment the gamekeeper stepped aside with a jeering laugh.

'Goo on up theer then, Mogg, if you wants a wasted journey.'

'What d'you mean by that?' Harry, wary of treachery, did not relax his body, but then the other man grounded the butt of his gun.

'Her arn't up theer,' he leered with patent satisfaction, 'so you'se walked out here for nothing, Mogg.'

'Then where is she?' Harry demanded, but White only shrugged his meaty, fustian-clad shoulders.

'I'll goo on up to the hall,' Harry growled, and a sneering grin bared White's teeth.

'Suit yourself, Mogg. But like I told you, her arn't there.'

Harry stood unable to decide whether or not the man was speaking the truth. The drumming of horses' hooves caused him to look back down the track and he grinned with satisfaction. Hugh Taylor, elegant in pearl grey riding clothes, polished kneeboots and a high-crowned, broad-peaked jockey cap was approaching fast.

Harry said nothing, only waited for the doctor to reach them, knowing that William White would not dare lie to the man.

Taylor reined in his cantering mount and halted by the two men, the horse snorting and striking sparks from the stony ground with its hooves.

'Is your master at home, White?'

The gamekeeper removed his moleskin cap respectfully. 'No Sir, he arn't. He's took the mistress and the nursing-'ooman to Henley-in-Arden.'

'To Henley?' Hugh Taylor's fresh-complexioned features were instantly suspicious, as if he already guessed at the reason for such a journey. 'Why to Henley?'

'The master's took the mistress over there to visit somebody, Sir,' White told him vaguely.

Taylor frowned impatiently. 'Damn you, White, spit it out! Whom has your Master gone to see? Don't fob me off with any protest of ignorance, man. I know well that Mr Dugdale will have told you.'

The gamekeeper's sullenness returned in full strength, but despite his obvious reluctance, he admitted grudgingly, 'Yes Sir, he told me. He told me he was agoing to take the mistress to see the gennulmen as looks arter the loonies there.'

The doctor's well-shaped lips twisted petulantly. 'Goddamn the man!' he swore softly, then asked White, 'How long ago did he leave?'

143

'Nigh on two hours since,' White informed him, and again Taylor swore.

'Goddamn and blast him!' Without another word he savagely tugged his horse's head around and spurred the hapless animal into a bolting gallop.

White's sneering chuckle followed him. 'That's upset the fuckin' pretty boy, arn't it? Dugdale's missus is kin to the Taylors. They'll not like her being put into a bloody loony-bin 'ull they, not one bit they wun't.'

He turned his head to look at Harry Mogg, but the young pointer, satisfied with what he had heard, was already walking quickly back to the turnpike road.

Chapter Seventeen

Henley-in-Arden was some seven miles distant as the crow flew from Redditch town. For three-quarters of a mile its buildings fronted the high road running between Birmingham and Stratford-upon-Avon. Apart from its two coach and posting inns the only other establishments of any commercial importance in the straggling village were the three private madhouses. They, together with another licensed asylum in the hamlet of Wootten Wawen two miles further southwards towards Stratford comprised the sum total of private madhouses in the whole county of Warwickshire. This singular attribute made the inhabitants of Henley the butt of cruel witticisms in the neighbouring settlements. It also evoked in the more sensitive or timid a superstitious aversion to the village. Tildy shared something of that aversion and this, coupled with the reason for the journey, caused her to feel increasingly depressed as they neared and finally reached their destination.

In the single-horsed trap Henry Dugdale was handling the reins, and his wife was crammed in between him and Tildy on the narrow seat. During the trip Henry Dugdale had maintained a morose silence, but Sybil Dugdale had wept and moaned continuously despite Tildy's constant attempts to soothe and comfort her. Now, at the crossroads which marked the southern entrance to Henley, Dugdale halted to allow a huge stage-wagon to precede them through the village, and for the first time he spoke to his wife.

'Now Madam, be good enough to dry your eyes, and cease from making such an unseemly spectacle of yourself.' He grated out the words, and his grey-hued face was grim and merciless as he went on to berate the weeping woman. 'Before God, Madam, I know well enough what an ill-fortuned day it was for me when I took you for wife. There is no need for you to so continuously remind me of that fact with your whining and wailing. Goddamn you, be silent!'

Tildy felt driven to protest. 'She can't help but be grieving, Sir. She knows well what an evil place you've brought her to.'

Sheer surprise caused the man to hesitate, then he asked grimly, 'Why do you call it evil, Crawford?'

'Because it is, Sir,' Tildy spoke out spiritedly. 'Everyone knows what happens here in these madhouses. Everyone knows how the poor afflicted souls are made to suffer.'

'Hold your tongue, you stupid bitch,' the man hissed savagely. 'Are you deliberately trying to distress your mistress still further?'.

As if to confirm what he accused, Sybil Dugdale's weeping became a wailing, shrieking outpouring, and swept by self-guilt Tildy could only draw the woman's veiled head against her breasts and desperately try to soothe her.

'God blast your eyes, now see what you've done, you thick-skulled yokel,' Dugdale muttered in disgusted anger, and shook the reins. 'Get on, get on now!'

Obediently the mare stepped out and the trap jingled along the village street. At first it seemed strange to Tildy that the sight and sound of a wailing woman being carried along in a trap as if against her will, attracted little or no attention from passers-by and loungers.

'But then, why should it do so?' she realized after some reflection. 'They must see sights like this every day of their lives. After all, it's a village of the mad, isn't it?' she sardonically acknowledged.

Dugdale brought the trap to a halt outside a three-

146

storeyed greystone house and beckoned to a blue-smocked labourer who was leaning against the side wall of the building.

'You there, is this the ''Stone House''?'

The man's broad red face regarded the trap's occupants speculatively. 'Ahr, it be,' he drawled. 'This be Sammy Brown's house.'

'That is Doctor Samuel Brown the surgeon?' Dugdale sought for clarification, and the man chortled derisively.

'Ahr, I reckon that's what he terms hisself, bloody surgeon. Bloody butcher, more like . . . 'Ull you be wanting me to look arter your horse and carriage, master? Only it arn't safe to leave 'um alone in this town. You knows that the place is full o' bloody loonies, doon't you?'

Dugdale nodded curtly. 'Very well, look to her head.'

Blue-smock tugged his forelock. 'I will, Sir, I will. You can trust me to do just that, Sir.'

As the man shuffled to hold the mare's bridle, Dugdale stepped from the trap, telling Tildy, 'Stay here with your mistress until I send for you, Crawford.'

With his long cloak swirling about his legs he went up the short flight of steps and hammered on the front door with the butt of his whip. The door opened, and after a brief exchange Dugdale entered and the door closed behind his top-hatted figure.

Blue-smock stared at the two women in the trap, and nodding his head towards Sybil Dugdale, he asked Tildy, 'Be her agoing to be took in here, my duck?'

Tildy, still cradling the woman against her breasts, could only shake her head. 'I don't know . . . I hope not.'

The man's answering grin was not unkindly. 'Ohh, it arn't so bad for them as can pay well, my duck. Mind you, Sammy Brown takes in a whole rake o' paupers, as well. They doon't get treated so good.' He looked about him with a conspiratorial air, and whispered, ''Ud you like to see 'um? They'm prime fun.'

'See who?' Tildy queried.

'Why, the bloody loonies, o' corst.' The man seemed aggrieved at her lack of understanding. 'Jesus Christ! Who

147

the bleedin' hell did you think I meant? Theer's no sport to be had in looking at normal buggers, is there?'

Tildy could not help being curious. 'How can they be seen?'

Blue-smock's broad red face became animated with pleasurable anticipation. 'You mun goo round to the side of the house theer,' he directed. 'Theer's a window that lets on to one o' the cellars. They'm chained up in theer. It's prime fun to tease the mad buggers, so it is. Why, they shakes their chains and bellows like bulls, and goes bloody mad at you.' He paused and grinned delightedly. 'Theer now, I'se just said a good thing, arn't I, when I said about the bloody loonies going bloody mad at you.' He screwed his eyes tightly shut and laughed uproariously, and Tildy found him such a bizarre character that she could not help but giggle herself.

'So theer you be, you bugger.'

Unnoticed by Tildy the house door had opened again and now a hugely fat bald-headed man also wearing a dark-blue smock was standing at the top of the steps.

At the sound of his deep voice the man at the horse's head let go of the bridle and scurried back to the side of the house, protesting vehemently.

'Joey Bates has done naught bad, Master Wilkins! Joey Bates has bin a good boy. He's done naught bad!'

The fat man, so short and broad that he appeared like some great round barrel on legs, skipped down the steps with a surprising lightness of foot.

'Has that bugger theer been a trouble to you, missy?' he asked Tildy, who could only stare bemusedly at what was happening.

'No, my master told him to hold the horse's head,' she answered. 'Why do you ask?'

'Because he's one of our loonies, missy,' the fat man told her. 'He's harmless enough, but sometimes he can get a bit saucy wi' females.' The puffy slit eyes measured Tildy appreciatively. 'Particular when they'm as sweet and toothsome-looking as you, missy.' Without shifting his gaze from Tildy he waved a pudgy hand towards Joey

148

Bates. 'Get back here and get hold o' the horse's yed agen, you great lummox.' And as Bates scurried back told Tildy, 'Youm to bring your mistress inside the house. Doctor Brown wants to have a look at her.'

'So this is the lady.' In height and rotundity Samuel Brown was the double of Wilkins, but his voice was high-pitched and fluting and his head was capped with luxuriant grey curls. His high cravat and silken shirt were ruffled with expensive lace, but his black swallow-tailed coat, his waistcoat and even his tight-legged pantaloons were thickly encrusted with the dried blood, pus-stains and body-fluids engendered by his surgical practice, and from his button-hole dangled the waxed threads of ligatures.

The room doubled as both office and surgery. A long troughed table stood against one wall, and Tildy gazed with queasy fascination at the collection of bottled gruesome-looking anatomical specimens, ancient yellow bones and human skulls which shared the shelves with assorted scalpels, saws, catheters, chisels, screw-tourniquets, mallets, jars of medicinal compounds, musty-smelling books and other assorted impedimenta.

'Will you seat Mrs Dugdale down there, girl,' Samuel Brown fluted, and pointed beringed fingers at a tall stool.

As she was lowered on to the stool Sybil Dugdale pressed against Tildy and clutched at her with such feverish strength that Tildy was not able to easily disengage. She looked in appeal at Henry Dugdale and he nodded.

'Stay close with her.'

Samuel Brown lifted the veil back from Sybil Dugdale's features then moved backwards and forwards in front of her, and circled her several times, examining her from all angles. Then he moved closer, and taking Sybil Dugdale's head between his hands he tilted it back and brought his tiny porcine eyes to within inches of her own. She was no longer weeping, now her wide-set grey eyes only gazed blankly into his questing stare. He made a great show of counting her pulse, and testing the heat of her skin, and then with the knuckles of his middle and forefingers he began tapping the sides of her temples where the rich chestnut hair was drawn back in loose-flowing waves.

'Take her hands and hold them down. Make sure you keep them so,' he instructed Tildy, and as she obeyed he gripped the back of Sybil Dugdale's skull with one hand, and began to intensify the force and speed of his knuckle taps. First to the right side, then to the left, then to the right again, faster and faster, harder and harder his knuckles drummed against the translucent, blue-veined skin.

The woman tried to pull away from the painful rappings but with surprising ease his pudgy hand kept her head immobile, his fingers whitening as he increased the pressure of his grip. At last she cried out in distress and struggled so violently against the restraining hands that the doctor released his grip and stepped back from her. Turning to Henry Dugdale he asked, 'May I speak openly, Sir, or might it be better that your nursing-woman leave us?'

To Tildy's surprise Henry Dugdale answered, 'You may speak openly in front of her, Doctor. I have complete trust in her discretion.'

The surgeon nodded his curly head. 'As you wish, Sir. I must tell you that your good lady is not labouring under a mere nervous affection. No doubt the Doctors Taylor acted to the best of their abilities when diagnosing the disorder as such, but I fear that diagnosis is sadly mistaken.'

He held up his hand as if to forestall any interruption.

'Nay Sir, hear me out, I beg of you. No blame can attach to those gentlemen and I impute none. After all, they lack my experience of mental afflictions.' Looking grave, he slowly lifted his hand and laid it on Sybil Dugdale's shoulder. 'I must tell you, Sir, that this poor creature is not merely melancholic, but instead is afflicted with a mania. To speak straight and plain, Sir, I fear she is truly mad.'

Henry Dugdale's eyes closed and his body swayed visibly. Then, opening his eyes again, he asked in a hoarse strained voice, 'Can anything be done to help her, Doctor?'

The surgeon now moved to stand closely facing the taller man, and again his hand reached out to rest on his listener's shoulder.

'I'll not make wild promises to you, Sir, but I will affirm that if there is one man in this country who can help your good lady, then I am that man. But I must warn you, the course of treatment will be long and arduous, and in all frankness, even I cannot guarantee a complete and permanent cure. I can however promise an improvement from her present sad condition.'

'Will the treatment cause her any pain or distress, Doctor Brown?' was Dugdale's next question, and again Tildy felt a shock of surprise as she detected the anxiety in his voice. This grim-faced man before her was showing a facet of his nature that Tildy would never have believed him to possess.

The doctor smiled condescendingly. 'Mr Dugdale, we are not dealing with normal bodily ailments in this case. Madness is a malignant incubus that permeates the mind and body of the afflicted person. It has to be mercilessly attacked on all fronts. It must be confronted and defeated throughout every ounce of tissue, every drop of blood, every inch of bone and marrow. I will not hide that fact from you, Sir.

'It might well be that during the treatment I shall have to resort to Draconian measures if I am to succeed in curing your good lady. But at the same time I shall of course always endeavour my utmost to limit any unavoidable distress or pain she may be called upon to endure.'

'And how long would the treatment last?' Dugdale's dark-ringed eyes were dubious.

Samuel Brown spread his hands and his smile held a suggestion of contempt for such a question. 'Why, for as long as necessary, Sir.'

Dugdale's grey-hued features darkened ominously as he recognized the veiled contempt. 'Do not try to treat me as if I were some cretinous chaw-bacon, Doctor,' he hissed. 'I asked you how long the treatment would take? How long it will be before you can judge whether or no it will prove successful? Kindly give me an estimate of length, and also some idea of what the treatment might entail.'

The medical man nervously hastened to mollify this suddenly menacing figure. 'I would think that four months would be the approximate duration of the treatment, Sir.' He paused, and Dugdale pressured immediately.

'And what will the treatment consist of, Sir?'

'Well, Mr Dugdale, as you will appreciate from what I have said previously, if I am to drive this malignant mania from your wife's mind, then I must treat the entire body. I normally commence the course by bleeding during late May and early June. Unfortunately we are now in October, but be that as it may, so long as the moon is full and the weather mild, then I can safely commence bleeding her. The course of bleeding will weaken the fibres of the body and loosen the grip of the mania, and this enables me to commence a vigorous series of attacks upon it by means of purging, vomiting and blistering for periods of up to six weeks' duration. All during the treatment I shall be administering various medicines of my own composition, the which, I may add, have proven so uncommonly efficacious that my fellow-practitioners are constantly badgering me to patent them so that they also might have them at their convenience.'

'But what if all this should fail, Doctor? What then?' Dugdale's stony expression had betrayed no emotion during the doctor's recital, but Tildy had seen how his hands clenched so fiercely that the knuckles stood out white beneath the skin.

Samuel Brown smiled confidently. 'I do not anticipate failure, Sir.'

'God willing, you will not fail, Sir, but if you should, what then?' Dugdale doggedly persisted, and Samuel Brown ahemmed impatiently, then blustered,

'I have other treatments, Sir, and some of them may be termed as of a revolutionary nature. But let me remind you of my reputation for achieving success in this most difficult field of medicine.' He paused, and then went on with an assumed air of casualness. 'My fees are also most reasonable. You'll not find the cost of your good lady's treatments to be prohibitive, I do assure you, Sir.'

'I am not concerned about cost, Doctor Brown,' Dugdale stated firmly. 'You may charge what you will, so long as you cure my wife.'

Satisfied that he had gained a customer, Brown's fat face beamed rubicundly. 'Be assured, Sir, that given God's help, I shall return your wife to normality.'

'When could you commence the treatment?' Dugdale appeared tense, as if he were trying to reach a decision.

'Almost immediately, Sir. If you cared to settle the details of fees etcetera now, then your wife could remain here this night, and tomorrow morning I could begin her cure.'

'Will I be able to visit her whenever I choose?' Dugdale still seemed uncertain.

Samuel Brown answered with apparent regret, 'Sadly, Mr Dugdale, it is not allowed.'

'What do you mean, Sir, not allowed?'

'Experience has shown us, Sir, that such visits cause considerable distress both to the patient and the visitors. Indeed Sir, it can be proven that visits positively retard the patient's progress towards normality. However, you will be kept constantly informed as to your good lady's well-being and progress,' Brown continued smoothly, 'but I am forced to be adamant on this particular point, Mr Dugdale. Your good lady cannot be allowed visitors, at least until the treatment had progressed sufficiently so that a visit will cause no harmful effects.'

A nerve began to twitch violently in Dugdale's left cheek, and with an exclamation of distress he clapped his hand against the writhing flesh.

Brown sensed that the time had come to make his next move. 'Do not decide anything in haste, Mr Dugdale. I shall leave you here for a while to reflect on the matter. I'm sure that a period of reflection will persuade you that your good lady's welfare demands that she stay here.'

The doctor glided discreetly away, leaving Dugdale and the two women to their troubled silence.

At length Dugdale sighed heavily and said to his wife, 'There is naught else for it, Madam, but to leave you here for treatment.'

Sybil Dugdale gave no indication of having heard him at first. She kept her head downcast and her eyes focused on her entwined writhing fingers. Then tears fell silently down her white drawn face.

Dugdale drew a sharp intake of breath and asked Tildy, 'Do you wish to remain in my employ, Crawford?'

'Doing what, Sir?' Tildy had not expected this question, having already accepted that with Sybil Dugdale entering this madhouse there would be no job left for herself.

'I want you to remain here with Mrs Dugdale. Mayhap it will ease her distress at being left here. I shall arrange matters with Doctor Brown regarding your bed and board, and you will of course carry out any duties he may expect of you. I will continue to pay your wages.'

Tildy was only too happy to accept. She desperately needed to go on working and earning, if only for little Davy's sake. The thought of her baby caused her to say aloud.

'There is something I must ask of you, Sir.'

'What is that?' Dugdale frowned, but Tildy was not deterred.

'It's about my child, Sir. I wish to visit him. I wasn't expecting to be this far distanced from him.'

The man shrugged uninterestedly. 'You will doubtless have opportunity to do so, Crawford, when you have ensured that Mrs Dugdale is well settled. Speak to Doctor Brown about the matter. I expect he will grant you a few hours leave of absence.'

'Yes, Sir, I thank you.' Tildy bobbed a curtsy and even as she did so a curious sense of duality seemed to divide her being, and in her mind she seemed to hear her own voice saying scornfully, 'Look at you now, Tildy. How submissive and humbly grateful you have become towards a man that you so reviled and despised. How the offer of a few weeks' extra work has changed your attitude. What happened to that Tildy who had such pride and spirit? What has happened to her?'

As she went out of the door Tildy muttered beneath her breath, 'Perhaps that Tildy has been forced to begin to grow up.' It seemed that the voice in her mind laughed and then rejoined, 'We shall see, Tildy. We shall see . . . '

On his journey back to Redditch Henry Dugdale met Hugh Taylor coming at a gallop some two miles out from Henley. The doctor reined in his lathered, snorting horse by the side of the trap as Dugdale also halted. Taylor's breathing was heavy and his face flushed and sweaty from the hard ride.

'Where is she?' he demanded, and his eyes were angry. 'Where have you left her?'

Dugdale was icily cool. 'If you refer to my wife, Taylor, then I have placed her under the care of Doctor Samuel Brown.'

'You had no right to remove one of our patients from our care.' Even as he said the words Taylor inwardly recognized his own inconsistency in the matter, but was able to disregard it.

'I have every right to do as I see fit with my own wife.' Dugdale's icy composure was unaltered. 'Your treatment of her was ineffective. I've spent a small fortune on your quackeries and Mrs Dugdale's mental condition has only worsened.'

'You've yet to pay for half the treatment, Dugdale, so it ill befits you to criticize,' Taylor was stung to reply.

'You will be paid in full, Taylor. A gentleman does not repudiate debts, even unjustified ones.' The grey features suffused with contempt. 'You are a worthy representative of your profession, Taylor. Ranting about payments due to you for treatments which have proven worthless. I'll bid you good day, Sir!' He lifted the reins and shook them. 'Get on! Get on now!'

But before the horse could move the younger man leaned from his saddle to catch hold of the bridle and stop the horse.

'No Dugdale, do not run away. I've something more to say to you.'

The grey-hued features twisted in fury, but Dugdale held himself in check. 'Then say it quickly, Taylor, for I've no more time to waste on you.'

Although Taylor's own fury was seething, outwardly he was controlled. 'I wish to speak now as Sybil's kinsman, not as her doctor. I wish to know what is your real reason for incarcerating her in a madhouse!'

'Incarceration in a madhouse!' Dugdale ejaculated, and laughed, but there was no mirth in the laughter, and his deep-sunk eyes burned with rage. 'What a dramatic turn of phrase you possess, Taylor. Incarceration in a madhouse, indeed.' He seemed to be savouring the description. 'Incarceration in a madhouse,' he repeated yet again, and then snapped out, 'I have placed my wife under the care of a reputable surgeon who boasts of considerable success in his treatment of the mentally afflicted.'

'I know of Brown's repute, Dugdale,' Taylor interrupted hotly, 'and I do not seek to impugn his reputation. What concerns me however, are your own motives for taking such a course of action. Do you hope to be rid of Sybil so that you may enjoy her money without hindrance from her? So that you may do as you will without being forced to endure the inconvenience of a wife in your house? Is that why you have incarcerated her in Brown's madhouse?'

For a few seconds it seemed that Henry Dugdale would leap at the throat of his inquisitor. His powerful hands bunched into white-knuckled fists and he drew breath in long shuddering intakes. The lust to destroy was so rampant in his eyes that Hugh Taylor, brave man though he was, released the bridle of the trap-horse and tensed himself against attack, his right hand reaching towards the saddlebag which held a ioaded pistol, the frequent accompaniment of travellers in these troubled times.

But Dugdale made no movement and no reply, only kept his ravening glare fixed on the younger man's face. When finally he did speak his voice was thick and guttural.

'If you were not my wife's kinsman, Taylor, I would kill you for what you have just said.'

With that he lifted the whip from its holder and flicked its long thong against the trap-horse's glossy rump. 'Get on,' he growled, and this time Taylor let him go without further hindrance, shakily aware of how close death had been for either one of them during those brief moments.

He sat his mount and watched the trap disappear from sight, trying to decide his next move. He sighed heavily, and asked himself, 'Why am I now so concerned about Cousin Sybil? I did not want her for patient, and God knows I've never had much liking for the woman. Why should I now bother my head? Is it because I dislike Henry Dugdale, and resent him having untramelled use of money which was a part of our family's inheritance? Is that the reason, purely and simply stated? Am I now concerned solely for mercenary motives?' Troubled and made uncertain by his own thoughts he turned his mount's head back towards Redditch.

Chapter Eighteen

'Now then, Tildy, 'ull you take another slice o' pork?'
Tobias Wilkins's head was a round pinkly glistening ball in
the candlelight, and as he smilingly proffered the thick slice
of meat on the prongs of his long-handled fork Tildy was
irresistibly reminded of a toby jug. She smiled at the
thought, and declined the offer.

'My thanks, Master Wilkins, but I'm full to bursting.'
She looked down at the remnants of roast potatoes, carrots
and peas swimming in the thick gravy on her plate, and felt
unaccountably guilty that she should have feasted so richly.
'I've stuffed myself like a pig. I declare you must think me
such.'

'Don't talk so sarft, my wench.' Amanda, Tobias
Wilkins's wife, who was as short-statured and rounded as
her husband, reached for the big stone jug of ale, and
despite Tildy's protests refilled the girl's leather drinking
jack. 'Get that down you, girl. Youm a pretty cratur, but
youm a deal too skinny. You needs to put a bit o' mate on
them bones.'

They were in the comfortably furnished parlour of the
Wilkins on the second floor of the Stone House. Three
doors away from them, having been soundly dosed with
Godfrey's Cordial, Sybil Dugdale was soundly asleep in the
bed she would share with Tildy for this night at least. In the
corner of the room the grandfather clock whirred and

chimed, and Tobias Wilkins listened to the resonating echoes with a smile of beatific satisfaction.

'Theer now, arn't that a wonderful sweet-toned bell?' he exclaimed as the last chimes died away.

He stared at Tildy as if inviting comment, and she nodded and smiled to congratulate him on his possession.

'Yes, it's truly fine, Master Wilkins, a truly fine chimer.'

The fourth member of the group around the table spoke out. 'Yes, Joey Bates reckons it's a fine chimer, as well.' His broad red face was greasy with the juices of the meat and the gravy.

'Be quiet now Joey, and finish your dinner.' Amanda Wilkins scraped the remnants of her food on to the lunatic's plate. 'Here, have this as well, my lad.'

She reached for Tildy's plate and gave those scraps also to Joey Bates, who screwed his eyes tightly shut and laughed uproariously.

'That's it, Missus! That's prime, that is! The more the merrier, Joey Bates says. The more the merrier.' He chortled delightedly. 'Joey Bates can ate the cupboard bare, Joey Bates can.'

'Shush now, and ate your grub,' the fat woman told him, and still chortling, the lunatic did her bidding, shovelling meat, potatoes, carrots, peas and gravy-soaked bread into his capacious mouth.

Since Henry Dugdale's departure Tildy had stayed with Sybil Dugdale in the room allotted to them and had not seen anything else of the house or its inmates. Now her curiosity could no longer be restrained.

'Can you tell me about this place, Master Wilkins? I've a great wish to know what happens here.'

The pink ball of his head tilted on his stumpy neck as he squinted questioningly at her. 'Theer's no call for you to be feared o' this place, Tildy, or of the loonies. They'm locked up secure.'

'But I'm not feared, Master Wilkins,' she hastened to assure him. 'I'm not feared at all, but I am curious about them.'

'Ahr, well now.' His lips pursed doubtfully. 'You knows

159

what curiosity did for the cat, doon't you, young 'ooman?'

His wife cut short his prevarication. ''Ull you stop blethering, Wilkins,' she puffed irritably, 'and tell the wench what she wants to know.'

He frowned. 'You knows that Doctor Samuel doon't like us to talk to anybody about what happens in here, Manda.'

'Don't talk so sarft, Wilkins, this wench is agoing to be living and working here, arn't her? So her's bound to see and hear what's going on. It's best to tell her about all such things now, so her 'ull understand.'

'I've no wish to pry into matters which don't concern me,' Tildy flustered defensively, and in her mind a tiny voice cried 'Liar!'

'Don't you moither your yed about prying, Tildy,' Amanda Wilkins reassured her. 'You'se got a right to know since youm agoing to be helping us out whiles youm here.'

'Oh yes, I'm very pleased to be helping you.' Tildy was genuinely anxious to help because she wished to learn how the mentally sick were treated in such a professional establishment, and how they could be cured.

After a pause, Tobias Wilkins's many chins nodded agreement. 'Ahr, I suppose youm right, Mrs Wilkins. She'll need to know, wun't her? And God knows we can allus find use for another pair o' willing hands, can't us?' He grinned at Tildy. 'You'll have to excuse me being a bit wary, Tildy, only there's a lot o' wicked tongues in this village as 'ud be only too glad to blacken the character o' this house, just for badness.'

'Wicked tongues are to be found anywhere, Master Wilkins,' Tildy replied, 'but my own tongue is not one of them – at least I hope and pray it's not.'

'I'm certain sure it arn't, my duck.' The bald pink head bobbed up and down. 'Let me see now, wheer's to start . . . Ahr, yes, well, we'em licensed for thirty, Tildy, that means we can take thirty loonies into this house. Ten paupers and twenty paying. They all has to be paid for, of course, but it's the parish that pays for the paupers. Twelve shillings and sixpence the week for each on 'um, so it arn't chape, is it? The private patients be charged whatever the doctor reckons their families can afford.' He winked slyly. 'And that's normally a sight more than they reckons they can afford. We tries to keep the paupers separate and to divide the rest up into their different types as well, but it's hard to keep strictly to that.'

'How many patients are here now?' Tildy asked.

'Seven paupers, and fifteen paying.'

'That's a large number for you to care for,' Tildy remarked.

'Oh, we get's help in when needful,' Amanda Wilkins answered. 'We'se got Joey here, and there's a couple o' women in the village we can call in iffen theer's an emergency like. And then Doctor Brown's got his young gennulmen students as well. They works a lot wi' the patients.'

'Do the paupers get differently treated from those who have money?' Even as she asked Tildy could guess the answer, and it was no surprise when the other woman clucked her tongue derisively and said, 'You doon't really need an answer to that 'un, does you girl? But in all truth, me and Tobias does our best for the poor buggers, so there arn't that much difference made atween all on 'um.'

'Does Doctor Brown live here at the house as well?' Tildy wanted to know, and Tobias Wilkins laughed.

'God's trewth, no! 'Ud you live in a bloody madhouse if you needn't? No, he's got a fine big house just outside the village. He's well set up, Tildy. This place is just one of his lines. He's got a practice, he does operations, and he teaches anatomy and surgery to his students. He's got money coming in from all over. But this pays him well enough, and he's got a lot of interest in treating the loonies and trying different cures on 'um, so he spends a good half of his time here.'

'Come on, girl, I'll show you over the place. You might as well see it now, when there's nobody to bother us.'

In the light of the lantern the winding brick-lined stair-well descending into the darkness beneath the vaulted roof was eerily forbidding, and Tildy's throat tightened with apprehension of the unknown. That apprehension deepened as she followed Tobias Wilkins down the stairs and a damp-fetid stench clogged her mouth and throat. A solitary voice was muttering unintelligible gibberish, and just as she reached the bottom of the stairs a harrowing shriek reverberated from the clammy darkness beyond.

'Dear God, who's that?' she gasped in fright, but the fat man only laughed.

'Pay no heed to it, Tildy. You'll get used to the skrawking. These be our cellers. We keeps most on our loonies down here.'

He lifted the lantern high and walked forwards, and Tildy hastened to keep close to him, nervous of standing alone in this depressing, frightening place. The cellars were four in number, two leading off each side of the central corridor which ran from front to rear of the building. As they moved along the corridor it seemed to Tildy that the air became even more dank and chill and reeking with the stenches of human sweat and excreta.

'Look here, Tildy.' Wilkins shone the light into the furthest cellar and Tildy peeped over his shoulder. There was no door and the cellar was some twenty feet long and six feet in width, its arched roof six feet high in the centre. On each side stone shelves some two feet wide ran the length of the walls and at the far end was an unglazed window covered by a thick iron grille. Wet, filthy straw was strewn thickly underfoot and on the shelves and in this straw were two lines of human figures.

As the pale light illuminated their heads and bodies Tildy moaned audibly in mingled pity and horror. These men and women seemed like creatures of a nightmare, some wholly naked, some half covered by one-piece smocks, their hair matted, tangled clumps on their gaunt and filth-caked heads. Some slept in unquiet muttering twitchings, some were awake, gazing blankly into the light, rocking backwards and forwards, crooning tunelessly, sobbing, laughing, gibbering. One man was masturbating himself, strings of mucus falling from his gaping, gasping mouth. Opposite him a woman spread her thighs wide, flaunting her bush of pubic hair in the lantern's glow, her hands beckoning in lewd invitation. Tildy could hear the dulled clankings of metal and as her eyes strained in the gloom she made out the chains and fetters which secured everyone of these tortured souls to the great iron rings embedded in the walls.

'These be our hopeless cases,' the fat man told her. 'There's naught to be done wi' 'um except sluice 'um down and feed 'um. Come on, I'll show you the others.'

The sights and smells, the low ceilings, the damp-running walls suddenly closed about Tildy, and she started to panic as a sensation of being trapped overwhelmed her. Her mouth opened and her breathing became a harsh panting as she desperately battled to draw breath into lungs that had seemingly ceased to function. Cold nausea invaded her; she felt as if she were suffocating, and in terrified escape she turned and ran towards the flight of stairs. She hurled herself up the winding steps, stumbling and bruising her knees upon the bricks, tearing the skin from her fingers as she scrabbled at the walls to heave herself upwards. She gained the ground floor of the house and slumped against the wall, her breath rasping, body shaking, her mind desperately fighting to regain control of her reeling senses.

The yellow lantern light bathed her and the fat man's deep voice came close to her ears.

'Come now, Tildy, calm yourself down. Theer's naught to fear. Them poor buggers can't harm you. They'm well-locked up, they can't get free. Come on back upstairs, I'll gi' you a drop o' summat to steady your nerves.'

Feeling weak and spent Tildy allowed herself to be helped back into the cosy parlour. Amanda Wilkins bustled to sit the younger woman down and pressed a small glass against her blanched lips.

'Here you be, my duck. You just take a sup o' this, it'll do you good.'

Tildy gulped and coughed as the raw gin burned her throat and her stomach heaved, but she swallowed hard and in moments the fiery spirit heated her belly and spread

163

warmth and strength through her clammy-sweated body. She felt herself calming and the trembling of her hands stilled.

'I'm sorry,' she mumbled shamefacedly. 'I don't know what made me go like that. I've never acted that way afore.'

The older woman clucked her tongue sympathetically. 'Theer theer, my duck, doon't let it moither you any. I'se sin it take folks like that a score o' times afore. Why, the fust time I went down theer to the cellars it gi' me a funny turn, I'll tell you. I threw up me breakfast all over the floor, arn't that right, Mr Wilkins?'

Her husband was quick to confirm what she said. 'Ahr, that's true that is, Tildy. My missus was took very queer her fust time down theer. But she got used to it real quick, as you 'ull, my duck.'

'Of course you 'ull.' Amanda Wilkins squeezed Tildy's shoulder encouragingly. 'It's like a miasma, you see, girl. That's what the loonies gives off, a sort o' poison miasma, but you gets used to it. You'll hardly notice it next time you goes down, you'll see.'

Tildy was much calmer now and was able to evaluate the woman's words. She found herself believing what Amanda Wilkins had said. What she had experienced in those cellars had indeed seemed like the effects of a poison miasma. She clutched at that explanation which would excuse what she could not help regarding as her own shameful weakness in behaving as she had.

'Yes, Mrs Wilkins, I'm sure you're right in what you say,' she agreed shakily. 'It'll not happen again. I'll be better prepared for it next time.'

Chapter Nineteen

'Theer, that don't look too bad, does it now?' Amanda Wilkins cut through the last long tress of chestnut hair, and with scissors held high regarded her handiwork with evident satisfaction.

Tildy could only think how sad and forlorn a picture Sybil Dugdale now presented. Dressed only in a long grey canvas smock which left her thin white arms and neck bare, and now shorn of her beautiful hair, Sybil Dugdale sat very still on the stool and kept her gaze fixed on the entwined writhing fingers upon her lap. Since her arrival yesterday at the Stone House the young woman had not spoken a word, not even to reply to questions. Also she had refused all food and had drunk only cold water.

'Did you really need to cut off all her hair?' Tildy asked, and Amanda Wilkins responded regretfully.

'Yes, it has to be done when they fust comes in, Tildy. The Doctor's very strict about that. Mind you, it makes it easier for us to keep the head-lice in check, and theer's some o' the treatments where long hair gets in the way o' things.

'It's a pity when they'se got nice hair, like this 'un had, but theer's naught else for it. Come now, Doctor Brown 'ull be getting aerated if we keeps him waiting much longer.'

She took Sybil Dugdale's thin arm and pulled her to her feet. The young woman was unresisting, allowing herself to be handled and directed as if she were a mindless passive creature.

'Here is our new patient, gentlemen.' Samuel Brown and three of his students were in the surgery/office on the ground floor. When Tildy entered the room behind the two other women the young men stared avidly at her and exchanged nudges and winks, but although her colour heightened, she did her best to ignore them.

'Ahahh yes, Crawford,' Doctor Brown smiled kindly at her. 'You will be assisting Mr and Mrs Wilkins whilst you remain here. I trust that your stay will be a happy one.'

'Thank you, Sir.' Tildy bobbed a curtsy, but even as she moved the doctor had switched his attention to Sybil Dugdale.

'You will observe the patient's bodily posture, and facial expression, gentlemen. Take particular note of her eyes, hands and fingers. You will observe her apparent lack of comprehension and her indifference to the fact that we discuss her . . . ' He carried on his dissertation for some time, and his students listened attentively. Tildy also listened, trying to store what he said in her memory. Finally he told his audience, 'This lady was diagnosed by other medical practitioners as suffering from a variation of nervous hysteria. That diagnosis is in error, gentlemen. She is not suffering from nervous hysteria, but from maniacal melancholia, a totally different malady. Now, Mr Fletcher, how would you prescribe her?'

Douglas Fletcher was clad like his fellow students in dark swallowtail coat and pantaloons, with a white waistcoat, linen shirt and cravat. His curly brown hair was close-cropped and powdered, his handsome face ruddy with good health, his strongly-built body standing a good six feet in height, making him easily the tallest person in the room. His blue eyes wandered towards Tildy and he smiled briefly as he caught and held her gaze.

'Come now, Mr Fletcher. We await your prescription,' Samuel Brown prodded, and the young man coughed, covering his mouth with well-manicured fingers, then questioned, 'Might I enquire as to the duration of time this patient has been so afflicted, Sir, and what other treatments she has undergone?' His voice was pleasant-timbred and well modulated with no trace of a local accent.

Brown nodded approvingly. 'Good, Mr Fletcher, good. Always ascertain a patient's previous treatments before prescribing.

'Apparently she has always been of a somewhat melancholic disposition, Mr Fletcher, but her present condition dates from a short time following her marriage, some one and a half years since. There are periods when she appears almost normal, but those periods are of short duration and occur only rarely.

'Her previous treatments have been medicinal – mainly various compositions containing roots of valerian, cassamunair and black hellebore, together with salt of steel, rectified spirit of wine, distilled vinegar and extract of saffron. In short, gentlemen, the standard types of elixir against the melancholy.'

Douglas Fletcher pondered gravely for some moments, and then asked. 'Has there been no attempt to shock the affliction, Sir?'

'To my knowledge, no,' Brown answered equally gravely, and the younger man then stated decisively.

'Then, Sir, I would prescribe immediate shocking of the affliction.'

'By what methods?' Brown probed.

'By bleeding, Sir, coupled with rigorous purging, followed by whipping and cold douches.'

Brown turned to the other students. 'Gentlemen, do you agree with that prescription?'

Peter Donovan, a puckish-featured, lean-bodied Irishman with a great shock of red hair was the first to answer. 'Yes, Sir, I think it suitable.'

The third student, small and thin with a pale disagreeable expression shook his narrow head. 'No, Sir, I do not agree.'

'Why not?' Brown's smile was encouraging.

167

'Because, Sir, the patient is not robust. She appears sickly and anaemic. I fear that a course of blood-letting and rigorous purging will gravely diminish her vital spirit and thus allow the malady to gain an even stronger hold.'

'Then what is your alternative prescription, Mr Fusey?'

'I would cup and blister initially, Sir, to draw the malignant humours into a position where they can be shocked with the galvanic battery.'

Brown nodded judiciously. 'There is much merit in your prescription, Mr Fusey, and indeed, I had myself considered galvanism coupled with blistering. However, in my judgement the patient is stronger in body than she appears. Therefore, initially we shall follow Mr Fletcher's proposed course.

'I realize that it does not have the attraction of novelty, as does the galvanic battery, but in my experience it is always the wisest thing to initially follow the old and trusty methods. Always remember gentlemen, that novel treatments, such as galvanism, are still not widely understood. They are a new frontier which must be explored with due caution. Therefore the wise doctor initially sticks to the well-trodden pathways of treatment, particularly in our most specialized field.'

He nodded at Fletcher. 'You will bleed the patient, Mr Fletcher. Draw ten ounces. And you, Mr Donovan, will administer the purge. Prepare a mixture, and make sure that it is of a drastic nature.'

The Irishman disappeared from the room and Douglas Fletcher took from the shelf a bronze bowl which on its inside surface was graded with measuring lines for fluid ounces. He also selected a short-bladed scalpel from a case of instruments, and a hinged metal ring some two inches broad and padded on its inner surface with thick cloth. He saw Tildy's interested gaze and smilingly demonstrated the object for her.

'See Crawford, it's a type of tourniquet.' He snapped it shut, tightening the open ends together with a brass butterfly screw. 'Ingenious, is it not?'

At first Sybil Dugdale paid no attention as the young

man placed the bowl beneath her left arm and then secured the tourniquet on that arm, just above her sharp-boned elbow. He tightened the screw and the veins visibly engorged and pulsed blue beneath the white skin of her forearm.

'Shall I continue, Sir?' Fletcher asked Doctor Brown, and receiving a nod of assent, he grasped Sybil Dugdale's arm firmly with his left hand, lifted the scalpel with his right hand and cut a neat longitudinal slit in the trunk vein.

Sybil Dugdale's eyes widened with horror as the blood jetted, then she screamed hysterically and tore free of the restraining grasp.

'God dammit, hold her still!' Samuel Brown shouted. 'Wilkins, Crawford, help Mr Fletcher. Keep that bowl under her arm Mr Fusey, we must have the measure of the blood.'

But even the combined efforts of Tildy, Amanda Wilkins and Douglas Fletcher could not keep Sybil Dugdale under control. Eyes bulging, teeth clenched and bared she screamed and struggled so violently that Brown himself was forced to come to their aid. Even as she fought to hold Sybil Dugdale, Tildy was fearfully awed at the strength contained in the thin sickly body of the woman. A wild kick sent the bronze bowl flying, blood gouted from the cut vein and within moments the skin and clothing of them all were smeared with its sticky redness.

'Get her on to the floor,' Doctor Brown panted, and as they wrestled the heaving, twisting body downwards he loosened and removed the tourniquet. 'We must bind the vein and place her under restraint. Fetch some manacles, Fusey.'

The pale faced student ran from the room to reappear within moments carrying fetters, chains and leather belts.

'Crawford, take her left leg! Kneel on it and hold it still, girl!' Brown instructed, gasping for breath. 'Wilkins, take the right leg. Fletcher, Fusey, see to her arms, and watch her teeth. She'll tear you to shreds else.'

Moving with the sure dexterity bred during years of

practise, Brown strapped a broad leather belt around the shrieking woman's waist and chained and manacled her hands to it. More manacles and chains fettered her legs. Then panting heavily Brown clambered to his feet and from one of his pockets produced a small cylindrical piece of wood that had stout leather thongs secured to each end.

'We'll need to gag her,' he told the two students. 'Press her chin down, Fletcher. Twist her nose closed and back, Fusey.'

As they obeyed him the fat man forced the wooden block between Sybil Dugdale's teeth and secured it in position by tightly tying the leather thongs behind her head. Then he bound the bleeding vein. Trussed and helpless as she was, still Sybil Dugdale's body heaved and fought, and half-strangled shrieks erupted from behind her wooden gag.

Tildy stared down at the horribly distorted features of her mistress and a sick wave of nausea overwhelmed her. Bitter bile seared her throat and she gagged violently, then sank to her hands and knees and vomited on to the blood-stained floor. Sick with shame and self-disgust she could only cover her face with her hands and sob helplessly.

'Take Mrs Dugdale down to the dark room,' Brown told his students. 'Secure her face downwards and wait for me there. I'll come presently.'

At this moment Peter Donovan appeared, carrying a large flask of dark-coloured, foul-smelling liquid. He stared with amazement as Fusey and Fletcher went past him carrying the twisting, struggling Sybil Dugdale by her feet and shoulders.

'Take the purge down to the dark room, Mr Donovan,' Brown ordered. 'And take also a glyster bladder and pipe. We'll administer a dose rectally; it will help to quieten her. Go with him, Wilkins.'

Once alone with Tildy, Samuel Brown lifted the sobbing girl to her feet. 'Come now, Crawford. Control yourself,' he told her sternly, and waited until her sobs lessened, then said, 'To be a good nursing-woman, Crawford, it is necessary that you become hardened to distressful sights and happenings. If you allow yourself to be overcome by

170

another's sufferings, then you will not be capable of aiding them. As a young student I was taught that the good surgeon inures himself to his patients' screams. You must learn to do the same, Crawford. Now dry your eyes and come with me, there is work to be done.'

Chapter Twenty

That evening Tildy lay alone in her room thinking of Sybil
Dugdale pinioned to the wall of the dark dank cellar, awash
in her own excrement. With closed eyes and trembling
hands Tildy mentally relived the events of the day. Seeing
again the soiled naked buttocks of her mistress as she lay
face downwards on the stone floor with the long thick pipe
of the glyster bladder thrust into her anal passage like an
obscene giant phallus.

Tildy moaned softly as she heard again Sybil Dugdale's
agonized shrieks when the students whipped her fragile
shoulders and back with long thin bamboo canes. As Tildy
had watched and heard what had happened in that cellar
she herself had gagged and retched again, her empty
stomach straining in futile agonies, her eyes blind with
tears.

'It cannot be right,' she whispered now into the stillness
of the room. 'I don't care what the doctors say, such
treatment can never be right. How can such cruelty cure
madness? How can it cure anything?'

Her miserable reveries were interrupted by a knocking at
the door, and Amanda Wilkins told her, 'Tildy, you must
come to the parlour now, youm wanted.'

'It'll be the doctor,' Tildy thought. 'No doubt he wants
to tell me to leave because I'm so useless at helping the
others. What will Mr Dugdale say, I wonder, me leaving
Mrs Dugdale alone here?'

'Tildy? Did you hear me? Youm wanted in the parlour,' Amanda Wilkins called again.

Tildy sighed. 'Ah well, if I'm to be given my sack, so be it,' she accepted resignedly, and answered aloud, 'All right Mrs Wilkins, I'll be along directly.'

Rising from the bed she tidied her hair and straightened her shabby old grey gown, then took her candle and made her way to the parlour.

When she opened the door the warmth and good smells of stew cooking and wood burning in the hearth met her, and someone totally unexpected was there to meet her also.

'Harry Mogg!' Tildy exclaimed in pleased surprise, then a sudden disquieting thought caused her to catch her breath. 'Is aught the matter with my Davy?'

'No, of course there arn't,' the young needle pointer hastened to calm her fears. 'The babby is thriving, Tildy. I bin up to see him this very arternoon so I could bring you news of him.'

'But how did you know where to find me?' Tildy queried, and he laughed at her puzzled face, then told her banteringly.

'Love allus finds a way, Tildy, doon't you know that yet?'

She was deeply touched. 'Oh Harry, have you walked all this way to bring me news of Davy? I'm really thankful to you, I really am.'

His piquant grin shone out. 'Good, I'm glad you're pleased, Tildy, and to tell you the truth, it warn't too hard to find you here. There arn't so many girls as pretty as you in these parts. I soon found a couple o' young bucks who'd seen you come into the village and knew where you was astaying. There arn't no secrets in villages, my duck.' He paused, and studied her with shrewd eyes. 'You arn't looking too bright and perky wi' yourself, Tildy. What's up?'

Returning his gaze Tildy gave in to the impulse to unburden herself. 'Truth to tell, I'm not very happy about being here, Harry. I think it's going to be very hard to do the work they want of me here. The treatment they give the loonies is cruel, Harry. I can't think it right to give the poor souls such treatment. I can't help but think the doctor's wrong when he says it will cure them.'

The young man tried to reassure her. 'The doctor must know what he's about, Tildy. I mean, life's cruel and hard, arn't it, and necessarily some o' the things that doctors does must seem cruel hard to us as doesn't fully understand what they be about.'

'I know that, Harry, and I know that when a woman is as ignorant as me, then it's easy to misunderstand, but, but . . . ' She hesitated with slightly parted lips while she searched for words to explain exactly what she felt, and the young man hungered to crush his own mouth to those moistly tempting red lips so close to his own.

'Tildy, listen to me,' he said urgently. 'Iffen you arn't happy here, my honey, then leave the place now and come back to Redditch. You can live wi' me in my cottage and bring your little Davy to live there as well. I'll be good to you both, Tildy.'

Her heart sank as she heard him. 'Oh no, Harry, don't fall in love with me because I can't leave here and come with you. I'm still married and it wouldn't be right.'

'Bollocks to what's right!' he ejaculated scathingly. 'In this life you must do what you wants to do, and fuck anybody else's ideas o' what's right and what arn't . . . ' She shook her head as again he urged her to come with him, and she began to experience an increasing sense of entrapment, as if he were physically binding her to do as he wanted her to.

'No, Harry! You don't understand me,' she burst out desperately. 'I don't want to live with any man. I like you a lot, Harry, and I want you for my friend, but I don't love you in the way you want me to, so I couldn't live with you.'

Now it was his turn to hesitate and to stare uncomprehendingly at her as he searched for words, and finally told her bluntly,

'But I arn't saying I loves you, Tildy. I arn't talking about love, that's summat in books, Tildy. Summat for the gentry to sing about and write verses about. Love arn't for the likes of us, Tildy, and I arn't offering you love. I'm offering you and your babby a roof over your yeds. I'm offering you full bellies and clothes on your backs. I'm offering you pleasuring in me bed, and protection agen what other men 'ud try to force on you. We can still be friends when we'em sharing a bed, Tildy. Friendship arn't agoing to stop because I'd be lying between your legs of a night-time, is it?'

His almost brutal frankness created a mixture of reactions in Tildy. Her vanity was piqued because he had stated that he did not love her romantically, but at the same time she felt relieved because however unwilling she was at times to acknowledge the fact to herself, she knew that whenever a man professed to love her, she then could not help but feel a sense of responsibility and of guilt if he should commit some foolish act because she had told him that she did not return his love.

'Thank you for being so honest with me, Harry.' She chose her words carefully. 'And thank you also for offering me and my Davy a home. But my answer must still be no. I must try and make my own way in the world, Harry, and learn to look for no man's help when that way becomes hard.

'I don't know why I am the way I am, Harry. I don't know what drives me to act as I do. I only know that there is nothing else I can ever do but to try to be my own woman – my own possession, and no one else's. But I still want you for my friend, as I am your friend.'

For a few moments he stared sombrely at her, and then his gap-toothed grin spread across his face. 'That's a fair enough answer, Tildy, and I reckons I can understand what it is youm saying. I'll stay your friend, my duck, and I'll prove a true 'un. But I'll tell you straight, Tildy, I'd like more than anything in this world to be in bed wi' you, and to gi' you and meself a pleasuring. So iffen you ever needs a man's loving, pretty girl, you just say the word.'

She could not help but blush hotly, but although he had embarrassed her, he had not offended her. There was nothing dirty or furtive about Harry Mogg's lust for her; it was open, honest and healthy, and Tildy could accept it as such without offence or fear.

The clock in the shadowed corner struck the hour and Harry grimaced. 'I'll have to leave you now, Tildy. I'se got to meet my new boss. He's agoing to gi' me a ride back to Redditch.'

'Your new boss?' Tildy questioned. 'Are you not doing the pointing at the forge now then?'

'I arn't doing the pointing anywheres now, Tildy,' he winked at her slyly. 'I works for a man name o' Jonas Crowther now, doing a bit o' this, and a bit o' that. It pays well, and it arn't so hard on me lungs. 'Bye for now, my honey, I'll see you soon.'

He had brushed her cheek with his lips and gone whistling down the stairs before the full import of what he had told her sank home to Tildy. Then she remembered the hard-featured, menacing man at Mother Readman's, and remembered also the old woman's words: 'Crowther's an evil sod . . . Him and his bloody gang . . . There's no devilment the buggers doon't get up to . . . Iffen there was any justice in this world, then Crowther would ha' bin hung years since, and his bloody bully-boys wi' him . . .'

'Oh my God!' Tildy breathed with fearful dismay. 'Oh God, Harry, what are you mixed up with? What are you doing with that evil man?'

Chapter Twenty-one

'The parson says 'ull you come to the chapel now, Master Cashmore. He says youm to come straight away. He says youm to leave whatever youm adoing and come straight away.' The shock-headed, barefoot urchin breathlessly gabbled the message and then scampered off from the doorway before Joseph Cashmore could even swallow the mouthful of food that bulged his weatherbeaten cheek. The constable gulped hard to dispose of the half-chewed bread and bacon and swore in loud disgust.

'Bollocks to it! Carn't a man have a bite to ate wi'out bleeding interruption? I'm buggered if I'll goo anywheres until I'se ate me bit o' grub.'

'But the parson says youm to come straight away, Joe,' Janey Cashmore standing behind her burly husband timidly ventured to point out. He swung on her and she quailed before his glare and flustered nervously, 'Well, I was only saying what the boy said, at least what I thought he said.'

'Don't you start trying to think, my wench, you arn't got the capacity for it. You leave all the bloody thinking to me.'

'Yes Joe, I'm sorry. I wasn't thinking,' Janey Cashmore whispered submissively.

'Well, doon't stand there like a bloody mawkin, 'oman! Fetch me me things,' he roared, and she ran to do his bidding.

* * *

'Ahhh, there you are at last, Cashmore. It's taken you long enough to arrive.' John Clayton was patently out of temper.

Standing in the chapel porchway with him was another burly-bodied man whose clothing was dusty-white with flour and who carried the long-crowned staff of a constable.

Cashmore nodded dourly at the man, for there was no love lost between himself and Edwin Ashwin, constable of Ipsley parish and proprietor of the Ipsley flour mill.

Cashmore raised his bushy eyebrows interrogatively. 'What's amiss, Parson Clayton, that I needs to be fetched from me breakfast for?'

'I am unable to tell you that myself yet, Cashmore,' Clayton snapped. 'The Reverend Wren has sent Master Ashwin to bring you and me down to Ipsley church immediately, but did not tell Master Ashwin the reason why.'

Cashmore nodded glumly and then peered up at the sky where black storm-clouds were ominously massing. 'It looks like we'em going to get a soaking as well, if them bloody clouds be anything to goo by.'

'No, we'll not, Cashmore.' Clayton's temper had not been improved by the constable's surly manner. 'I've sent word to Master Smallwood. He'll be bringing his carriage, and we shall ride in that . . . '

In the yard of St Peter's Church at Ipsley another small group of men were waiting for the arrival of the Redditch party. As William Smallwood's carriage rattled to a halt outside the lich-gate the Reverend Phillip Wren, incumbent rector of Ipsley parish, came to meet it. Small and ample-paunched, his watery-blue eyes were worried behind their square-lensed spectacles, and his short fat fingers toyed nervously with the heavy gold watch-chain hanging across his dark waistcoat.

'Good morning, Reverend Clayton, thank you for coming so promptly,' he welcomed his fellow clergyman, and John Clayton bowed in reply.

'Good morning to you, Sir. Now, what's amiss?'

The watery blue eyes blinked rapidly and the little man told him with great agitation, 'It is terrible, Reverend Clayton, terrible! But come, you shall see for yourself.'

The three other men in the yard were stocky, ruddy-faced farmers, dressed in thick fustian coats and leather-gaitered, with wide-brimmed, shallow-crowned hats. Wren made brief introductions.

'These are my church wardens, Reverend Clayton, Master Whittington and Master Whitehouse, and this gentleman is Master Spiers, my sexton.'

Clayton nodded. 'Gentlemen,' and they muttered their greetings.

The small clergyman led the combined parties around to the opposite side of the ancient church and even as they rounded the squat bell-tower John Clayton saw and understood the reason for the urgent summons.

A fresh grave had been tampered with, its wilting posies of flowers and evergreen wreaths piled to one side, and the head of the raw clay mound dug into.

A concerted growl of outrage came from the throats of William Smallwood and the two constables, and Clayton felt his own throat thicken with anger.

'Resurrection men!' he stated flatly, and beside him Phillip Wren nodded his plump head so vigorously that his white tie-wig slipped sideways.

'Exactly so, Reverend Clayton. There were body-snatchers here last night.'

Clayton advanced to the edge of the grave mound and stared down into the cramped shaft sunk into the heavy red clay. His eyes roved around, noting the tarpaulin sheeting carefully placed to catch the excavated earth, the shovels, the crowbar and mallet, the voluminous hessian sack and the strong rope with the viciously spiked iron hook spliced to its end.

'Thank God they did not have time to break into the coffin,' Clayton murmured, and then in a louder tone asked, 'Who was it that disturbed them?'

''Twas me, Parson,' Spiers, the Ipsley sexton answered.

'I was acoming along the Watery Lane about half-past midnight and I see'd a light abobbing about, so I snuck around the hedges and come upon the wicked bastards from the field side theer.'

'How many were there?' Clayton wanted to know.

'Two that I saw, Parson.'

'Could you recognize either of them?'

'No Parson, 'twas a clouded sky, there was no moonlight, and they doused the glim as quick as lightning when I shouted.'

Again Clayton's eyes went back to the articles the would-be grave-robbers had abandoned. 'Judging by these they were men who knew what they were about,' he mused aloud. 'A short while longer left undisturbed and they would have broken open the coffin lid, hooked out the corpse and refilled the hole. Once the wreaths and flowers were replaced, then no one would have been any the wiser.' Again he looked directly at the sexton. 'You are lucky that they did not attack you, Master Spiers. Men who commit such sacrilege as this are normally desperate characters who do not shrink from violence.'

'I'd got me fowling-piece wi' me, Parson, and I shouted and let fly at 'um from the other side o' the hedge theer. The rattle I made they must ha' thought theer was a whole troop o' dragoons acoming.'

'You fired at them?' Clayton said eagerly. 'Do you think you might have scored a hit?'

The bovine features were doubtful. 'I can't rightly say that I did, Parson. One of 'um cried out, but it might ha' bin in fright at being so disturbed. They scarpered like bats out o' hell, I'll tell you.'

'You did well, Master Spiers, and played the man,' Clayton congratulated. 'I shall make it my business to bring that fact to the attention of the Reverend the Lord Aston. I trust that the Reverend Wren will do the same.'

'Oh indeed, Sir, indeed I shall,' Phillip Wren flustered, and the sexton beamed with pride and pleasure, until Edwin Ashwin whispered in his ear.

'What was you adoing at half-past midnight in the

Watery Lane wi' a fowling-piece, Josh Spiers? Bit o' poachin' was it?'

Lightning streaked, thunder cracked and black storm-clouds lashed the land with hail and rain.

'Come gentlemen, we'll take shelter.' Clayton led the group back around the bell-tower and they hurried through the porch and into the gloomy interior of the small church.

'What's to be done, Sir?' Phillip Wren was almost pleading, and his fat fingers tugged fretfully at his watch chain. 'What's to be done?'

'Precious little until this storm passes, unless you wish a soaking to add to our troubles,' Clayton told him with jocular grimness. 'When it has passed you will take steps to notify the bishop and also the Warwick magistrates of what has happened here. Sadly Sir, although body-snatching is almost endemic these days, I fear the judiciary will pay but little heed to your tidings. In the eyes of the law, to steal a corpse is not a criminal offence. Ridiculous, is it not? We can have a man transported if he steals the shroud the corpse is wrapped in, but if he takes only the corpse, then we can do little or nothing against him in the way of punishment.' He sighed wearily, and then asked, 'How many burials have you performed here this last sennight?'

'One other apart from the one we have just seen,' Wren informed him, and then his chubby features became woeful. 'Oh dear Lord, I pray not.' He groaned his distress and Clayton voiced his agreement with that sentiment.

'I pray not also, Reverend Wren, but sadly we will need to make certain that the other grave has not already been emptied.'

He frowned unhappily as he considered the three burial services he had himself presided over at the parish church in Tardebigge hamlet and the burial yard at Redditch during the previous fortnight. 'At least it has been a very low rate of burials for the time of year,' he comforted himself, and said aloud, 'It's a bad business and a grievously sad one also for the bereaved families.'

A murmur of agreement greeted his words and he continued, 'Until such time as we bring these damned rogues to book, we shall have to institute a grave-watch gentlemen. I shall suggest to the vestry that a reward be offered for these body-snatchers, and as soon as I return to Redditch I shall set about informing our neighbouring parishes of what has occurred here.' He lapsed into silence, appearing to be considering something, and then said, 'I wish to suggest something, gentlemen. I wish to suggest that we each one of us makes discreet enquiries as to the possible purchaser of a cadaver in this neighbourhood. It is in all likelihood a Birmingham surgeon, or Warwick or Worcester, mayhap even further afield, but nevertheless there are surgeons in our own neighbourhoods, and many of them have a use at times for anatomical specimens.'

An uneasy silence followed, a silence which lengthened almost unbearably, until Joseph Cashmore questioned, 'And if we did find such a surgeon locally, Parson, what then? What can we do? There's no law agen buying a body, so what can we do?'

'What do people always do when cases of this kind are discovered, gentlemen?' Clayton said grimly. 'They rise up and drive the offender from the parish. We shall have to do the same. We want no body-snatchers here, or their employers.'

A growl of agreement came from his listeners, and one of them said amid plaudits, 'That's it, Parson. We'll drive the bastards out, lock, stock and barrel . . .'

Chapter Twenty-two

Tildy was deeply troubled. For ten days she had witnessed and aided in the treatment of Sybil Dugdale. She had been able to steel herself to endure the shrieks of the tormented woman as the cane bit into her flesh, to wash her soiled body following the dosing with violent purges, to hold the bronze bowl beneath the bleeding veins and measure the amounts of blood drawn from the thin arms, all these things Tildy could endure. But, before her eyes Sybil Dugdale's condition, both mental and physical had visibly worsened almost daily.

'The treatments that the doctor has prescribed are useless,' she told herself now as she paced the floor of her room, her mind in turmoil. 'Worse than that, they are damaging Mrs Dugdale. They might even end in killing her. I've studied what Buchan says in his book. He advocates kindness and gentle exercise and peaceful surroundings. Of course, he says that in some cases bleeding, blustering, purges and vomits are good, but nowhere does he say that loonies should be beaten with canes, or chained up in cold dirty cellars like wild beasts.'

Tildy came to a halt, wrestling mentally with her own self-doubts. 'But I'm so ignorant. How can I dispute with Doctor Brown? He is so educated and has so much experience in these matters. He is successful too. Have I not heard him talk of the wonderful cures he has effected even with the most deranged maniacs . . .'

'Tildy? Tildy, where be you?'

It was Amanda Wilkins calling from the ground floor, and Tildy hastened to go down to the other woman. During her time in the Stone House she had become friends with both the Wilkins, and had also become very fond of Joey Bates. Now, as she descended Tildy made up her mind to speak to Amanda Wilkins about what was troubling her.

'Ahhh, theer you be. Come on, my duck, we'se got a lot o' work to do. The visitors am coming this arternoon, so we needs to get the cellars cleaned and freshened, and the loonies as well.'

'The visitors?' Tildy was puzzled. 'But I thought that Doctor Brown did not allow visitors . . . '

'Oh, these arn't them sort o' visitors, Tildy. These be official 'uns. They'm appointed by the magistrates under some act o' the London parleyment, or so I'm told. One on 'um is the preacher here at Henley, Parson Ward, and the other's a medical gentleman from Stratford. He's named Conolly. They goes round all the madhouses in these parts three times a year.'

As Amanda Wilkins bustled about to collect brushes, mops and buckets she gossiped non-stop, her pink-mooned face beaming happily as she told her stories. 'That Doctor Conolly, he's a paddy, he is, and a real paddy of a temper he's got as well. Him and Doctor Brown don't half goo at it, I'll tell you. They'm like a pair o' fighting dogs ready to fly at each other's throats.'

'Why do they quarrel?' Tildy's interest was taken.

'Well, it's mostly because they don't agree on the right way to handle the loonies. Doctor Conolly reckons that we shouldn't chain 'um up, and that we oughtn't to use the cane on 'um. He's a sarft silly bugger if you asks me. How else am we agoing to stop the loonies from hurting themselves, or anybody else who comes nigh 'um, iffen we don't keep 'um well fettered? And as for the caning, well, that's a proper medical treatment, that is, everybody knows that.'

Tildy seized her opportunity. 'But it doesn't work, Mrs Wilkins.'

The older woman came to a standstill, her arms loaded with mops and brooms and stared at Tildy with a shocked expression.

'Don't work? Is that what you reckons? Or did I not hear you right?'

Once begun, all Tildy's doubts seemed to leave her, and she repeated with a fast-increasing confidence. 'No, it doesn't work. Look at Sybil Dugdale. She's been caned every day, along with the other dreadful things being done to her, and she's getting worse because of it.'

The older woman's jowls shook from side to side as her head rocked agitatedly. 'You don't know what youm atalking about, my girl. Does you think a great man like Doctor Brown 'ud prescribe a treatment that don't work? God's trewth!' She expelled a noisy snort of derision. 'Youm only a bloody "Johnny come lately", you am. How the bloody hell can you know what's right for treating loonies?'

'I've read books about it,' Tildy reported spiritedly, 'and those books don't say that loonies should be chained and striped with canes.'

A mounting hostility crept into Amanda Wilkins's manner. 'Books, is it?' she sneered. 'And what does a bloody nussing-'ooman want wi' books? I canna read nor write, girl, but I'm a good nuss-'ooman, and I'se bin nussing loonies for a sight more years nor you. Why, youm still but a slip of a girl. Youm hardly out o' your babby-clouts yet.' The woman's indignation boiled over. 'Who the bloody hell does you reckon you am, Tildy Crawford? You arn't bin here a sennight yet, and now youm atelling me that you knows better nor me how to look arter loonies.'

Tildy had no wish to quarrel with a woman who had shown her nothing but kindness, and she hastened to try and calm the explosive atmosphere. 'No, Mrs Wilkins, please don't even think that I'm saying such a thing. I know that you know better than me about such things, and I'm really sorry if I've upset you. I meant nothing against you personally when I said that chaining and striping with canes should be done away with, and that they do no good for Sybil Dugdale.' She lifted her hands palm uppermost in an appeal for understanding. 'You just said yourself that Doctor Conolly also thinks that striping and chaining should be stopped – that they do no good.'

'Huh, Conolly, is it!' Again Amanda Wilkins vented a snort of derision. 'And who is bloody Conolly, when he's about, I'd like to know?' Without pausing for breath she answered her own question. 'Another ''Johnny come lately'' like yourself, that's who he is, and a bleeding bog-trotting papist to boot. The bugger knows naught,' she ended vehemently. 'He knows bloody naught!'

Tobias Wilkins, together with the three students and Joey Bates were already down in the cellars. At the rear end of the central corridor a door opened on to a large sunken area outside of which a flight of steps led up into the rear yard of the house. This door was now open and shafts of the early morning sun lanced through into the dank corridor. The five men were busily unshackling the lunatics and leading them outside, where they could be re-shackled to more iron rings bolted into the brick lining of the sunken area.

Pallid-skinned from their subterranean confinement, their eyes squinting against the unaccustomed glare of the sunlight, shaggy-headed and foul-smelling, the lunatics reacted in their various ways to this disruption. Some snarled and fought, others capered wildly, some shambled dazedly and yet others remained cocooned in their fantasy worlds.

Such a one was 'Crystal' Arnold, a grotesquely tall, emaciated man with long straggles of grey hair and beard. He whimpered as Douglas Fletcher led him from his cellar. Tildy had come down the stairs behind Amanda Wilkins, both laden with cleaning articles, and in the narrow corridor, a broom handle carried by the older woman struck 'Crystal' Arnold's thigh in passing.

He screamed and bellowed, 'She's trying to break me! She's trying to break me! Did you see what she did, she's trying to break me!'

Further along the corridor Joey Bates screwed his eyes tight shut and laughed uproariously. 'Just hark to that mad bugger! That's prime fun, arn't it? That's prime fun. Just hark to that loony sod. Crystal Arnold is getting broke up. That's prime that is, that's prime!'

'Take care, I beg you take care,' the tall man pleaded piteously. 'If you strike me I'll break to pieces. Take care, I beg you.'

Douglas Fletcher chuckled at Tildy's concerned expression. 'Don't worry your pretty head about him, Tildy. He'll come to no harm. He only thinks that he's made of glass. I do assure you he is flesh and blood, just as you are . . . look!' Playfully he lifted the hem of the man's trailing smock and slapped sharply at the lean buttocks. The man jumped high in the air, bawling, 'Murder! Murder! I felt it crack then! I felt my arse crack right across. Murder! Murder! Someone help me!'

Tildy didn't know whether she most wanted to laugh or cry, and Douglas Fletcher, still chuckling, stroked the distraught man's head.

'Calm yourself, my dear fellow,' he soothed. 'There is no crack in your arse. The glass is very thick there, so it won't break easily. Calm yourself and come with me now.' The young man winked at Tildy who could not help but return his smile. 'Come with me and I'll wrap you in a thick eiderdown to protect you.'

He led the lunatic on as Peter Donovan came up behind him leading 'Anne Boleyn' by her hand. 'Anne Boleyn', sixty-three years old, almost bald, and grossly obese, was weeping and demanding to be taken back to her cellar to collect her head.

Again Tildy smiled, excusing her sense of guilt for laughing at the afflicted, by the thought that if she didn't laugh, she also would be weeping.

'Shall I go and clean Mrs Dugdale?' she asked Amanda Wilkins. The other woman, still disgruntled by their earlier contretemps, only nodded brusquely without speaking.

Sybil Dugdale was in the smallest of the cellars. A room which had no window, or even a grille to let in the outside air. Tildy pushed open the door and the light admitted from the corridor enabled her to see the far end wall where Sybil Dugdale was pinioned.

'Oh dear God, what are we doing to this poor creature,' Tildy murmured aloud in pity and remorse as she looked at the pathetic physical wreckage that confronted her. Sybil Dugdale's eyes were black deep-sunk pits in a shorn skull-head. She crouched on a small heap of filthy mouldering straw, her smock drawn back to display legs and feet caked thick with her own excrement. A broad leather belt encircled her waist, iron rings clamped her wrists to that belt, and a short chain ran from the rear of the belt to secure her to the wall. Her bony ankles were close-fettered and saliva dribbled from her gaping, blue-lipped mouth.

'This is evil. Truly evil.' Tildy's eyes blurred, and she dashed the hot tears away with knuckled fingers. 'I'm going to get you out of this, Mrs Dugdale,' she whispered as she went to the crouching woman, who seemed unaware of her presence. 'Do you understand what I'm saying to you, you poor soul? I'm going to get you out from this evil place.'

In the dull light she saw the raw bleeding sores on ankles and wrists caused by the constant chafing of the iron fetters, and a sudden white heat of anger coursed through her being. 'I'll swear on my babby's life that I'll get you away from here, cost me what it may.

'Don't talk such rubbish. Don't promise what you can't perform,' the demon of doubt jeered in her mind. 'How can you, a nursing-woman, a virtual pauper, a nobody, get her away from this place where her own husband has put her. You can do nothing. Nothing!'

Tildy drew a deep breath and summoned her faithful ally, stubbornness, to her aid. 'I will. I've sworn to get this poor soul out from here and I will.

'Then tell me how.' Doubt sneered and challenged. 'Just tell me, how?

'I will get her away. I will. I will. I will,' stubbornness reiterated doggedly over and over again until doubt was driven back in retreat.

'Is the lady ready for a breath of fresh air, such as it is?' Peter Donovan entered the cellar and came to stand at Tildy's side. He stared down at Sybil Dugdale and said in a low voice, 'You're looking peaked, Ma'am, to say the least. You come on with me now and take some sunlight.'

He reached towards the sick woman but she shrank from his hands, pressing her shoulders back against the wall, her skull-like head rocking wildly from side to side and moans of fearful distress bubbling with the saliva from her cracked lips.

The spectacle was too much for Tildy to bear with equanimity, and she turned aggressively upon the student. 'Leave the poor creature be, can't you?' she hissed. 'Haven't you made her suffer enough already with your cruel treatments? Must you torment her even further?'

He straightened upright and regarded her silently for some moments, his elongated freckled features impassive, but his eyes gleaming with both sympathy and understanding.

'I know, Tildy, I know how you feel, and sure now who wouldn't feel that way.' His musical Irish accent was pleasant to the ear and Tildy found his voice acting soothingly upon her strained nerves. 'I've been watching you closely these last days, Tildy. I know how it upsets you to see Mrs Dugdale being given her treatments. But you listen careful now, Tildy.' He lowered his voice, as if fearing to be overheard. 'You'll do no good for this poor woman by giving way to your own pity for her. Doctor Brown prescribes what must be done to cure her, and no matter what you or I might think, what he prescribes will be done. The only person who can put an end to these treatments, or remove her from here is her own husband . . . '

Tildy opened her mouth to speak, but he gently placed his forefinger against her lips and smiled. 'No, don't talk, just listen . . . '

She nodded in mute acceptance, so he took his finger away and went on.

'Like you, Tildy, I think that Mrs Dugdale is deteriorating because of what is being done to her. But I'm only a penniless student, and also an employee of Doctor Brown. He is a wonderful benefactor to me, and it is only because of his kindness and with his help that I can ever hope to become a doctor. So I will never, ever, publicly go against him. And despite my own misgivings concerning this woman, I shall keep my mouth shut and do as I am told.

'Because I like you, Tildy, I'll give you some advice, and that advice is to say naught to Doctor Brown or anybody else in this house about what you think concerning Mrs Dugdale's condition. They all think they are right in what treatments they are using. The only chance you have is to go and tell Henry Dugdale what you think and urge him to remove her from here.

'There is a man coming here today, a doctor, who also disagrees with the treatments we sometimes use here. His name is John Conolly and he lives at Stratford. Why not have a quiet word with him when he comes here? See what his opinion is.'

'I will,' Tildy answered emphatically, and she felt a great warmth of gratitude flood through her towards Peter Donovan. 'And I thank you for your kindness, Master Donovan. I am truly grateful to you.'

'That's all right, Tildy.' He appeared gratified by her words. 'But remember, what I've said remains purely between you and myself. I shall categorically deny ever having spoken with you if I'm asked about it. My first loyalty lies towards Doctor Brown and towards my own interests, of course, for the two are indivisible.'

'I won't involve you ever, Master Donovan,' she assured him fervently, and he smiled again.

'That is understood then. Right, I'll leave Mrs Dugdale in peace, and you must just clean the place around her as best you can. Make sure that you put a fresh smock on her, and put some bandages and salves on those fetter-sores.'

'I will, Master Donovan,' she smiled, and with a last wink he left her.

She briefly ran through in her mind what he had advised, and felt as though a great burden had been lifted from her.

'I'll do it,' she muttered, 'I'll do what he said.'

Chapter Twenty-three

Late that afternoon Doctor John Conolly and the Reverend Paul Silas Ward, perpetual curate of Henley-in-Arden parish church, walked together along the straggling rutted High Street towards the tall grey Stone House.

This was the last asylum on the visitors' list. During the course of the day they had already inspected in Henley the houses of Thomas Burman, surgeon, with its thirty-seven inmates, Benjamin Gibbs, gentleman, with five inmates, William Roadknight, gentleman, with sixteen inmates, and in neighbouring Wootten Wawen, the house of Mary Gibbs, widow, with five inmates.

Now the middle-aged clergyman sighed wearily. 'I shall be happy when this day is done, Doctor Conolly.'

The tall raw-boned Irishman, who had the craggy weather-beaten features and reddened shovel-like hands of a navvy, agreed with his companion's sentiment, but for very different reasons. The soft-bodied, overweight cleric disliked the physical effort of traipsing up and down numerous flights of stairs, and subjecting his senses to the varied and violent assaults made upon them in the different establishments. He was also more than a little afraid of being thrust into close proximity with potentially dangerous maniacs.

John Conolly, on the other hand, would be happy to be done with his visitation because he found it almost intolerably difficult to hold his temper in check. The treatment he saw being meted out to the confined lunatics in every madhouse offended both his intelligence and his sense of humanity. Added to this, he was frustrated in any attempt he made to alter the mode of treatment. So long as the licensee of the private madhouse paid his yearly licence fee of ten pounds, plus ten pounds to the county clerk of the peace, each Michaelmas, and a further ten pounds to each of the separate official visitors again at Michaelmas, the licensee could do virtually as he chose with the unfortunates entrusted to his care.

Of all the madhouses in the district John Conolly disliked that of Samuel Brown's the most strongly. In the other madhouses close confinement, fettering, purging, vomiting, dosing with drastic medicines and canings were virtually standard practice, but Samuel Brown added further refinements to torment both the inmates and John Conolly's sensibilities. The man was an inveterate experimenter, forever seeking a miracle cure, a panacea for mental afflictions. He subjected his unfortunate inmates to treatments that were at times, in John Conolly's view, barbaric in their cruel savagery. On one occasion, following what the Irishman considered to be the untimely death of one of Brown's patients, Conolly had laid a complaint before the justices of the peace and had opposed the renewal of Brown's licence to keep a madhouse. But the complaint had been ignored and the renewal granted. From that date onwards personal enmity had coloured every aspect of the two men's professional and personal relationship.

Conolly peered at the sinking sun low down in the western sky and pulled out his hunter-watch to check the time.

'We should not be too long in finishing our business at Doctor Brown's house,' he remarked. 'I hope not, for I've an operation to perform this night back at Stratford.'

'Speaking of cutting people up, Doctor Conolly, has there been any incident of grave-robbing reported in the Stratford area of late?' the cleric asked.

'What do you mean by grave-robbing? Is it body-

193

snatching you refer to?' The doctor spoke curtly. He had little liking or respect for his present companion, or for any other type of priest, come to that.

'Yes, mayhap I should have said, body-snatching, but I understand you in the medical line are chary of using that expression.' Ward's puffy features bore a sly expression and there was more than a hint of malice in his tone as he went on, 'There's talk that some wicked surgeon hereabouts has been employing resurrection men in these parts. A grave was tampered with at Ipsley some days past, and upon investigation another grave at Tardebigge churchyard was found to have been desecrated also, and the poor sinner whose final resting place it was has been stolen from it.

'In my opinion there is no punishment too great for the resurrection men, or for those who employ such depraved animals. They should all burn together in hell for eternity.'

'How can you say such men deserve to burn in hell,' Reverend Ward?' Conolly found the cleric's manner irritating, and made no attempt to keep that irritation from his voice. 'A dead body feels nothing and only rots in the ground.'

'The human body is formed in the likeness of God, Doctor Conolly,' the clergyman intoned sanctimoniously, 'and the grave is a consecrated resting place. Our Lord did not intend Christians to be butchered like beasts on slabs for the amusement of degraded minds.'

The doctor grimaced wryly. 'I do not condone resurrection men, or those who employ them. But let me remind you that the only way a medical student can learn how to carry out operations is by practising the necessary techniques, and by dissecting anatomical specimens. A surgeon instructing his pupils in anatomy and dissection does not butcher corpses on slabs to provide amusement for degraded minds. Under the present system the medical profession cannot obtain a sufficient supply of human cadavers for its instructional needs. Ergo, surgeons are driven to break the laws of morality in order to meet those needs. They do this in the long run to aid humanity. To help those in pain and suffering, and to cure the lame and the sick.'

'To rob a grave is an abomination in the sight of God,' Ward said heatedly.

'It is a greater abomination to allow ignorance and superstition to hinder the progress of medical knowledge,' Conolly riposted with equal heat.

'The anatomist desecrates the temple of the soul,' Ward countered.

'The temple of the soul can have its fabric torn and mutilated. The anatomist seeks knowledge so that he may repair and restore that fabric.'

'The human fabric is of no importance,' Ward replied loftily. 'I care not a fig for the sufferings of men's mortal bodies; it is the redemption of their immortal souls that concerns me, and that should be the sole concern of each and every one of Our Lord's humble servants here on earth.'

Conolly laughed with a bitter contempt. 'It is a sad fact, Reverend, that those of you who wear the cloth are invariably among the most concerned for the comfort and well-being of your own physical bodies. Priests of all denominations are, in my personal experience, the very first to come pestering we wicked body-snatching surgeons for cures for their bodily ailments. I suggest that the next time you suffer from a megrim, you ask your Lord for a cure, and not approach those whom you so quickly condemn to eternal hell-fire.

'Anyway, let us put an end to this fruitless argument. We are arrived at Stone House.'

With a sulky sniff the cleric nodded agreement, and the doctor mounted the steps and tugged on the bellrope at the side of the massive front door.

When the visitors came down into the cellars in company with Samuel Brown and the students, John Conolly only glanced perfunctorily into the larger rooms. He knew well that all would have been cleaned, the lunatics washed and the bedding straw changed well before his arrival. When the party came to the small cellar where Tildy and Sybil Dugdale were inside, however, Conolly spent some considerable time studying Sybil Dugdale.

'She is a newcomer, is she not, Doctor Brown? And since she's separate, I'll wager she's not a pauper,' he stated.

With a touch of smugness Brown told him, 'Of a certainty she is no pauper, Sir. Her husband is Henry Geast Dugdale, a gentleman who has considerable landholdings around the area of Redditch. He was recommended to me and I decided to try and help him.'

'She appears to be in a sorry state, whatever her station in life may be,' Conolly observed coolly. 'What treatments are you subjecting her to that leave her this way?'

'The standard treatments to enable us to diagnose and evaluate her deepest mental condition, Sir,' Brown told him with a touch of asperity. 'Lunatics must be physically taxed if they are to be cured.'

'How long has she been here?'

'Some ten days.'

'Humph!' Conolly vented a contemptuous ejaculation. 'Judging by her appearance the wretched creature is not benefiting from such an evaluation.'

'She is a most difficult case, Sir.' Samuel Brown refused to be goaded into anger. 'However, my evaluation of her condition is now completed and I intend to commence a course of treatment this very day which I am confident will prove most salutary.'

'And what course of treatment will that be, Sir, double whippings and extra chains?' Conolly queried scathingly.

Knowing that his refusal to be goaded only goaded the Irishman the more, Brown smiled maliciously and replied with an equable tone, 'Indeed no, Sir, I have something in mind which is a little more scientific than the course you have just suggested we use.'

Conolly's craggy features reddened as the thrust sank home, and with resentful awareness of the amused smiles directed at him, he growled, 'I would like to see this new treatment, Sir.'

Brown beamed expansively. 'And so you shall, Sir. You may even learn something from it.' He turned away, adding soto voce, 'If it's possible for anything to penetrate that thick skull.'

The rest of the party tittered, and Conolly's fists clenched, but he forebore to challenge Brown, realizing that that was precisely what the man wanted him to do.

Despite his intense dislike of the man and his methods, Conolly was forced to admit that Brown had achieved some remarkable cures of mental afflictions, and he was now curious as to what method he proposed using with Sybil Dugdale.

Brown told Tildy, 'You will bring Mrs Dugdale up to my surgery in a few moments, Crawford. I shall be ready for her by then . . . ' He turned to the rest of the party. 'If you will kindly accompany me, gentlemen . . . '

Tildy bobbed a curtsy as they left, and her thoughts were troubled. She had studied Doctor Conolly closely and was not happy with what she had seen of him. 'He looks and speaks as rough as a pointer,' she felt with dismay. 'And he's so grim and thunder-looking. I reckon he'd bite my head off if I spoke to him about Sybil Dugdale. But yet, he was quick to tell Doctor Brown that she didn't look well. Who knows, mayhap his bark is worse than his bite.'

Pushing the man from her thoughts, she knelt by Sybil Dugdale's side and stroked the ragged-cropped hair. 'Never you mind, my dear, I'll get you from here no matter what. Never you mind now.'

The woman gave no sign of understanding, only moaned and dribbled, and scratched with broken fingernails at the leather belt around her waist.

The four wooden troughs, each some two feet long, ten inches wide and six inches deep were arranged in a hollow square. Each was filled with liquid and contained close-set rows of metal plates slotted crossways and covered by the liquid.

'This gentlemen, is my battery of voltaic piles,' Samuel

197

Brown announced proudly. 'You see what they consist of? Alternate plates of copper and zinc immersed in a five parts dilution of muriatic acid. Each separate pile generates its own electrical fluid and by means of these connectors,' he indicated the pairs of copper wires which ran from each box to its fellows, 'I collect all the fluids so generated and combine them together into a single powerful force which can be discharged through these negative and positive conductors.' He pointed at two wires running from one box, each ending in a tiny copper ball, which were lying upon a circular pad of resin. 'The resin is a non-conductor of electrical fluids, gentlemen, so nothing can be lost through the conductors when they are so placed.'

'I thought you said that you had something new to show us?' Conolly was openly sneering. 'I've seen demonstrations of galvanism before, Brown. On almost every fairground in the country there's a cheapjack with a galvanic battery making dead frogs' legs jump about.'

'That may well be so, Conolly.' For the first time Brown gave way to open pique and his plump round cheeks quivered as he excitedly answered the Irishman's sneers. 'But you have not yet seen galvanism cure madness, have you? You have not seen any fairground cheapjack utilize a powerful faradic current to stabilize a derangement of the intellect. You have not yet seen . . . ' Tildy's knock came at the door and Brown broke off his diatribe to call her in, then continued. ' . . . You have not yet seen what I can do with this fluid. I know well that you have always been jealous of my success, Conolly.' As he spoke he ran his hand repeatedly across his curly grey cap of hair. 'Well Sir, after today I'll warrant you'll have even greater cause to be so.

'Lay Mrs Dugdale down upon the operating table, Crawford,' he instructed Tildy, who was staring with wide eyes at the arrangement of troughs and wires on the floor.

She dragged her gaze away from the weird looking contraption and obeyed him, murmuring soothing reassurances to Sybil Dugdale, as she gently guided her on to the table and straightened out legs and arms so that she lay comfortably. But the woman was totally immersed in her own confused reality and paid no apparent heed to Tildy, only allowed her body to be moved and arranged as if it were something that had nothing to do with her.

Tobias Wilkins came into the room carrying a large tray on which was a bowl of hot water, a towel and shaving implements.

'Good,' Brown nodded to the man, and then said quietly to the three students, 'Strap Mrs Dugdale down, gentlemen, and one of you stand near to hold her head still while Wilkins shaves her.'

With the dexterous speed of long practice, the students used long leather straps to secure Sybil Dugdale to the table, then Douglas Fletcher cupped her face in his strong hands, and held her head immobile while Tobias Wilkins used the cut-throat razor to shave away the soapy hair, leaving the unfortunate woman completely bald, and her scalp an obscenely pallid fish-belly white. Tildy's heart sorrowed for the grotesque spectacle the once pretty Sybil Dugdale now presented as she lay whimpering, her deep-sunk black-ringed eyes rolling from side to side.

Samuel Brown had busied himself in attaching resin-coated insulated handles to the conducting wires of the battery so that he could lift and manipulate them without suffering shocks himself. He now lifted the conductors and stood behind Sybil Dugdale's head.

'Mr Fletcher, you will assist me,' he instructed, and nodded towards a thick pad of silk cloth. 'When I give the word you will hold the patient's head still, using that pad to insulate your hands.'

'Very well, Sir.' The young man seemed gratified at being selected, and despite her own uneasiness about Sybil Dugdale, Tildy found herself becoming fascinated by what was to take place before her.

'Now gentlemen,' Brown assumed a lecturing manner, 'since we are all concerned with the care and treatment of the insane, I take it that we all share a knowledge of Doctor Andrew Combes's admirable treatise on insanity. Also I shall assume that you all have cognizance of Doctors Gall and Spurzheim's system of phrenology. Based upon their separate teachings, and my own experience, I have diagnosed this patient's condition as being a manic derangement of her organs of cautiousness, located in the parietal lobes of the external brain within the superior marginal convolution and posterior to the horizontal fissure of sylvius.'

He pointed to a spot some three inches above and slightly to the rear of Sybil Dugdale's ear.

'You may see clearly the deformity caused by the derangement.'

Tildy stared hard but try though she might could not persuade herself that the area indicated looked any different from the surrounding scalp. Despair at her own ignorance swept across her and she thought hopelessly, 'How will I ever be able to obtain the knowledge these people have?'

'Therefore, gentlemen,' although he addressed the room at large, Brown's eyes sought out John Conolly in visual challenge, 'I propose to use a revolutionary method of treatment in this case. I intend to pass electrical fluid through the patient's organs of cautiousness in a series of carefully structured faradic interrupted currents. This will shock the senses from their present derangement. Whilst they are in disorder, I shall cup and blister the nape of the neck and the base of the occiput, and thus draw out from the body the malignant humours which are the primary cause of the present derangement.

'Within a very short space of time, gentlemen, I am confident that the senses will settle once more into equilibrium, and this unfortunate creature will be fully cured.' He paused, and still with his eyes locked on Conolly's, asked slowly, 'Has anyone any opinion to offer concerning either my diagnosis, or my proposed method of treatment?'

Tildy sensed the battle of wills between the two doctors, and waited curiously for its outcome. The silence lengthened, broken only by the whimperings of Sybil Dugdale and the loud chesty breathing of Tobias Wilkins. Within John Conolly's mind a tremendous struggle was raging.

200

He lusted to challenge and debunk Samuel Brown's diagnosis. To wipe the smile from the fat smug face. But to his chagrin he realized his own impotence to do that. He lacked the necessary knowledge to contradict the diagnosis, and indeed, was inclined to agree with the diagnosis himself. As to the proposed method of treatment? His fists clenched in frustration. It could well work. Brown had undoubtedly achieved some remarkable results with his experimental methods in the past. He might well achieve success with this one.

Conolly's eyes broke contact from Samuel Brown, and moved to Sybil Dugdale. 'I must not let my personal dislike for Brown stand in the way of a possible cure for this woman,' he accepted, and with an almost imperceptible shake of the head, he declined to pick up the figurative gauntlet the other man had flung down before him.

Samuel Brown recognized his victory, and burgeoning elation caused him to smile broadly. 'Very well, gentlemen, I shall commence the treatment,' he announced. 'Mr Fletcher, be kind enough to take up the pad and exert pressure against the patient's forehead during my initial contact. She must not move as I apply the conductors. After the initial contact, it should no longer be necessary for you to aid me.'

'Very well, Sir.' Fletcher, radiating his own keen antici-pation, carefully put the pad in position and pressed his palms down upon it. Sybil Dugdale wailed in fear as her head was crushed upon the wooden table, and then Samuel Brown lifted the conductors and carefully positioned them so that the copper balls aimed directly at the areas he had designated.

'Take care that no part of your body comes into direct contact with her,' he warned Fletcher, and jabbed the copper balls against the sides of the shaven skull.

There was a flash and a crack and Sybil Dugdale's face distorted horribly and crimsoned as her body jerked violently and stiffened. Brown pulled back the conductors and the rigid body slumped. Then again he jabbed, and again there came the flash and crack and again the limp body stiffened, straining against the leather strappings. This time a pungent odour of seared flesh filled Tildy's nostrils, and she wanted to scream out in shock and protest.

Each time the copper balls flashed and cracked and the limp body on the table jerked, and the lolling head thumped dully against the wood, Tildy also jerked and her own body stiffened.

Again the crack and flash, Sybil Dugdale's eyes were white bulging orbs in the vile rictus spasming of her face, and Tildy thrust her own knuckles between her teeth and bit down hard to stop herself crying out in outrage. 'The doctor knows what he is about,' she recited in silent litany. 'The doctor knows what he is about. You know nothing. You are ignorant. The doctor knows what he is about.'

The passage of time ceased to exist for Tildy. All she was aware of was the crack and the flash, the jerking and stiffening, the thumping of the shaven head against the wooden table, the pungent smell of seared flesh. 'Let it end! Please God, let it end! Let it finish!' Tildy begged silently, and tasted the warm saltiness of her own blood as her sharp teeth bit into skin and flesh.

Then, abruptly, it was over, and she heard Samuel Brown's calm voice issuing further instructions.

'How can he be so calm?' she wondered incredulously. 'How can he be so calm and easy?'

'Keep her upright, Fletcher. Have you the cups ready, Fusey? Good! Apply them there, there and there. Hold her steady, Fletcher . . . Good. Hand me the blisters, Donovan. They are cantharides, are they not? Good. Remove the top cup, Fusey. God dammit, hold her steady, Mr Fletcher! Don't worry about that blood from her mouth, man. She's merely bitten her tongue.'

Brown took the squares of calico cloth spread thickly with a paste of Spanish fly, and pressed them firmly upon the raised lumps of flesh left by the application of the heated cups on the slender nape of Sybil Dugdale's neck, and the base of her narrow skull.

The woman was comatose, her head slumped forwards against Douglas Fletcher's chest, and the blood seeping from her slack mouth running down his white shirt front and ruffled cravat.

'There, it is done,' Brown smiled. 'Lay her chest downwards, Mr Fletcher, and turn her head sideways. We do not want her to choke on her own blood, do we?' He turned to Tildy. 'You will stay here with her, Crawford, until she regains her senses and you must see to it that I am informed immediately she does so. Come gentlemen, let us adjourn to the inn for some refreshment.' He spoke directly to Conolly. 'That is unless you wish to make further inspection, Doctor Conolly.'

'No, I have seen sufficient for the day,' the craggy-featured Irishman answered grimly. 'I would greatly appreciate your keeping me informed of this patient's progress however, Doctor Brown. I am interested to study the efficacy of this new-fangled treatment of yours.'

'But naturally, Sir,' Brown smiled spitefully. 'And I've no objection to your utilizing the treatment for your own practice, Conolly. It will do wonders for your reputation.'.

'As to that, Sir, my reputation suffices me well enough.'

They moved from the room and Conolly spoke again. 'I must make use of the offices, Doctor Brown, so I'll bid you a good bye now.'

'Very well, Doctor Conolly, they're out back.'

The group separated in the hallway and Tildy listened carefully for the Irishman's return from the outdoor privy. When she heard his footsteps she went into the hallway to intercept him.

'Please Sir, might I speak with you?'

'What is it you want?' He glared unwelcomingly down at her from beneath his bushy brows, and she felt nervous of him.

'It's about Mrs Dugdale, Sir. I'm not happy about her treatment. She seems to be getting worse because of it.'

His craggy features became a granite-like mask and he growled, 'I'll pretend I've not heard that, young woman, and you may think yourself lucky that I am such a forbearing man.'

She stared in wide-eyed incomprehension and he

scowled, 'An ignorant female domestic, such as yourself, has no right to voice opinions on matters concerning her betters. You'd do well to bite hard on that loose wagging tongue of yours, girl, and do not provoke me by further impertinence, or I shall report your behaviour to Doctor Brown.'

He walked on, leaving a downcast young woman behind him . . .

Chapter Twenty-four

Though it was long after midnight Tildy still lay sleeplessly staring into the darkness, her mind too full to permit her to rest. The sudden clattering of small pebbles against the window caused her to start in surprise. Another rattling and another, each following the other in scant seconds brought her from her bed, and she peered through the leaded panes. The moon was full and bright, silvering the roofs of the town, and Tildy could see clearly the man standing beneath her window, his face lifted upwards to her.

'Harry Mogg! Oh my God, has something happened to my Davy to bring him here at this hour?'

She opened the casement and called down anxiously, 'Is my Davy all right?'

His low-pitched chuckle answered her. 'Well, he was bloody thriving when I saw him a few hours since.'

Relief for her child mingled with a compound of pleasure and irritation. The pleasure of seeing Harry Mogg, and the irritation for the potential embarrassment it could cause her if anyone was to see him beneath her window.

'What do you want here, Harry?' she questioned, and again he chuckled.

'I needs to talk to you, Tildy, but it arn't no good trying to hold a conversation like this.' His voice was hoarse as he strained to whisper, yet still be heard. 'I'll come up.'

Suiting action to words he swarmed up and into her window as lithe and agile as a cat.

In the shadows of the room they faced each other, and he gently took her chin between his thumb and fingers and turned her head so that the moonlight fell across it. His eyes drank in her beauty, the glossy dark hair piled up on her head, the luminous brown eyes, the flawless skin, the delicate structure of the oval face, the firm shapely body beneath the simple white nightshift. 'By God, but youm a beautiful wench, Tildy,' he murmured huskily. ''Tis small wonder that youm always in me thoughts.'

Almost forcefully she struck his hand away and retreated back into the shadows.

He stared hard at her. 'What's troubling you, Tildy? Be you angered with me for coming here?'

'No, I'm not angered for that, Harry. But I'm angered at what I've seen here this day, and I feel that if I don't tell somebody about it, then I'll burst wide open.'

'Then tell me, Tildy,' he answered instantly, and reached for her hand. 'Here, come sit down beside me and you tell me anything that you'se got a mind to.'

She allowed him to keep hold of her hand as they sat side by side on the bed she had once shared with Sybil Dugdale, and Tildy let everything flow from her. She told him of the awful sight of Sybil Dugdale's body jerking and stiffening as the electrical fluid jolted through her. She told him of the whitely bulging eyes, the stench of seared flesh, the hideously distorted features, the blood seeping from blue lips to stain the white shirt of Douglas Fletcher. And then she told him of her long vigil in the surgery beside the comatose woman. Of the heaving, vomiting arousal, and of the blank, dazed incomprehension of Sybil Dugdale as Tildy had pleaded with her for some sign of recognition or awareness of where she was, who she was, and what had been happening to her.

'I fear that they've destroyed her mind, Harry.' Tildy was near to tears by now and her whispers were shaky and broken. 'She's like a breathing dead thing and they've chained her up again in that stinking cold cellar. In the dark without a spark of light, and the rats running over the floor. I argued with Doctor Brown about it, and I told him the treatment was no good for her, but he only shouted at me and told me not to be so insolent to my betters. He said I was just an ignorant chaw-bacon, and he'd a mind to dismiss me for being so saucy.

'He said that the electrical fluid had improved her mental condition immensely. Those were his very words, Harry.' She mimicked the high fluting tones of the doctor. 'I see immense improvement in her mental condition, Crawford. I'll have her fully cured before the end of the month.'

Harry put his free arm around Tildy's trembling shoulders and hugged her gently to him. 'Theer now, my duck, don't upset yourself so. Mayhap he's right. Mayhap he 'ull have her cured afore next month comes.'

Now Tildy wept openly, 'But he will not, Harry. He will not!' Her voice rang out high in distress.

'Hush now, you'll wake the bloody house up else.' Harry Mogg squeezed her hand. 'You canna know for certain that he wun't cure her, Tildy. Arter all, he's a proper doctor, arn't he, and youm only a nussing-woman.'

'Don't you think I know that?' Tildy rejoined angrily. 'Of course I'm only a nursing-woman, but I'm not stupid, Harry. Ignorant and lacking schooling, yes. But I'm not dense. I can read and write, and I can see things and understand them. My brain is as good as any man's and I can use it. I've seen how Sybil Dugdale has got worser and worser ever since she was brought to this terrible place. I've got to get her out of here, Harry, afore they end by killing her with their cures.'

'But her arn't your concern, Tildy,' he argued vehemently. 'Her's no kin to you, and no friend neither. Her's done you no favours in the past, nor shown you no kindnesses. You'se only known her for a few weeks, and bugger me, she arn't even your sort, is her? Her's bloody gentry; her arn't one of us.'

'She's a poor tormented soul!' Tildy hissed with a vehemence to equal his own. 'She's a pathetic, pitiful

207

creature who's got nobody here to care what becomes of her. Nobody except me.'

'Don't talk so bloody sarft, girl,' Mogg exclaimed furiously. 'Her's got kin, and her's got a husband.'

'Yes, and truth to tell I don't think that any of them care a damn what becomes of her,' Tildy cut in. 'But I care, Harry. Don't ask me for the reasons why, I don't rightly know myself why I care so much. But care, I do, and I'll not stand by and let them destroy the poor soul.'

'You'll not be able to do much alone,' he reminded her, and for a moment her heart sank as she considered the odds ranged against her. But she refused to allow that moment to lengthen, and told him determinedly,

'I'll manage, Harry. I'm not feared to be alone.'

'Well, you arn't alone, Tildy because I'm with you. Whatever you wants to do, I'll stand wi' you.'

'Will you, Harry? Will you really?' Gratitude and fondness suffused her, and she allowed herself to relax against his taut muscular body, enjoying the warmth and the sensation of security his enfolding arms created in her.

'O' course I will, honey. I'll always stand wi' you, I'll swear to that.' His voice was husky, and with a swift movement of his head he bent to kiss her. Her hands moved to push him away, but there was no real volition to give them force, and their mouths remained locked together. All the sexuality that Tildy had for so long repressed burst out from its enforced bondage, and a terrible hunger for his lips on her lips, his hands on her skin, his throbbing maleness enfolded and entrapped within her own body clamoured for satiation, and she experienced a mental and physical surrender to her own all-conquering needs.

With a tender strength he moved her back on to the bed, his lips and tongue drinking the sweet juices of her mouth, his gentle hands searching and finding and fondling the soft moist yielding heat between her thighs. Her own desires drove her as he slowly lifted the nightshift from her body, and her fingers loosened and removed his clothing. Naked they twined, breast to breast, belly to belly, mouth to mouth, and Tildy felt him enter her hungering emptiness, and she moaned throatily as his hard maleness filled that emptiness and began to satisfy that hunger.

Her throat, her breasts, her nipples, her belly, her thighs trembled to the sucking heat of his mouth, and in her turn she tasted the clean tangy flesh of his body. Crying out she squeezed his lean thrusting hips and waist with her thighs and arms and drove her hips to match his pulsing rhythms. Shivers of exquisite pleasure racked her flesh and as his hands enfolded her buttocks, lifting her upwards so her own fingers clutched and kneaded his small hard round buttocks and strained to draw him deeper and deeper within her. Panting and writhing their mutual rhythmic thrustings became faster and faster, harder and harder, deeper and deeper until with an unbearable throbbing of delight they achieved the climactic release they so desperately sought.

Slowly Tildy's pantings eased as she lay beneath the slumped body of the man, his maleness softening inside her, his harsh breathing also quieting as he murmured into her ear.

'I love you, Tildy. I really do love you. Come and live wi' me. Please come and live wi' me. I'll be good to you, you'll want for nothing. I love you truly, my honey, I love you truly. Only say that you'll come and live wi' me.'

Afloat in the pleasing drowsy haze of satisfaction, Tildy's tongue and lips began to form the words of acceptance, but then the realization of what she was about to do jangled through her mind, and in sudden alarm she wriggled out from under him and rose from the bed. Her hands lifting and tugging the nightshift over her head and body to cover her nakedness.

'What's the matter?' Harry also rose and stood to confront her, his body a luminous paleness in the shadowed room. 'What's up, Tildy, is it summat I'se done?'

She softened to the concern and anxiety in his voice. 'You've done naught, Harry. At least, naught that was bad.'

He reached out for her, but she stepped back from his seeking hands.

'By the Christ, girl, what's wrong wi' you?' There was annoyance tingeing the puzzlement in his voice now.

Tildy breathed in deeply as she tried to marshal her thoughts. 'Don't be angry with me, Harry,' she pleaded. 'I'll try and explain to you in a minute when I've got my head clear.'

'Then you'd best get your yed cleared quick, my wench,' he said grimly, and her own fiery spirit rose in instant resentment at his tone.

'Don't you start telling me what I'd best do, Harry Mogg,' she retorted hotly. 'I'm not your wife to be ordered about.'

'Maybe not, but youm my woman now, arn't you?' he growled, and Tildy could not hold back a spasm of incredulous laughter.

'Your woman?' She shook her head emphatically. 'Oh no, Harry, I'm not your woman. I'm not any man's woman. I'm my own woman and nobody's property.'

'How can you say that?' he demanded, and it was his turn to demonstrate incredulity. 'How can you tell me that you arn't my woman, arter what we'se just done?'

'I can say it, and I do say it,' Tildy spoke as adamantly as she felt. 'I'm my own woman, Harry Mogg, and if you think that because I've just made love with you I'm become your property, then you're sadly mistaken and you'd best leave here right now.'

Sudden angry suspicion caused him to step towards her. 'Has you bin playing the whore wi' me, Tildy Crawford?' he demanded menacingly. 'Be I just one among many that you opens your legs for?'

Tildy flared into fury. 'Don't you dare to say that to me, you stupid, thick-headed . . . ' Words failed her, and she pushed him hard on his chest, causing him to fall back a pace. 'I'm no whore and I've never been loose-living. Don't you dare to say such things to me.'

Taken aback by the savagery of her reaction Harry Mogg became flustered, and then he tried to calm her. 'I never meant it that way, Tildy, so don't take it so. You got me so roiled up that I didn't know what I was asaying. But I meant no insult. I knows youm a good-living girl. I knows that.'

But his words did nothing to calm Tildy's agitation. For now her anger was turning against herself for her own weakness, and with it, came self-disgust. 'I'm forever saying that I'm no whore,' she castigated herself bitterly, 'and yet I've just played the whore. I'm fond of Harry Mogg, but I'm not in love with him, so I can't use that as an excuse; and like it or not, I'm still a married woman.' Although Tildy had little liking or respect for organized religion, and scant credence in the sanctity of priests of any denomination, yet her childhood conditioning still held her partly in thrall. She still felt it was a wickedness and a degradation of a woman to indulge herself in sexual relationships outside the marriage bond.

'Come on now, Tildy, don't act this way.'

She could hear Harry Mogg's pleadings.

'We arn't done aught that's bad, girl. We'se give each other a bit o' loving, a bit o' comfort. What's so wrong in that?'

She dragged deep breaths into her lungs in an effort to calm her rampaging emotions, causing her full breasts to rise and fall rapidly, and the man saw the erect nipples pressing through the thin cotton shift, and desire flooded through him once more and he moved to take her in his arms.

'No! Damn you, no!' This time her hands did push him away with force, and he stared at her in half-angry bewilderment, shaking his head slowly as he told her,

'I reckon it arn't only them buggers down in the cellars whom bloody gone in the yed, girl, from the way youm acting.'

Hot words sprang to her tongue, but she bit them back, understanding why he was angered. 'Listen to me, Harry.' She tried to speak calmly. 'Perhaps for you what we just did together was nothing bad . . . and I'll not be a hypocrite and say that I didn't want to do it. It gave me release, and it gave me pleasure, but having admitted that, I still have to say that for me it was a wickedness and a degradation of myself to have given in to my own weakness and my desires like I did, even though I found it a sweetness to lie with you.

'I can't help the way I'm made, Harry. It's naught against you, or wrong with you, that makes me refuse you my kisses now. It's just the way I'm made, Harry, and at times I think it's a curse on me.' She sighed sadly. 'But I fear that I'll always be this way, and there's naught you or anybody else can ever do that will change me. If you can't accept me as I am, then you must go from me and leave me be.'

He snatched eagerly at this apparent softening in her attitude. 'Youm a bit upset right now, my honey, and arter all, it's only natural that you should be so, and I respects you all the more for it. But you'll think different about it, come tomorrow, you see if you wun't. So make me happy, Tildy, and tell me that you'll come and live wi' me.'

'I cannot do that, Harry,' she told him quietly, but adamantly. 'It would be easy for me to lie to you and send you happy from here. But I'm too fond of you to do you such a wrong. I cannot say what the future will bring. If someday I am free, if my husband should die, or find some way of ending our marriage properly, then mayhap you and I could live together, mayhap we could marry. But as things stand now, I cannot come to live with you, and I cannot be your woman.'

She reached out and took his hands between her own, as if by physical contact she could pour understanding of how she felt into him. 'The way I feel deep inside me, my dear, is that I cannot ever become any man's woman, any man's property. I have to belong only to myself, Harry, please try and understand what I am saying. Please try, I beg you.'

He stared down at their clasped hands for long, long moments, and sighing harshly he slowly shook his head. Still staring at their hands, he told her,

'No Tildy, I canna understand. I fear I arn't clever

212

enough to understand what youm saying.' Now he lifted his head and met her eyes. 'I knows only that I wants you, Tildy. That I hungers for you. That my body and soul cries out for you, and I'd do anything to have you for mine.'

'It cannot be, Harry,' she whispered. 'It cannot be.'

'Don't say that,' he answered sharply. 'Anything can be, and might be, so don't say that to me.'

She made no reply and after a time he said, 'Listen, girl, for the present let's stay as good friends. We'll just forget all about what's happened atween us here tonight, and we'll be like we was afore . . . Only promise me one thing, and that is if there should come a day when you wants a man agen . . . ' He reddened and broke off, momentarily disconcerted, then went on hurriedly, 'Don't take it amiss what I'm going to say, 'ull you, Tildy. I means no offence or insult.'

'All right Harry, I won't.' Despite her mood a smile of wry amusement curved Tildy's lips, and when he saw that smile Harry Mogg's piquant grin shone out at her, and he chuckled.

'Well, I reckon you knows already what I'm agoing to say, Tildy, and say it plain and open I 'ull, because I loves you, my honey. If ever youm in need of a man's loving, then come to me, and if ever you feels a fondness for some other cove, which God forbid, then tell me straight and open so that I shan't have to go on eating me heart out for you all the days o' me life.'

Tension abruptly dissolved between them, and with a giggle Tildy nodded her agreement, and Harry Mogg laughed with her. Then Tildy sobered abruptly.

'But what am I to do about Mrs Dugdale, Harry?' The question was rhetorical because before he could formulate any reply, she went on, 'I'm going to Bordesley Hall tomorrow morning to see her husband, and tell him what's happening to her here. He must take her away from here. He must.'

'But what if he wun't, honey?' Harry Mogg's tone was cynical. 'What if he's put her here to be rid of her? What can you do then?'

Tildy's lips tightened as he voiced what she had until now refused to admit as a possibility.

'Well then, Harry,' she murmured softly, 'what I could do then just remains to be seen, doesn't it . . .'

Chapter Twenty-five

'What's this youm asaying, girl?' Tobias Wilkins's fat face was bemused. 'Youm telling me that youm agoing to see your master and ask him to take his missus out from here?'

In the grey dawn Tildy faced the man in his parlour, and reiterated doggedly, 'Indeed I am, Master Wilkins. Mrs Dugdale has got worse here, instead of better. Doctor Brown will end by killing her with his contraptions.'

Tildy's own face was grey and drawn in the gloom of the room. After Harry Mogg had left her she had slept but little, and that little had been broken and disturbed by troubled dreams.

'And when does you intend leaving here then?' Tobias Wilkins demanded to know.

'Right now,' Tildy informed him firmly.

'And you intends going wi'out so much as a by your leave to the doctor?'

'It's not necessary.'

'You hold hard now, young 'ooman, because it bloody well is necessary.' The fat man slammed one meaty fist down on to the table causing the breakfast platters and cups to jump and rattle. 'It bloody well is necessary to have words wi' the doctor afore you goes gallivanting around the country saying such things agen him.' The huge pink face twisted in a scowl. 'Asaying such things agen all on us in this house, come to that.'

'No Master Wilkins, you do not understand,' Tildy

215

shook her head in denial. 'I'm not against anyone here. I'm not against the doctor or anyone else of you, but I don't think that Mrs Dugdale should remain here any longer. It's doing her great harm.'

'And who the bloody hell be you to say what's doing what?' Wilkins shouted angrily, his deep voice thundering so loudly that Tildy involuntarily flinched back from him. Yet despite the physical flinching she spoke out clearly and strongly.

'I'm a woman who has eyes to see with and ears to hear with, Master Wilkins, and what my eyes and ears tell me, my brain can understand. This place is no good for Mrs Dugdale and I'm going to tell her husband so, and come the devil or high water, I'll not turn aside from my purpose.'

'God's trewth, girl, youm as daft as the rest on 'um down in them cellars.' Amanda Wilkins had come to the door of the room and had listened to Tildy speaking. Now she entered fully and came to stand at her husband's side. They made a large and fearsome couple.

'Does you think that a gentleman is agoing to listen to you atelling him that a great man like Doctor Brown don't know what he's about? Youm bloody daft iffen you thinks he'll believe you, girl.'

Tildy could only shake her head again. 'I don't know whether Henry Dugdale will believe me or not, Mrs Wilkins, but I do know that he must be told.'

The normally placid, kindly features of Amanda Wilkins were now a mask of savage hostility. 'Jesus Christ on the cross!' she spat out. 'We'se took you into our parlour and treated you like you was blood-kin to us, and this is how you repays us, by going tittle-tattling round the country telling everybody that we'em wicked cruel and bad to the loonies here. How can you tell such lies, girl? How can you?'

'No, Mrs Wilkins, no!' Tildy protested in shocked dismay. 'That's not my intent or my belief at all. I know that you care for the loonies well, and I know that you don't treat them cruelly. But Mrs Dugdale has got worser here,

216

and it's no good for her to stay in this place. By saying that I'm not blaming you or Mr Wilkins in any way. I'm only saying that the doctor's treatment is no good for her. She needs a different sort of treatment.'

'I'll say no more to you, Tildy Crawford,' Tobias Wilkins loured at her. 'It's a wonder that the doctor didn't turf you out from here yesterday for your sauciness to him. Youm turned out to be a bad lot, girl, a nasty piece of work, and you'd best get from here right now. But I'll tell you this much, you'll not put a foot over this door ever agen, and when I tells Doctor Brown what youm adoing, then you can be sure that you'll never find work as a nussing-'ooman in this parish, or any of the other parishes round about here, not iffen you lives to be a hundred, you wun't.'

'Mr Wilkins is speaking true, my wench,' Amanda Wilkins added her grim assurances to her husband's. 'Any nussing-woman who speaks badly about the doctor who employs her, never finds work wi' any other doctor. So you think well about what youm adoing, girl, because youm cutting your own throat by doing it, and for no good reason either.

'No matter what you tells him, that Henry Dugdale 'ull not take his missus from here because this is where he wants her to be. Youm still green as the grass, my wench. You'se got a lot to learn about men and women and the things they'll do agen each other.' She grimaced contemptuously. 'He's a bad bugger is Henry Dugdale, and youm acting like a bloody fool iffen you does what you intends. You could stay here and live well for weeks to come, and then get other work easy with our reference for your good character. Still, you'll live and learn. But youm making a terrible rod for your own back, girl, just see if you arn't.'

For a while Tildy remained silent, her own doubts about what she was intending to do sent flooding through her once more by the massive confidence with which the woman had spoken. She thought also of what might happen to her and her baby if she could no longer find work, and briefly she weakened, hovering on the verge of

217

abandoning her planned course of action. But then in her mind's eye she saw the pitiful spectacle of Sybil Dugdale's shorn head and emaciated, bruised body, and the rampaging floods of doubt stilled and ebbed. She drew a deep breath and answered quietly,

'I'm sorry that you think so badly of me, both of you. I truly do wish you both well, and I'm more than grateful for the kindness you've shown towards me. But I'm going to tell Mr Dugdale what's in my mind.'

The other woman sniffed in loud derision. 'Then it's your own funeral, you daft silly cow, and I wish you naught but bad luck of it . . . '

With a heavy heart Tildy picked up her small bundle of belongings, and escorted to the door by the scowling Tobias Wilkins, she left the Stone House.

Outside the street was quiet. Only a few be-smocked labourers were going to their work, and here and there a diligent housewife scrubbing her windows or doorstep moved in the stillness of the dawning day. Tildy trudged slowly along the rutted roadway, her mind filled with forebodings that she could not dispel, but her determination unwavering.

She had almost reached the crossroads where she would turn towards Redditch when she heard her name called, and turned to see the broad red grinning face of Joey Bates.

'Why Joey, where have you been? Did you not sleep at the Stone House last night?' she asked with surprise.

He winked slyly, and then screwed his eyes tight-shut and chortled gleefully. 'Not me, Tildy. Joey Bates was a wicked dog last night, Joey Bates was, and he's had some prime fun, just prime.'

His comical manner brought a smile to Tildy's lips and a momentary lightening of her depressed spirits.

'Spending the night with a girlfriend, were you, Joey?' she joked.

Again his eyes screwed tight and he laughed unroariously and capered about her, slapping his hands against his sides.

'. . . was prime fun, Tildy. Just prime it was.' He halted

218

and looked from side to side, then with a grotesquely sly expression he tapped his broken-nailed forefinger against his big pimpled nose. 'Joey Bates bin peeking into windows, Tildy, and I saw summat at Doctor Sam's house that was prime fun. Prime fun it was.' Again the tight-shut eyes and the chortling of sheer pleasure. 'It was prime. Prime it was.'

Intrigued, Tildy questioned, 'And what did you see, Joey?'

Once more the sideward look and the tapping of forefinger against nose, then he chortled and capered about her. 'Joey saw a dead bugger jumping, so he did. A dead bugger come to life.' He stood still, and in a delighted whisper told her, 'Joey laughed when he saw it, Tildy. It was prime fun. Doctor Sam used his 'letric fluid machine and made a dead bugger come alive and jump about, and there was pictures on him as well. All sorts o' pictures. By Christ, Joey laughed when he see'd that, I'll tell you, it was prime.' Shouting with glee the simpleton left her and ran with a shambling gait towards the Stone House, leaving Tildy staring after him in bewilderment.

'What can he have seen?' she wondered. 'What in heaven's name was Doctor Brown doing with his electric fluid and a dead body?' Mentally she shrugged. 'Ah well, it's not the dead who concern me, it's the living.'

Settling her bundle comfortably across her shoulder, and drawing her shawl close around her head against the clammy chill of the air, she took the road westwards towards Redditch.

As she trudged along she saw around her the work taking place upon a land now shorn of its harvest. Here a gang of women and children dug and collected potatoes, their clothing thick with muddy clay, their voices loud and tuneful in the still air as they sang and bantered. Further on, two-wheeled carts drawn by single horses carried piles of steaming manure to the meadows, their rustic drivers sitting stolid and unconcerned in a reeking mist of stench. A plough team of great black oxen plodded massively over a raw-stubbled field, and on one sweeping stretch of hillside

Tildy saw a line of wheat-sowers moving like soldiers with synchronized steps and sweeps of casting hands, their broad-brimmed hats bobbing in unison with their measured strides. She drew great draughts of the damp earth-scented air, and the oxygen surged through her blood to energize her muscles and send her legs thrusting over the miles of road.

It took her some two hours to reach Redditch, and as she climbed the sunken lane known as the Holloway which would bring her through the Bredon fork and into the town centre, her longing to see her child burgeoned unbearably. Even before she reached the stagnant stinking Big Pool she knew that instead of swinging towards Bordesley Hall, she would instead continue southwards up the steep Back Hill and gentler-sloping Mount Pleasant, through Headless Cross and on to Crowther's Row at Boney's Point.

'Well now, you'se gi' me a surprise, Mistress Crawford. I warn't expecting to see you for some whiles.' The rosy wrinkled face of Widow Fairfax beamed at Tildy from beneath the snowy white mob-cap. 'Come you in, young 'ooman, come you in.'

She invited Tildy into the warm room with its mingled smells of dried herbs and woodsmoke and clean baby flesh. The burnished kettle sang merrily on the bright-flaming grate, the toddlers and infants lay peacefully in their individual boxes ranged around the cluttered room, and the old woman's pink gums glistened toothlessly as she told Tildy,

'Here they be, all my little morsels, swate and comfortable. Now then, which is yourn?' Clucking her tongue in her mouth the Widow Fairfax moved along the rows of boxes, squinting short-sightedly, and muttering, 'No, t'ain't that 'un. Nor that 'un either. Nor that 'un. Ahhh, here you be, my little morsel, here you be, and I'se got a surprise for you, my lamb. Your mammy's come to see you.'

'ldy's heart was thumping fiercely, and she was forced

to swallow hard to ease the stricture of her throat as the old woman gently lifted her child from his box. The hunger to hold her baby close to her heart, to kiss, to cuddle, to caress, made Tildy impervious to anything other than that hunger, and in a daze of loving thankfulness she cradled her baby to her breasts, her lips touching his dark hair, her breath drawing the scents of him deep inside her. She crooned gentle words of love and longing and immersed herself entirely in the moment's needs, but then a sense of disquietude began to assail her. The child showed no awareness of her, only lay limp and flaccid-bodied in her arms.

'Davy?' she said sharply. 'Wake up, Davy. Wake up my honey-lamb and see your mammy.'

'Lord love you, girl, you'll not wake him now. He's only an hour since had his poppy syrup.'

Tildy gently pushed open one of Davy's closed eyelids and saw that the pupil of his eye was contracted almost to pinpoint. Alarm jolted her, and anxiously she felt for his pulse, ejaculating with relief when she felt it beating slow and heavy. Now she saw that his breathing was stertorous and also slow, and his skin felt moist and cold to the touch.

'He doesn't seem right, Widow Fairfax,' she told the woman. 'He doesn't seem to be well.'

The rosy wrinkled face chuckled back at her reassuringly. 'Theer now, just hark to the wench. Your babby's thriving, girl. He's as plump as a capon. You young 'uns doon't have the knowing o' babbies and their funny ways, like we old 'uns does. They'm always a bit stupefactious arter they'se had their feed and their syrup. 'Tis natural so. See now, you give him back to me for a minute.' She took the baby and clucked at him. 'Theer now, you naughty boy, you'se put the frits up your mam wi' your old sleep yeddedness. But youm all right, arn't you? Youm a proper little grenadier, so you am, a proper little bacon-bolter. You lie back down for a bit, now.' She laid him into his box and turned to Tildy, saying kindly,

'You looks fair washed up, my wench. That's what is making you so worried about the babby. It's because youm tired yoursen. You set yourself down by the fire for a bit, and we'll have us a dish o' tay. That'll perk you up, girl, and ease your mind as well, you see if it wun't.'

Her words forced Tildy to acknowledge her own weariness, what with the lack of sleep and the long walk, and she allowed herself to surrender to the necessity of a brief rest.

An hour later Tildy came away from the small cottage, her body rested, but her mind uneasy about her child and filled with the sadness of having to part from him again.

'This life is not good for him, and it's not good for me either. We should have a proper home where I could care for him.' Then she thought of her scant financial resources and experienced a sensation of hopelessness. 'I've hardly a guinea left of the money Anna Coldericke gave me. Still, there's near a sovereign of wages owing to me.' She grimaced in a flash of sardonic humour. 'But added together they don't amount to enough to live on, even though they're too much to die with.'

She passed by the White Hart Inn at Headless Cross and knowing that Harry Mogg's cottage was close by she was tempted to call and see if he might be home. But after a moment's reflection she decided not to. 'I'd best get this business of Mrs Dugdale sorted out afore I do anything else.' Disquiet invaded her. 'For all I know I might well be handed my sack by Henry Dugdale for acting as I am . . . And what will I do then for work, especially with the winter coming on . . . '

By the time Tildy was trudging up the rising ground of the Pot End lane, beyond which Bordesley Hall awaited her, the disquiet she felt concerning Henry Dugdale's reaction to her appearance had crystallized into a definite sense of foreboding. She slowed and halted on the crest of the rising ground and stood inwardly debating the wisdom of what she was about to do – before her the tall, ornate chimney ˙acks and gables of the hall enshrouded by its woodlands, ˙ˑ˙ˑ˙ d her the distant buildings of Redditch town on their woody hillsides. She stared for long moments at the hall, then turned to look back at the town.

'I could go back and ask advice. Mayhap Doctor Taylor would tell me what I might best do.' She caught her full lower lip between her teeth and bit down hard upon the tender flesh, as though the pain that action caused might enable her to make a final decision. 'Henry Dugdale might go mad at me for what I'm doing,' she thought apprehensively. 'He's a man of violence, he could well turn that violence against me.'

In this moment it seemed that she might well give way to her fears and retrace her footsteps. Then, deliberately she invoked the mental image of Sybil Dugdale chained in that foul smelling cellar in the darkness, with only the scurrying, squeaking rats to keep her company, and Tildy's resolve hardened and she fought away her nervous tremors. 'No, I'll not turn back. I'll not leave the poor soul to suffer so.'

Outside the great barred gates Tildy tugged hard on the bell-rope and heard the loud janglings of the doorbell. She waited a few seconds then tugged the bell-rope again. There was something missing, which for a brief while Tildy could not grasp, and then the realization came. There was no scrabbling of paws upon gravel, no snarls or deep-toned barkings of mastiffs.

'Mayhap they've all been sold,' she hoped, for she feared the savage beasts.

There was a sound of footsteps crossing towards the gate from the house, and then the small hatch in the gate opened and a female voice questioned, 'Who might you be?'

For a moment Tildy was shocked to silence by this unexpected happening, then she told herself, 'Mayhap Henry Dugdale's engaged a domestic.' Aloud, she said, 'I'm Tildy Crawford, I'm Mrs Dugdale's nursing-woman, and I'd like to speak to Mr Dugdale straight away.'

The hatch closed and Tildy heard the lock-bar being lifted, then the huge gate creaked slightly open.

'You'd best state what business you have with Mr Dugdale, Tildy Crawford.' The woman was tall and slender, her hennaed hair frizzed into tight curls only half-covered by the small cornette cap tied with ribbons beneath her chin, and her blue and green striped silken dress was ruffed and vandyked at her long throat and flounced around her silken slippers.

Tildy judged the woman to be in her late twenties, and thought her attractive, even though the hard lines patterned around her eyes and mouth could not be fully hidden by the artfully applied rouge and enamel.

'Might I ask who you are, Ma'am?' Tildy queried, and the woman nodded.

'Yes, you might ask, girl, but whether you'll be told is quite another matter. You wait here for a minute or two, I'll be back directly.'

She turned on her heel and re-crossed the gravelled fore-court to disappear through the open front door of the hall.

Tildy was bewildered by the strangeness of her reception, and could only wonder helplessly at what was happening inside the house. On impulse she started to cross to the open front door, then halted again, racked by indecision.

The woman reappeared and came towards Tildy with one clenched hand outstretched. 'Here Crawford, these are the wages owing to you. Now you must leave here.'

'What?' Tildy stared at the sovereign in her fingers. 'But I didn't come here to collect this. I've come to see Mr Dugdale.'

'Well, you can't see him, and you are no longer in his employ.' The woman glanced back over her shoulder at the house, then satisfied that she was not being watched, told Tildy in low urgent tones, 'Listen well, girl. A messenger came on horseback from Doctor Brown at Henley afore you reached here. Mr Dugdale went half-mad when he heard what the man had to say. I can't tell you what was said because I wasn't in the room, but suffice to say that you are finished with this family now, girl, finished for good. So now you've got your money, you'd best leave.'

The fact that she had been dismissed did not greatly ꞏꞏꞏldy. She had, after all, had the presentiment that

that would happen. But her familiar demon of stubbornness caused her to stand her ground.

'I want to see Henry Dugdale myself,' she stated doggedly. 'I want to tell him what is happening to his wife.'

The other woman became nervous. 'Look, girl, if you keep on arguing, then you'll have that bastard White and the dogs let loose on you? He's up in the woods with them now, but he'll be back soon. So you just go from here.' As her nervousness increased so did the woman's sing-song Welsh accent become more pronounced. She gnawed at her lips, then went on, 'Look now, go quick because Henry Dugdale is in such an evil temper that God only knows what he might do. I've known him for years, girl, and I know to my own cost what he's capable of doing when he's like he is now.' Again she looked back anxiously at the open front door, then turned again and now Tildy could see the fear in the other's eyes. 'Just go, good girl, for pity's sake, go. If I'm not back inside in a few seconds then he'll come looking to see where I am, and then it'll be God help us both. So for my sake, if not your own, just go now . . . go!'

Sympathy impelled Tildy to accede. 'All right then, Ma'am, for now I'll leave. But I'll return here because I must see Mr Dugdale, and I must try and make him understand what is being done to his wife.'

'Do you think he don't know well what's being done to her, you bloody little fool?' the woman hissed, and grasping the edge of the great gate threw her weight upon it and slammed it shut in Tildy's face. The lock-bar thudded home, there were retreating footsteps over the gravel and then the slamming of the front door.

Tildy sighed downheartedly. 'Is everyone stark raving mad in this place, I wonder?' She began to walk slowly away from the hall, but despite the rebuff her determination to somehow get her message through to Henry Dugdale was unshaken.

'I'll go to see Doctor Taylor, and I'll ask him to come up here with me and speak to Henry Dugdale. Surely even

Dugdale will not refuse to listen to his own wife's kinsman.'

The longer she dwelt on the idea the more feasible and promising of success it became, and with this new hope to hearten her she stepped out for Redditch town.

At that same moment, both Taylors, father and son, together with their fellow practitioner, Doctor Alexander Pratt, and the Reverend John Clayton were seated around the table in the small vestry room of St Stephen's Chapel. The atmosphere in the room was tense and acrimonious and John Clayton's rugged features mirrored the grimness of his mood as he spoke to the three doctors.

'The fact remains, gentlemen, that the night before last at Feckenham burial yard another grave was opened and the body of Henry Stoddart was stolen.'

'God dammee, Sir . . . have you not told . . . told us this already?' Alexander Pratt delivered his words in short staccato packages.

John Clayton glared angrily at the lanky, sallow-faced medical man who made a funereal figure with his tall black hat and black clothing.

'Indeed I have, Sir,' he retorted heatedly, 'and I shall continue to repeat it until I at last bring you to the gravity of what is happening. Two bodies have now been stolen in this area. If it had not been for the timely arrival of the Ipsley sexton, it would have been three bodies stolen.'

'But how does . . . that concern me . . . might I ask . . . Sir?' Pratt demanded.

'It concerns you, Sir, because resurrection men act on behalf of medical men,' Clayton spat in reply.

The other's sallow face darkened in rage. 'Do you suggest . . . that I . . . am employing body-snatchers?' he roared.

Before Clayton could answer Charles Taylor intervened. 'Gentlemen! Gentlemen!' He rapped the table with his gold-topped walking cane. 'We are not ignorant labourers. . . s conduct our discussion in a seemly and proper . . . beg of you.'

John Clayton reined back his galloping temper and inclined his tie-wigged head in a stiff bow. 'Quite so, Sir, and I apologize if my words have caused offence. They were most certainly not intended to do so. I cast no aspersions upon you, Doctor Pratt, and I trust you will accept that fact.'

Equally stiffly Alexander Pratt accepted the apology, and Charles Taylor then enquired,

'Why was there not a watcher appointed for Stoddart's grave, Reverend Clayton? After all, in view of the previous occurrences at Ipsley and Tardebigge I would have thought a watch would now be maintained for the necessary period following any fresh interment.'

'There was a watcher, Sir,' Clayton sighed wearily. 'A tramper, but the fellow got swinish drunk and fell asleep. While he was snoring like a pig the outrage was perpetrated.'

'Can you be sure that the tramper was not in league with the resurrection men, John?' Hugh Taylor, a handsome dandy in his plum coat, lavender pantaloons, gaudy cravat and waistcoat, his hair scented and curled, entered the discussion for the first time.

Again Clayton vented a weary sigh. 'Indeed he might well have been so, Hugh, but how could we prove that? And of course, he might well be telling the truth.' The clergyman swung his glance to each of the other men in turn. 'Gentlemen, the very fact that I requested you to meet with me is a measure of my desperation. As a Christian and as a clergyman, these wicked crimes fill me with horror, and the grief caused to the bereaved families almost defies description. I know that you gentlemen are above reproach in all aspects of your character, but I must speak plainly and state my belief that it is a member of your profession who is employing these vile body-snatchers, and I also believe that that person could well be found in one of our neighbouring parishes.'

'God dammee, Sir . . . and he could . . . be equally well found . . . in Brummagem . . . or Worcester . . . or even Coventry, or Warwick . . . It don't take . . . an over-large hamper . . . to carry a corpse . . . and there's carts aplenty . . . journeying to those cities . . . from these parts.'

Both the Taylors nodded their agreement with Pratt's statement and Clayton himself accepted the possibility of its truth.

'Indeed, Doctor Pratt, the person I spoke of could well be found in one of those cities, but I'm of the firm opinion that we shall discover him nearer home. But to do this, I need your assistance, gentlemen.'

He paused, as if awaiting their reaction, and it was Charles Taylor who gave it.

'I believe that we have already given our assistance, Reverend Clayton. We have each one of us contributed to the offered reward money for the apprehension of those responsible. What else would you ask of us?'

'I would ask you, Sir, to pursue your own enquiries among your fellow medical practitioners. You have much intercourse, one with another, you assist each other to perform operations, and you assist in consultations also. You are more likely to discover the person responsible for these evil outrages than the parish constables, or indeed, even the magistrates themselves.'

Charles Taylor's customary benevolent expression metamorphosed into a stern distaste. ''Pon my soul, John!' he ejaculated. 'You are asking us to play the spy!'

'No Sir, I do not ask you to play the spy.' Clayton knew immediately that he had overstepped an invisible line of etiquette, and now tried to repair the damage he had done. 'Never would I ask you to behave so ungentlemanly, Sir. I merely wish you to enquire of your fellow doctors as to the identity of a rogue.'

'By God, young man, you go too far!' Taylor's temper exploded. 'You are now saying that we doctors are rogues!'

'Sir, I beg you, do not think that.' Clayton's rugged features were scarlet with embarrassment.

'I'll hear no more!' Charles Taylor stood up and taking his tall hat from the table crammed it hard upon his head. 'I bid you a good day, Reverend Clayton.'

The old man stamped from the room, to be instantly

followed by Doctor Pratt. Still seated opposite the clergy-man, Hugh Taylor burst into a shout of laughter.

'By the Christ, John, if you could but see your face,' he gasped, and dissolved into helpless laughter at his friend's mortified expression.

After a while he calmed and sobered. 'John, listen well,' he told the clergyman. 'You must understand that although we doctors may dispute and fight with each other like so many cats and dogs, we stand locked together like a band of brothers against those outside the profession who attack us.

'Doctors are so sadly vulnerable to insult and abuse from those whom we fail to cure, that we have to shield each other's mistakes and ignorance, if only for our own individual protection when we ourselves happen to fail. And concerning the practice of body-snatching, I have to tell you, that although in public we may condemn it, yet in private we condone it and accept that it is a necessity.

'So I would suggest that you endeavour to mend the bridges you have today cast down between yourself and my fellow practitioners, and try to ensure that a good watch is maintained upon every fresh interment in this area. After all, John, after nine days and nights the cadaver is too rotted to be of any use either to us, or to the sausage-makers.'

'You are saying that I should shut my eyes and pretend this evil does not exist hereabouts,' Clayton rejoined indignantly, and his friend shrugged and smiled.

'No John, do not shut your eyes; merely focus them on attainable objects. At this moment the abolition of resur-rection men is not an attainable object . . . A good watch over a grave is.'

Together the young men left the chapel and John Clayton invited, 'Come to the house, Hugh, and take a glass of wine with me. Mrs Hemming presented me with a half-dozen of fine port.'

Hugh Taylor was happy to accept and they strolled arm in arm along the Green and down the Fish Hill. As they reached the gate of Clayton's home the young doctor halted and swore quietly.

'God blast my eyes, there is just the one I wanted to see.'
He stared down the hill at the young woman with a bundle
on her back who was beginning the ascent towards them.

Clayton recognized her also. 'That's the Crawford girl,
is it not?'

Taylor nodded. 'It is indeed, and once again she has
succeeded in creating upset. A messenger came from
Doctor Brown at Henley just before I came up to the
vestry. I'll hold here for a moment, John, and have a word
with her.'

Tildy looked up the hill and saw the two men standing
higher up. She smiled her pleasure at seeing that one of
them was Hugh Taylor and quickened her pace. She
reached them slightly out of breath and before she could
speak Hugh Taylor told her curtly, 'I have already received
the message concerning you, from Doctor Brown,
Crawford. Suffice to say that he has my full approval for
dismissing you, and you will receive no further employment from my father and myself, and I shall ensure that no
one among my acquaintances shall employ you in future
either.' He jerked his head in dismissal. 'Now be on your
way, girl.'

Tildy's utter shock at this unlooked for reception left her
momentarily lost for words, and by the time she had begun
to formulate any reply she was alone and the two men were
walking up the pathway of the house.

'Wait!' she shouted after their retreating figures. 'Wait,
Doctor Taylor, and tell me why you are treating me in this
way, and why you believe the lies told you. Don't just run
from me as if you're frightened of me.'

Now it was Hugh Taylor's turn to be shocked. He swung
on her incredulously. 'Who the devil d'you think you are
addressing with such insolence, girl?' he demanded.

'I'm addressing you, Sir,' Tildy answered spiritedly.
'And I demand that you listen to me.'

'You demand?' The young man stared at her as though
he could not believe the evidence of his own senses. 'You
demand?' he repeated, and looked at his companion as if
seeking confirmation of what he was hearing.

John Clayton grinned wryly. 'Did I not once tell you how forward and impertinent towards her betters, this one was, Hugh?'

'Indeed you did, John, and I see now precisely what you meant.' Taylor faced Tildy once more. 'Doctor Brown has already informed me that he dismissed you for insolence, Crawford.' His eyes were bleak. 'That same insolence you now display towards me. He informs me also that if your behaviour were not already sufficiently heinous, you now propose to go proclaiming to the world that Doctor Brown is mistreating his patients.

'I warn you now, girl, that if any word of such behaviour on your part reaches my ears, then I shall see to it that Doctor Brown is immediately informed, and I shall recommend to him to take whatever course he deems necessary to punish you for your wickedness. Now go from here before I send for the constable and have you taken up for insulting behaviour.'

He turned on his heel and in company with the clergyman entered the house.

Tildy stared helplessly at the closed door with a tumult of emotions rampaging through her mind - anger, humiliation, disgust and frustration all battling for dominance.

'They treat us worse than dogs,' she muttered to herself, and tears of chagrin filled her eyes. 'Their lies are always believed before our truths. I try to help a gentry woman, and her menfolk turn on me as if I were the wickedest creature in all creation.'

Inside the house John Clayton looked questioningly at his friend, and the young doctor shrugged his elegant shoulders.

'I suppose I'd best tell you what that was all about, John. As you know, much to our family's shame, Henry Dugdale committed my cousin Sybil into Sam Brown's madhouse at Henley. It's a sore point with both my father and myself, you may be sure, and we prefer not to discuss it or have it discussed. Such a shame on a family needs best be buried and forgotten.

'Still, Brown is highly reputable and has achieved some remarkable cures. Keeping that fact in mind, we have been able to bear with dignity what has happened, and to hope that some good may eventually come out of it.' He smiled grimly. 'And of course, there is naught that we can do about the situation anyhow. Henry Dugdale has the right to do whatsoever he pleases with his own wife. Now, after our thinking that the whole sorry business is well along the road to being forgotten and no longer talked about in polite society, lo and behold, along comes this damned pauper bitch and tells Sam Brown in so many words that he's a fool and a charlatan, and has the audacity to tell him also that she intends to bring Sybil Dugdale's plight to the world's attention and have her removed from his establishment to boot.' He chuckled mirthlessly, shaking his powdered, curly head. 'God dammee, what's the world coming to, John? We've now got damned pauper bitches trying to tell us what we may and may not do.'

'She can do nothing,' John Clayton assured his friend. 'And if she continues to pester her betters about this matter, then you must have her committed to the Bridewell as a public nuisance.'

Hugh Taylor's normal good humour was fast returning, and now he grinned and said jocularly, 'The trouble is, John, and forgive me for saying it in front of a man of the cloth, but she is such a toothsome piece of flesh that I could hardly bear to have her shut away when there are so many other things I'd prefer doing with her, only think what a waste of beauty it would be . . . '

They laughed together, and the faint echoes of their laughter reached Tildy's ears. Her face flaming with anger and shame, she turned from the gate and slowly walked on up the hill.

Chapter Twenty-six

Mother Readman's kitchen was full. Rain and chill winds had driven the loungers from the streets and they came to the lodging house in search of warmth, shelter and company. Mother Readman sat enthroned by the fire, presiding like some beggar queen over her ragged court, and little Apollonia scurried around the room serving out bowls of stew and tankards of porter and cider to those who had money or credit. She was also using the opportunities to bargain with prospective clients for her own services later that night. By the fat old harridan's side Tildy sat on a three-legged stool and poured out her story to this woman who had been a good friend to her.

' . . . and so Mrs Readman, Brown's now told the world that he dismissed me when in truth I left of my own accord, and he's made sure that I'll get no more work as a sick-nurse around these parts.'

'Don't you worry your yed about that, my duck. You'll find other work, iffen that's what you've a mind to do,' the old woman comforted, and added, 'but why a pretty wench like you wants to work like a dog when you could easily get a man to keep you beats me, I'm fucked if it don't.'

Tildy caught her lower lips between her white teeth for a moment, then said reflectively, 'It's not being given my sack that worries me so much, Mrs Readman, but the knowing that I've failed poor Sybil Dugdale. I can't see what I can do to help her now.'

Mother Readman puffed out her cheeks until they resembled vast balloons of blue-streaked tallow, and then exploded the trapped air in one mighty gust. 'Pheww! You don't want to moither your yed about that, my duck. You must look to yourself fust now. How be you fixed for the rhino? Has you got enough to see you through?' The hard eyes, slitted in their puffy balls of fat, softened as they studied the girl. 'Iffen you arn't got any money, Tildy, then you can find your bed and board wi' me. You can help in the house here for your keep, Ahr, and have your babby here wi' you as well.'

Tildy felt a warm gratitude towards the old woman. 'Thank you kindly, Mrs Readman. Truly I'm grateful for the offer, but I've a couple of sovereigns with me, and I've paid for my Davy to stay another two weeks at the Widow Fairfax's. But if you can find me a bed I'd like to stay here for a few days until I can sort myself out.'

'Stay and welcome, girl. There's a spare bed in my room you can use. I'll charge you a shilling the week, and if youm short, then take a bowl o' stew whenever you've got the hunger on you. You needn't pay for the bit o' grub. But let me give you a bit of advice, my duck. Keep them two sovereigns for your own use. Don't you goo throwing good money arter bad, like you did last time. That old bugger's back agen, and his pockets be as empty as ever, and his thirst as strong.'

'Do you mean Marmaduke Montmorency?' Tildy asked with eager pleasure. 'I'd love to see him again, I really did like him for all his nonsense. Did he go to London? Did he get work as an actor? When did he come back to Redditch?'

'Hold your horses, girl,' Mother Readman held up her grimy fat paws as if to fend off the avalanche of questions. 'Bite on your tongue for a minute and I'll tell you,' she chuckled hoarsely. 'I can understand you aliking the old bugger. Truth to tell, I'se always had a soft spot for him meself. Anyways, he come back last week, drunk as a lord, arse out of his britches. The bugger ne'er went up to London, he only got as far as bloody Evesham, and when

234

he'd drunk away all the money that you'd give him and whatever else he could borrow, beg or steal, then he turned up here agen like a bad penny, and he's bin on me rope ever since. He'll be the ruin o' me, so he will,' she mock grumbled. 'He arn't paid me yet.'

Tildy could not hold back and interrupted, 'Where is he now, then?'

Mother Readman swore and cackled with laughter simultaneously. 'Fucked if I knows wheer the bugger is. I sent him to Alcester wi' a parcel, so he's more nor likely lying in a ditch right now, pissed out on his bloody mind. Mind you, Tildy, we'se had a grand bit o' fun wi' him this last day or two.' Again she wheezed for breath and again the raucous laughter cackled from her, shaking her billows of flesh.

'He got hisself some work the other day, Tildy. He went to Feckenham to Grave-Watch over Henry Stoddart because the family was feared o' the resurrection men alifting him up. You knows they bin about these parts of late, don't you?'

Tildy nodded. The subject was common knowledge in the district and had been a main topic of conversation.

'Anyways,' Mother Readman went on, 'theer's our Marmaduke watching over the grave and somebody gives him some drink. O' corst the bugger ends up gettin' stoatious and he falls asleep by the side on the grave. While he's snoring, along comes the bloody resurrection men and lifts old Henry out. When Marmaduke wakes up he gets such a shock that he falls down into the hole hisself, and it being so narrow and him still so drunk, he can't push hisself back up out on it, and when the people comes to see who's screaming and hollering they finds Marmaduke headfust down on the empty coffin, shouting that the devil has come to the churchyard and took Henry and chucked him into the grave as a replacement.'

Wheezing and gasping, tears streaming from her eyes, Mother Readman rocked in her chair, helpless with laughter.

Despite the gruesome content of the story Tildy was

swept along by the other woman's infectious merriment and was laughing hard herself.

'Everybody's bin ribbing Marmaduke ever since and asking if he'd sold old Henry for a panorama,' Mother Readman cackled.

'A what?' Tildy gasped.

'A panorama,' Mother Readman wheezed, and she wiped her eyes on her dirty grey apron. 'You see, old Stoddart had bin a naval man, and from all accounts his whole body was covered wi' them tattoos. You knows what they be, don't you? Them pictures o' ships and girls and suchlike that the jack tars likes to ha' put on their skins.'

Tildy gasped with shock as memory jolted her and she sobered instantly.

The old woman stared in puzzlement at this abrupt change of mood.

'Why Tildy, what's up wi' you, my duck? You'se gone as pale as a ghost.'

Wordlessly Tildy shook her head, her mind a maelstrom, and then managed to say, ''Tis nothing, Mrs Readman, I'm all right. I just had a bit of a funny turn, that's all. I think perhaps I need a breath of air, it's very hot and close in here.' Without waiting for answer she rose and hurried from the room, leaving curious looks behind her.

Outside the Silver Square was sordid and depressing in the dark drizzle of the afternoon, but Tildy was unnoticing of her surroundings. She walked slowly out of the square and along the narrow muddy fetidness of Silver Street, her mind trying desperately to marshal and evaluate what she had just heard.

'Covered in pictures!' That was what Joey Bates had said. 'A dead bugger jumping about, coming to life, covered in pictures. Covered in pictures! A dead man jumping about in Doctor Brown's house. A dead man who was covered in pictures!'

'Can it be Stoddart's corpse that Joey Bates saw?' Tildy asked herself over and over again. 'Can it be? And if it was, then how did Samuel Brown come into possession of it? Was it he who was employing the body-snatchers? If it was he, and that fact came out, then Samuel Brown would be in serious trouble. It could well ruin him.'

Tildy's thoughts suddenly veered at a tangent, and an idea burst upon her that was frightening in its connotations. If it should really be Stoddart's corpse in Doctor Brown's house, and if he had purchased that corpse from the resurrection men, then could she use that knowledge to force Samuel Brown to release Sybil Dugdale from his madhouse, and instead place her under the care of her kinsmen, the Taylors?

Tildy swallowed hard. 'I'll have to be sure that it really is Stoddart's corpse in Brown's house.' Her heart began to thump. 'Oh God help me,' she whispered. 'Give me the courage to do it . . . Please, give me the courage . . . '

Chapter Twenty-seven

The night was well advanced. Heavy clouds obscured the moon, and the drizzle of misty rain had soaked through Tildy's shawl and bodice and caused the folds of her skirt to cling heavily and clammily around her legs. She crouched in a clump of bushes, her eyes fixed on the house some twenty yards distant from her, and nerved herself to move towards it yet again.

By careful questioning to avoid any suspicion as to her intentions she had managed to obtain a fuller physical description of Henry Stoddart from Mother Readman, and now she intended to make certain that the dead man Joey Bates had told her of was the tattooed ex-sailor.

It seemed to Tildy that she had been hiding near to the house for hours without end and she had lost all track of time as she shivered with the cold, her muscles cramping painfully, only moving whenever a light was lit in one of the downstairs rooms to creep up to its windows and peer in, hoping to discover in which room the corpse lay.

Now only one room remained to be checked. Shuttered, and until a few moments ago remaining in darkness. But then light had appeared from between the slats of the wooden shutters, and so Tildy, wincing at the wrenching in her cold-stiffened joints, crept slowly and cautiously forwards. She pressed her eyes to a wide crack where the wood had warped from the frame, and felt a surging satisfaction. Several candles made the interior well lit, and although her view was restricted, Tildy could see the sheet-covered body on the narrow trestle table, and a section of the voltaic piles of a galvanic battery beneath one end of that table. Several men were moving in and out of her line of vision, and Tildy recognized Samuel Brown, Peter Donovan, Doulgas Fletcher and the barrel-like figure of Tobias Wilkins. Their voices were too muffled by the window and shutter for Tildy to hear clearly what was being said, but there was much laughter and apparent banter taking place.

Samuel Brown drew the sheet from the table, and Tildy clearly saw the naked corpse. It had grey hair on its head and its brawny chest and arms, and from neck to ankles it was patterned with a mass of interwoven blue, black and red tattooing.

Although she was almost certain that it was indeed the corpse of Henry Stoddart still Tildy needed to see one thing more to give her an absolute certainty. According to Mother Readman, Henry Stoddart's right hand was missing three fingers, blown off in a sea-fight during the war. It was the left-hand side of the corpse which presented itself to Tildy, so she waited where she was.

Samuel Brown had the conductors of the galvanic battery in his hands now, and standing behind the head of the table he carefully positioned them above the dead face. His companions were out of Tildy's view, so she had an unobstructed view of what was to happen. She saw the blue flash of the spark, and she moaned in horror as the dead man's jaw quivered and gaped wide, the whole face contorting in a fearful grimace, and then nausea threatened to overwhelm her as the bleared dead eyes opened and stared sightlessly upwards. Tildy wanted to turn and flee, and she felt herself bathed in cold sweat as the waves of sick horror broke over her. She thrust her knuckles between her teeth, biting hard and fighting for control.

Brown was moving around the body until he now faced Tildy almost directly opposite where she stood, his head bent low, his gaze intent on the effects the electrical discharges were causing. Now it was the thighs and legs moving as the blue sparks flashed upon them, the muscles twitching and jerking, the limbs contorting, the heels thumping upon the table top.

'Oh God help me!' Tildy feared she might faint as her sight swam giddily, and she gagged helplessly. 'God help me,' she moaned deep in her throat.

Again Samuel Brown changed position, again sparks blue-flashed, and the right arm of the corpse raised up, the fingers spasmodically clenching and relaxing and clenching once more, and Tildy groaned in mingled horror and relief as she saw the mutilated hand.

'It is him. It is Henry Stoddart,' she told herself with a fierce certainty, and sagged back from the window. With instinctive caution she crept stealthily away from the house and once on the roadway grabbed her skirts high with both hands and ran headlong, not stopping until her straining lungs could no longer drag in sufficient oxygen to fuel her labouring flagging muscles. Then she sank down against the wet-dripping hedgerow and waited pantingly for her over-taxed nerves and strength to recoup themselves.

When her breathing had eased and her jangled nerves calmed, Tildy trudged on through the murk and drizzling rain. As she walked she came to the realization that she did not know how best to make use of the knowledge she now held.

'I need to talk to someone who's got more experience of the world than me. Someone I can trust. Perhaps Mrs Readman . . . No . . . She's got more than enough on her plate already, she wouldn't thank me for adding this to her load . . . Harry? Harry Mogg! Of course. Harry will be able to tell me the best course to take . . .'

Footsore, wet and weary, Tildy knocked on the door of Harry Mogg's cottage. The cottage was in darkness, no light shone from its windows and there was no sound of movement from within. Again she knocked, louder and longer this time.

'Where can he be?' she wondered. 'Is he out with the Rippling Boys, up to some mischief or other?'

At Tildy's level of society, morals and mores had their

own peculiar structure, and what would in polite society be considered unlawfully wicked was not necessarily regarded in the same light by the labouring classes. Tildy was not repelled by the unlawful activities of the Rippling Boys. She found it hard to condemn men who stole from the wealthy, or poached the gentry's game. Even though she herself was scrupulously honest, she accepted that necessity was a harsh taskmaster, and that many men, women and children became criminals in order to fill their empty bellies. There was one cardinal rule, however, that when transgressed was universally condemned among the poor, and the transgressor damned. That unspoken rule was that you never stole from your own kind, those who had little or nothing themselves.

The cottage remained still and dark and Tildy was about to turn away when Harry Mogg's voice came from behind her.

'It's you, is it, Tildy?'

Startled, she swung to face him. 'Harry, you scared me creeping up like that,' she remonstrated, and he laughed softly.

'I don't answer the door at night, Tildy, unless I knows for certain who's knocking on it. I always comes out through me little tunnel to see who's acalling on me.'

'Your tunnel?' she queried, and again he laughed.

'It's me secret way in and out o' the house, honey. I'll show it to you someday. Now come on inside out o' this damp.'

He led her into the cottage and used flint and steel to kindle his tinder-box, and lit the rushlights in their iron holders. In their pale wavering glow he studied her face.

'What brings you here at this time, my honey? Has you decided to come and live wi' me?'

He reached out for her, but she moved back from his questing arms.

'No Harry, don't start that now. I need to talk to you and get your advice.'

Good naturedly he accepted the rebuff and told her, 'Sit you down then, my duck, and say on.'

The room was sparsely furnished with a table and rush-bottomed chairs, and Tildy seated herself on one of these. She lifted her shawl back from her glossy hair, and Harry Mogg's throat tightened as he saw her beauty.

'By God, Tildy, I wish you'd come and live wi' me,' he said huskily. 'I've a powerful love for you.'

'Leave it now, Harry, please, and listen to what I have to tell you,' she begged, and went on to relate all that had happened.

He heard her out in silence, his expression deliberately neutral.

' . . . and so what's best for me to do now, Harry?' she finished.

For a while the young man gave no answer. Then he drew a chair nearer to her and sat on it facing her, taking her hands within his own.

'Leave it lay, Tildy,' he said emphatically. 'Youm treading on terrible thin ice, girl. You could get yourself into some awful trouble.'

'I know that, Harry, that's why I need you to tell me how to go about using this knowledge I now hold over Samuel Brown. I want to get Sybil Dugdale out from that place and back in her own home where she belongs.'

'But her husband don't want her back, honey,' Harry protested. 'You said yourself that theer's another 'ooman in the hall now. That's his fancy-'ooman from Brummagem, Tildy. He's bin agoing wi' her for years. Brought her out from Wales when her was a young girl, so they say, long afore he knew his missus. It's common knowledge in these parts that Henry Dugdale only wed his missus for her money.'

'That's as maybe,' Tildy argued back, 'but I think he's got some feeling for his wife. He was really upset when we took her to Henley.'

'Was he now? Well, he warn't too upset not to bring his whore from Brummagem, was he? By Christ, Tildy, youm really green about some things, arn't you?'

'Perhaps I am, Harry, but I'm not green about what's happening to Sybil Dugdale. That man Brown is driving her to destruction with his experiments, and I'm not going to stand by and let him do that to the poor creature, especially not now when I've the means to ruin him in my hands if he won't do as I want him to and leave the poor soul in peace.'

Harry Mogg's expression was dour and grim. 'Leave it lay, Tildy. Forget what you've seen in Henley this night. Put it right out from your mind, and put Sybil Dugdale out along wi' it. She's not your concern.'

Staring at him with puzzled eyes, Tildy said, 'I thought you would be happy to help me, Harry. Why are you acting in this way?'

'Because I know's what's best,' he told her forcefully. 'Youm agoing to turn all the gentry agen you, girl, if you brings this out into the open. They don't take kindly to a pauper trying to bring ruin down on one of their own kind.'

'But I'll not need to ruin him. I'll not need to bring it out into the open if he does what I want him to.'

'Fuck me blind, Tildy!' he burst out in sudden temper. 'Be you bloody simple in the yed? What youm talking of doing is committing a blackmail, and you'll be putting yourself in mortal danger if you does that.'

'He'll not dare to go to the constables or the magistrates,' Tildy said positively. 'He'll only bring ruin down on himself if he did that, wouldn't he?'

'I warn't meaning magistrates, nor constables neither,' Harry growled. 'You see it 'udden't be only Sam Brown that you was threatening, 'ud it? Youm threatening them who supplies him wi' the meat as well, arn't you? And they'll be the sort o' coves who'll shut your mouth for good and all.'

This statement momentarily disconcerted Tildy, but then she rallied. 'I'm not feared of the resurrection men. I'll get protection from the constable against them,' she spoke out bravely, but inwardly trembled at the thought of this fresh danger. But now her familiar demon of stubbornness had her in its grip and she would not be swayed from her purpose.

243

Harry Mogg regarded her closely for some moments, then in a softer tone he asked her, 'Be you really determined on doing this thing, Tildy? Even though it'll bring terrible danger for you?'

She drew a deep breath, and nodded. 'I am, Harry. I'm frightened I'll admit, but I can't leave Sybil Dugdale to be destroyed. No matter what risk I run from the resurrection men. I'll have to risk that because if I don't do all that I can for that poor woman, then I'll never be able to rest easy in my mind again.'

He sighed heavily, and then in a hoarse whisper he told her, 'Then youm agoing to ruin me as well, Tildy, and get me driven out from this parish. But I love you too much ever to harm you, and I'll not let me mates harm you either.'

Tildy's eyes became huge dark pools of sick despair as instant realization burst upon her. 'You're one of them! One of the resurrection men!' she ejaculated, and snatched her hands from his enfolding fingers.

'I'd no other choice than to do it, Tildy,' he cried out. 'I couldn't let me sister and her kids starve, could I? And what'll become of them if you informs on me? Answer me that?'

She could only gaze at him without speech, and he complained, 'Don't look at me like that, girl. Lifting a dead 'un arn't that evil. It don't make me the devil, does it?'

Tildy's mind was numbed as she struggled to comprehend what this shattering revelation would mean, but even in the maelstrom of mental confusion now engulfing her, one fact was already glaringly apparent. Sybil Dugdale was doomed to remain in the Stone House. Tildy knew that she could never bring herself to place Harry Mogg in any danger of phsyical harm, or being driven from his home.

He sat gazing at her with tormented eyes, and Tildy felt that she could not bear to remain with him a moment longer. She stood up, and told him hastily,

'Don't worry, Harry, I'll leave it lay. I'll not breathe a word of what I know to any living soul, not ever. God help

244

Sybil Dugdale now, for I cannot. But I've no wish to speak, or even see you, ever again.'

He went to reply, but she snapped, 'No! That's final, Harry. You are dead to me from this moment on.' Before he could move to stop her, she ran to the door and flinging it wide was gone from his sight and swallowed by the mists of the night.

Chapter Twenty-eight

The wind was from the north-east and carried swirls of snow on its bitter cold gustings to layer the iron-frosted ground with a white carpeting. Tildy stood just inside the gate of St Stephen's Chapel yard, shivering as the cruel wind struck through her threadbare clothing and brought tears from her dark-shadowed eyes.

On the road outside the chapel fence the black-cloth covered hearse and its attendant carriages stood in a long line, the horses snickering and whinnying and tossing their black-plumed heads as the scurries of snow lashed across them. Huddled in the lee of the carriages the hired mourners, holding their own long-shafted plumes of black feathers, stamped their feet, wiped runny noses on their sleeves, and muttered their miseries about the weather of this day, the twenty-eighth of December, 1821.

Despite the wind and snow Tildy stood stiffly erect, head held high, intent on the mass of people around the open grave in the centre of the yard. Even here, they were divided by the social order – the gentry forming the inner circle, the lesser breeds ranged around them, forming a living barrier against the onslaughts from the winter sky. Tildy's lips twisted in scorn and contempt as she studied the inner circle. The tall hats of the men wrapped around with the crêpe mourning scarves, the fur-lined collars of the paletots, the black veils and cloaks and jet mourning jewellery of the women.

A final sentence from the Reverend John Clayton, and the mass moved, eddied and broke into separate particles as they left the graveside to the ministrations of the undertaker's porters.

Tildy's gaze fixed on the leading group, dominated by the tall figure of Henry Dugdale, flanked by the Reverend John Clayton and closely followed by both the Taylors and the portly figure of Doctor Samuel Brown. Henry Dugdale presented the classic image of the bereaved husband, his tall hat massively swathed with crêpe, another scarf of crêpe tied around the sleeves of his black paletot, his face as grey and sombre as the day. His deep-sunk eyes noted Tildy, but he would have moved past her without acknowledgement if she had not stepped directly into his path.

'Do you know what day this is, Mister Dugdale?' Tildy's voice was tremulous, but it rang out determinedly. 'And I wonder if any of you others,' she pointed her fingers at the three doctors, 'I wonder if any of you know what day this is?'

John Clayton's shock and anger were clearly visible on his wind-reddened face. 'How dare you accost Mr Dugdale in such an insolent manner, Crawford?' he frowned. 'And at such a time?'

'I dare to because of what I must and will say.' She was now shaking violently in her agitation.

'Where is Cashmore?' Clayton looked about him for the constable, and by now the mourners had ranged themselves in a semi-circle around Tildy and the group with Dugdale. Their eyes avid with curiosity and gleaming with the anticipation of what this slender, shabby-dressed young woman might say.

Henry Dugdale lifted his black-gloved hand. 'No, Reverend Clayton, there is no need for Cashmore. Let this slut say whatever it is she wishes to,' he openly sneered at Tildy. 'But make it short and sharp, Crawford. I'll not have my guests detained by such as you in this inclement weather.'

'It will take only a moment.' Tildy fought to steady her voice and to overcome the timidity engendered in her by being the cynosure of all eyes. 'Today is Childermas, the Holy Innocents Day.' She found her breath catching in her throat, and her face flamed and crimsoned as her emotions threatened to overcome her. 'It was on this day that Herod ordered the killings of the children, and sent their innocent souls from this earth. Well you, and these others with you, have just buried what is left of the innocent soul you sent from this world. You and them are as evil and sinful as Herod.'

There was a concerted gasping and hissing of outrage, and the elder Taylor shouted,

'You saucy, wicked-tongued slut! I'll have you whipped for this criminal slander. Cashmore, get here and remove this slut. Get here this instant, man!'

Bulky in his caped winter cloak, the constable pushed through the crowd and grabbed Tildy with rough hands.

'Put her in the lock-up, Cashmore. We'll deal with her later,' Charles Taylor ordered, and other voices added their outrage to his.

'Yes, lock her up.'

'The slut's gone mad.'

'It's a disgrace.'

'It's shameful.'

'She should be whipped till she bleeds, for this.'

'Poor Mr Dugdale.'

'Poor man.'

'Poor suffering man.'

The heavy iron-studded door slammed shut, there was a rattle of bolts being thrust home, the hollow-sounding echoes of Cashmore's boots across the stone flags and the slamming of the outer door. Tildy looked about her at the mildewed stone walls of the cramped cell, the wooden pillow-block and pallet with its single filthy torn blanket, and her own breath misting in clouds before her in the freezing air. A lump rose to her throat and then the damn of self-control gave way and the sobs tore from her. Deep sunk in lonely misery she slumped down on to the damp pallet and let her grief pour out unrestrained.

A terrible guilt had gnawed at her since the night Harry Mogg had confessed what he had done, and so prevented her from making any attempt to force Doctor Brown to cease his treatments of Sybil Dugdale. Then a week ago she had heard of Sybil Dugdale's death in the Stone House. A sudden inflammation of the brain was the official and fully accepted verdict on the cause of death, but in Tildy's mind she regarded the woman's death as almost deliberate murder in which she shared the responsibility and the guilt, and that guilt had oppressed her with an all-consuming torment which had at last driven her to speak out as she had this day.

Time wore slowly on and at last her racking shuddering sobs hiccuped to an end, and for the first time in many weary days she felt an easing of the burden oppressing her mind, as though the weeping had acted as a catharsis. But then a fresh worry came to torment her. What would become of Davy now that she was here in the town lock-up?

For herself she was not unduly concerned. She felt that she had sufficient strength and courage to endure whatever might befall her now, but the thought of her baby left alone and unprotected brought more tears streaming down her wet cheeks. Davy was still at the Widow Fairfax's cottage. Tildy had thought it healthier for him to remain there, rather than bring him to share her own unhealthy quarters at Mother Readman's, and daily she had gone to visit him in between her searchings for work.

Now she berated herself angrily for giving in so shamelessly to what she perceived as her own weakness.

''Tis no use you bawling and crying now,' she told herself furiously. 'You've brought this present trouble on yourself, and instead of giving way to self-pity, you'd best be thinking of how to get out of this mess.'

Night had fallen, the cell was almost pitch-black, and only the moanings of the wind penetrated the arrow slit in the thick wall that cut her off from the world outside. The cold seemed to seep into her very bones, and teeth chattering in her head, she began to pace up and down the restricted space in an effort to warm her body. Anxiety throbbed through her mind no matter how hard she tried to rally her courage, but that anxiety was not for herself, only for her child.

. 'Oh God, don't let him suffer because of me,' she begged over and over again. 'Don't let harm come to him because of what I've done.'

Eventually sheer weariness forced her to sit and rest, but within scant minutes the aching cold in her bones drove her to pace once more. Seated again she wrapped the filthy blanket around her, necessity overcoming her innate fastidiousness, and swathed in its rank greasy folds she dozed fitfully. The hours passed with a grinding slowness and she drifted into a stupor engendered by exhaustion and cold.

The door of her cell crashing open penetrated that stupor and she blinked blearily at the lighted lantern carried by Joseph Cashmore.

'Come girl, rouse yourself,' he bade her harshly. 'It's gone six o' the morn. Time you was up and about. Here's the Reverend Clayton come to see you. Stand up and greet him respectful, girl.'

She pushed herself painfully to her feet, and stood swaying and shivering violently.

John Clayton experienced a rush of pity as he saw the forlorn bedraggled girl before him, and gently he told her, 'Be seated, Crawford, and listen very carefully to what I have to say to you.'

'Very well, Sir,' Tildy obeyed docilely, her fighting spirit temporarily chastened by the hardships of the night.

'Now listen to me, Crawford.' Clayton tried to speak harshly, but the pity he felt softened his tone. 'For your actions of yesterday, serious charges could be laid against you, which upon conviction at the quarter sessions would mean your imprisonment in the county gaol.'

Limpid, dark-ringed eyes blinked up at him from the wan, drawn face.

'You could also be whipped, if we so desired. You have

250

committed the criminal offences of lewd and disorderly conduct, and disturbing the public worship, and if that were not grievous enough, you have also committed a verbal libel against Mr Henry Dugdale and certain medical gentlemen. For that you could have a civil action brought against you in the courts, as well as the other charges.' He paused deliberately, to allow his words to sink fully into her understanding, then shrewdly hit on her weakest point. 'I know that you have an infant to maintain, Crawford, and it is that infant's welfare you must consider in regard to your future conduct. We have decided to show mercy to you this time, Crawford. No charges will be brought against you but I must warn you, that any repetition on your part of your disgraceful behaviour of yesterday, or any repeat of the shameful slanders made anywhere in anyone's hearing, will be punished with the utmost rigour that the law allows us. Now go from here and repent your wickedness.'

Utter relief was the paramount emotion in Tildy's mind. Utter relief that she would not be parted from her child. Too full to be able to reply, she rose and with bowed head walked past the two men and out from the open door of the lock-up. As she looked at the empty dark street, mortified sobs shook her frame and her eyes blurred with tears that she could not control; she stumbled away from the louring castellated building.

Final Chapter

Three weeks had passed since the day of Sybil Dugdale's
funeral, and for Tildy it had been a time of tribulation. Her
attack upon Henry Dugdale and the medical men had had
serious repercussions for her. The local gentry had closed
its ranks and none of them would give her work, not even
of the most menial kind, and when she had gone into the
surrounding farmlands seeking for employment at stone-
picking in the fields, she had been turned away as soon as
the farmers had discovered her identity.

Mother Readman had proved a staunch friend, but
Tildy's own pride forbade her from taking advantage of
that friendship and she had insisted on paying for her bed
and whatever food or drink she took in the lodging house.
Today, however, Tildy was forced to face the fact that her
situation was fast becoming desperate. The few shillings
she had remaining to her were needed to pay the Widow
Fairfax for Davy's keep, and after paying that Tildy would
have only pennies left.

She sat on her narrow bed and stared at her scant
belongings. The only articles that were saleable or even
pawnable were her beloved books. Sadly Tildy bade her
dreams goodbye as she parcelled up the four leather-bound
volumes in rags and carried them with her from the lodging
house.

The savage grip of winter was on the town and there

were few people in the wind-swept streets. Tildy's thoughts were sombre and her spirits depressed as she picked her way over the icy ruts of the road.

'Even if I manage to sell or pawn my books the money won't be much. And what will I do when that is spent also? It doesn't seem that I'll ever be able to find work in this town again. The whole world seems ranged against me.' For a moment she felt dangerously near to tears, but she bit her lips and summoned her pride, holding her head high. 'I'm not done yet,' she told herself stubbornly. 'If there is no work for me here, then I'll use the money I get for my books to go to Brummagem and seek work there.'

She reached her destination, the shop of Charles Burke Bromley, and went in. The interior did not appear to have changed since her last visit. It was still a hopeless confusion of jumbled articles and a mixture of smells. The proprietor himself was not present, however, only a tiny, bent-bodied old woman, wearing a huge floppy mob-cap and muffled in a profusion of vari-coloured shawls and scarves was in the shop sitting in a wooden-wheeled invalid chair, squinting at Tildy with a suspicious glare.

'Charlie? Charlie, come here.' The cracked old voice was surprisingly loud and penetrating. 'Charlie, wheer bist you, boy? Come here now.'

'I'm coming, Mother, I'm coming. Calm yourself do.' Charles Burke Bromley was just as Tildy had remembered him. Still swathed in his long white apron, his few oiled strands of hair slicked across his shiny pink scalp, his watery eyes blinking behind the thick-lensed spectacles.

He smiled with delighted surprise when he saw Tildy. 'Well, it is Mistress Crawford, is it not? How may I help you, Ma'am? I've often thought of you and wondered how you were progressing in your studies.'

Despite his being a comparative stranger, there was such palpable warmth and friendliness radiating from him that Tildy felt instantly at ease in his company.

'My studies were progressing well, Master Bromley.' She smiled back at him. 'But I fear they must now end for a while.'

His high forehead creased in a concerned frown. 'Well, I am most sorry to hear that, Ma'am.'

'What's this youm atalking about, boy? For pity's sake spake up, for I canna hear you plain,' the old crone's cracked voice interrupted the conversation. 'And wheer's me dinner, boy? I'm fair clemmed, so I am. Wheer's me dinner? Youm atrying to starve me, arn't you?' she accused angrily. 'Youm atrying to starve me to death.'

Her son reddened with embarrassment. 'Now please, Mother,' he remonstrated gently. 'Calm yourself. Your dinner is still cooking. It'll not be long.'

'And a pretty mess o' slops it 'ull be, as well,' the old crone grumbled, and said to Tildy, 'The boy is a fool, young 'ooman. He canna cook, he canna spin, he canna sew, and wuss than all that, he canna look arter me properly. The boy is a fool.'

Tildy lifted her hand to her mouth to hide a smile of amused sympathy for Charles Bromley.

'Pray excuse me, Mistress Crawford.' He bustled the invalid chair with its passenger out to the rear room of the shop, and Tildy could hear him saying, 'Now here is some fresh beef-tea, Mother. Drink it up, like a good soul. It will stay you until your dinner is ready.'

Flushed and perspiring he reappeared in the shop. 'Now, Ma'am, how may I help you?'

'If you please, Master Bromley, I wondered if you might buy these books back from me at whatever price you think fair.'

Understanding gleamed in his watery eyes. 'But of course I will, Ma'am,' he answered without hesitation. 'Forgive me if I intrude, but I know something of your difficulties since the incident at Mrs Dugdale's funeral.' He blushed and added hastily, 'It is a small town, Ma'am, and there is little that remains secret here, and always an abundance of gossip.'

It was Tildy's turn to blush with embarrassment. 'Then you will know why I needs must sell my books, Master Bromley. I'd appreciate whatever sum you could afford for them.'

He stared at her for what seemed a long time, then nervously coughed and asked, 'Might I enquire if you still seek for work locally?'

'Yes, I'm still seeking, but I fear I'll not find any employment hereabouts. I think that I shall have to go to Brummagem and look about there for something.'

Again he stared for a long silence, and then swallowed hard and blurted in a rush, 'Would you like to work for me, Ma'am, as my housekeeper, and to help care for my mother? I cannot pay very much for salary, but you and your child would be very comfortable here, and you would have your own pair of rooms. There is ample space – it's quite a large house, although narrow-fronted.' He hesitated a moment, and then added, 'And you can keep your books as well. You would be able to continue your studies.' He waved his hands in vague indication. 'The house is full of books; you can read them whenever you like.' He smiled at her almost timidly. 'And you'll not find me a hard master, Ma'am. In fact, I'll make so bold as to say that I'll prove a most considerate employer towards you.' He rubbed his hands together anxiously. 'Please say that you will come, Ma'am. I am in sore need, and you and your child will find a real home here with my mother and me.'

Tildy was both surprised by his offer, and uncertain. It promised a solution to her immediate problems, but still she hesitated to commit herself. 'But perhaps I may not be what you need, Master Bromley. You may not think me suitable when you come to know me better. I am assured that I'm too forward and impertinent towards my betters.'

'I'll chance that,' he replied softly, and urged, 'Please come. You will be performing a great service towards me if you did so. Situated as I am, I cannot care for my mother properly, or attend to all her needs. It wants a woman for that.'

Tildy thought of her child, lying in that box at Widow Fairfax's, stuporous with the poppy syrup every time she saw him, and her mind abruptly clarified.

'Very well, Master Bromley. I will come as your house-keeper.'

'Then when can you come?' he pressed eagerly, his beautiful teeth gleaming in a happy smile.

'This very day, when I have fetched my baby from Boney's Point.'

'I'm so glad.' Charles Bromley took her hand in his and shook it vigorously. 'And I do promise you, that you and your child will find a real home here.'

'I hope we do,' Tildy murmured, as if to herself. 'For we both sorely need a real home. We've never yet known one . . .'

Outside in the street once more Tildy's heart was full and her spirits soaring. 'I'll work hard and do my best for Master Bromley and his mother,' she vowed. 'I'll make sure that he'll not regret taking me in.'

She passed two men and caught a snippet of their talk.

' . . . so it's like I allus says, Jem – whilst theer's a breath left in your body, then theer's hope.'

Tildy could not help herself. She turned and told the speaker, 'I'll vouch for the truth of that, Sir,' and walked on giggling helplessly as the two men stared wonderingly after her.